I0647787

American Hero-Myths

Daniel G. Brinton

Contents

AMERICAN HERO-MYTHS

BY

Daniel G. Brinton

TO
ELI K. PRICE, ESQ.,

PRESIDENT OF THE NUMISMATIC AND ANTIQUARIAN SOCIETY OF PHILADELPHIA, WHOSE ENLIGHTENED INTEREST HAS FOR MANY YEARS, AND IN MANY WAYS, FURTHERED THE PROGRESS OF KNOWLEDGE, THIS VOLUME IS RESPECTFULLY DEDICATED BY THE AUTHOR.

PREFACE.

This little volume is a contribution to the comparative study of religions. It is an endeavor to present in a critically correct light some of the fundamental conceptions which are found in the native beliefs of the tribes of America.

So little has heretofore been done in this field that it has yielded a very scanty harvest for purposes of general study. It has not yet even passed the stage where the distinction between myth and tradition has been recognized. Nearly all historians continue to write about some of the American hero-gods as if they had been chiefs of tribes at some undetermined epoch, and the effort to trace the migrations and affiliations of nations by similarities in such stories is of almost daily occurrence. How baseless and misleading all such arguments must be, it is one of my objects to set forth.

At the same time I have endeavored to be temperate in applying the interpretations of mythologists. I am aware of the risk one runs in looking at every legend as a light or storm myth. My guiding principle has been that when the same, and that a very extraordinary, story is told by several tribes wholly apart in language and location, then the probabilities are enormous that it is not a legend but a myth, and must be explained as such. It is a spontaneous production of the mind, not a reminiscence of an historic event.

The importance of the study of myths has been abundantly shown of recent years, and the methods of analyzing them have been established with satisfactory clearness.

The time has long since passed, at least among thinking men, when the religious legends of the lower races were looked upon as trivial fables, or as the inventions of the Father of Lies. They are neither the one nor the other. They express, in image and incident, the opinions of these races on the mightiest topics of human thought, on the origin and destiny of man, his motives for duty and his grounds of hope, and the source, history and fate of all external nature. Certainly the sincere expressions on these subjects of even humble members of the human race deserve our most respectful heed, and it may be that we shall discover in their crude or coarse narrations gleams of a mental light which their proud Aryan brothers have been long in coming to, or have not yet reached.

The prejudice against all the lower faiths inspired by the claim of Christianity to a monopoly of religious truth--a claim nowise set up by its founder--has led to extreme injustice toward the so-called heathen religions. Little effort has been made to distinguish between their good and evil tendencies, or even to understand them. I do not know of a single instance on this continent of a thorough and intelligent study of a native religion made by a Protestant missionary.

So little real work has been done in American mythology that very diverse opinions as to its interpretation prevail among writers. Too many of them apply to it facile generalizations, such as "heliolatry," "animism," "ancestral worship," "primitive philosophizing," and think that such a sesame will unloose all its mysteries. The result has been that while each satisfies himself, he convinces no one else.

I have tried to avoid any such bias, and have sought to discover the source of the myths I have selected, by close attention to two points: first, that I should obtain the precise original form of the myth by a rigid scrutiny of authorities; and, secondly, that I should bring to bear upon it modern methods of mythological and linguistic analysis.

The first of these requirements has given me no small trouble. The sources of American history not only differ vastly in merit, but many of them are almost inaccessible. I still have by me a list of books of the first order of importance for these studies, which I have not been able to find in any public or private library in the United States.

I have been free in giving references for the statements in the text. The growing custom among historians of omitting to do this must be deplored in the interests of sound learning. It is better to risk the charge of pedantry than to leave at fault those who wish to test an author's accuracy or follow up the line of investigation he indicates.

On the other hand, I have exercised moderation in drawing comparisons with Aryan, Semitic, Egyptian and other Old World mythologies. It would have been easy to have noted apparent similarities to a much greater extent. But I have preferred to leave this for those who write upon general comparative mythology. Such parallelisms, to reach satisfactory results, should be attempted only by those who have studied the Oriental religions in their original sources, and thus are not to be deceived by superficial resemblances.

The term "comparative mythology" reaches hardly far enough to cover all that I have aimed at. The professional mythologist thinks he has completed his task when he has traced a myth through its transformations in story and language back to the natural phenomena of which it was the expression. This external history is essential. But deeper than that lies the study of the influence of the myth on the individual and national mind, on the progress and destiny of those who believed it, in other words, its true *religious* import. I have endeavored, also, to take some account of this.

The usual statement is that tribes in the intellectual condition of those I am dealing with rest their religion on a worship of external phenomena. In contradiction to this, I advance various arguments to show that their chief god was not identified with any objective natural process, but was human in nature, benignant in character, loved rather than feared, and that his worship carried with it the germs of the development of benevolent emotions and sound ethical principles.

Media, Pa., Oct., 1882.

CHAPTER I.
INTRODUCTORY.

SOME KIND OF RELIGION FOUND AMONG ALL MEN--CLASSIFICA-
TIONS OF RELIGIONS--THE PURPOSE OF RELIGIONS--RELIGIONS
OF RITE AND OF CREED--THE MYTH GROWS IN THE FIRST OF
THESE--INTENT AND MEANING OF THE MYTH.

PROCESSES OF MYTH-BUILDING IN AMERICA--PERSONIFICATION.
PARONYMS AND HOMONYMS--OTOSIS--POLYONOMY--HENO-
THEISM--BORROWING--RHETORICAL FIGURES--ABSTRACT EX-
PRESSIONS. ESOTERIC TEACHINGS.

OUTLINES OF THE FUNDAMENTAL AMERICAN MYTH--THE WHITE
CULTURE-HERO AND THE FOUR BROTHERS--INTERPRETATION
OF THE MYTH--COMPARISON WITH THE ARYAN HERMES MYTH-
-WITH THE ARYO-SEMITIC CADMUS MYTH--WITH OSIRIAN
MYTHS--THE MYTH OF THE VIRGIN MOTHER--THE INTERPRETA-
TION THUS SUPPORTED.

The time was, and that not so very long ago, when it was contended by some that there are tribes of men without any sort of religion; nowadays the effort is to show that the feeling which prompts to it is common, even among brutes.

This change of opinion has come about partly through an extension of the definition of religion. It is now held to mean any kind of belief in spiritual or extra-natural agencies. Some learned men say that we had better drop the word "religion," lest we be misunderstood. They would rather use "daimonism," or "supernaturalism," or other such new term; but none of these seems to me so wide and so exactly significant of what I mean as "religion."

All now agree that in this very broad sense some kind of religion exists in every human community.[1]

[1: I suppose I am not going too far in saying "all agree;" for I think that the latest study of this subject, by Gustav Roskoff, disposes of Sir John Lubbock's doubts, as well as the crude statements of the author of ***Kraft und Stoff***, and such like compilations. Gustav Roskoff, ***Das Religionswesen der Rohesten Naturvoelker***, Leipzig, 1880.]

The attempt has often been made to classify these various faiths under some few general headings. The scheme of Auguste Comte still has supporters. He taught that man begins with fetichism, advances to polytheism, and at last rises to monotheism. More in vogue at present is the theory that the simplest and lowest form of religion is individual; above it are the national religions; and at the summit the universal or world religions.

Comte's scheme has not borne examination. It is artificial and sterile. Look at Christianity. It is the highest of all religions, but it is not monotheism. Look at Buddhism. In its pure form it is not even theism. The second classification is more fruitful for historical purposes.

The psychologist, however, inquires as to the essence, the real purpose of religions. This has been differently defined by the two great schools of thought.

All religions, says the idealist, are the efforts, poor or noble, conscious or blind, to develop the Idea of God in the soul of man.

No, replies the rationalist, it is simply the effort of the human mind to frame a Theory of Things; at first, religion is an early system of natural philosophy; later it becomes moral philosophy. Explain the Universe by physical laws, point out that the origin and aim of ethics are the relations of men, and we shall have no more religions, nor need any.

The first answer is too intangible, the second too narrow. The rude savage does not philosophize on phenomena; the enlightened student sees in them but interacting forces: yet both may be profoundly religious. Nor can morality be accepted as a criterion of religions. The bloody scenes in the Mexican teocalli were merciful compared with those in the torture rooms of the Inquisition. Yet the religion of Jesus was far above that of Huitzilopochtli.

What I think is the essence, the principle of vitality, in religion, and in all religions, is ***their supposed control over the destiny of the individual***, his weal or woe, his good or bad hap, here or hereafter, as it may be. Rooted infinitely deep in the sense of personality, religion was recognized at the beginning, it will be recognized at the end, as the one indestructible ally in the struggle for individual existence. At heart, all prayers are for preservation, the burden of all litanies is a begging for Life.

This end, these benefits, have been sought by the cults of the world through one of two theories.

The one, that which characterizes the earliest and the crudest religions, teaches that man escapes dangers and secures safety by the performance or avoidance of certain actions. He may credit this or that myth, he may hold to one or many gods; this is unimportant; but he must not fail in the penance or the sacred dance, he must not touch that which is ***taboo***, or he is in peril. The life of these cults is the Deed, their expression is the Rite.

Higher religions discern the inefficacy of the mere Act. They rest their claim on Belief. They establish dogmas, the mental acceptance of which is the one thing needful. In them mythology passes into theology; the act is measured by its motive, the formula by the faith back of it. Their life is the Creed.

The Myth finds vigorous and congenial growth only in the first of these forms. There alone the imagination of the votary is free, there alone it is not fettered by a symbol already defined.

To the student of religions the interest of the Myth is not that of an infantile attempt to philosophize, but as it illustrates the intimate and immediate relations which the religion in which it grew bore to the individual life. Thus examined, it reveals the inevitable destinies of men and of nations as bound up with their forms of worship.

These general considerations appear to me to be needed for the proper understanding of the study I am about to make. It concerns itself with some of the religions which were developed on the American continent before its discovery. My object is to present from them a series of myths curiously similar in features, and to see if one simple and general explanation of them can be found.

The processes of myth-building among American tribes were much the same as elsewhere. These are now too generally familiar to need specification here, beyond a few which I have found particularly noticeable.

At the foundation of all myths lies the mental process of ***personification***, which finds expression in the rhetorical figure of ***prosopopeia***. The definition of this, however, must be extended from the mere representation of inanimate things as animate, to include also the representation of irrational beings as rational, as in the "animal myths," a most common form of religious story among primitive people.

Some languages favor these forms of personification much more than others, and most of the American languages do so in a marked manner, by the broad grammatical distinctions they draw between animate and inanimate objects, which distinctions must invariably be observed. They cannot say "the boat moves" without specifying whether the boat is an animate object or not, or whether it is to be considered animate, for rhetorical purposes, at the time of speaking.

The sounds of words have aided greatly in myth building. Names and words which are somewhat alike in sound, ***paronyms***, as they are called by grammarians, may be taken or mistaken one for the other. Again, many myths spring from ***homonymy***, that is, the sameness in sound of words with difference in signification. Thus ***coatl***, in the Aztec tongue, is a word frequently appearing in the names of divinities. It has three entirely different meanings, to wit, a serpent, a guest and twins. Now, whichever one of these was originally meant, it would be quite certain to be misunderstood, more or less, by later generations, and myths would arise to explain the several possible interpretations of the word--as, in fact, we find was the case.

Closely allied to this is what has been called ***otosis***. This is the substitution of a familiar word for an archaic or foreign one of similar sound but wholly diverse meaning. This is a very common occurrence and easily leads to myth making. For example, there is a cave, near Chattanooga, which has the Cherokee name Nik-a-jak. This the white settlers have transformed into Nigger Jack, and are prepared with a narrative of some runaway slave to explain the cognomen. It may also occur in the same language. In an Algonkin dialect ***missi wabu*** means "the great light of the dawn;" and a common large rabbit was called ***missabo***; at some period the precise meaning of the former words was lost, and a variety of interesting myths of the daybreak were transferred to a supposed huge rabbit! Rarely does there occur a more striking example of how the deteriorations of language affect mythology.

Aztlan, the mythical land whence the Aztec speaking tribes were said to have come, and from which they derived their name, means "the place of whiteness;" but the word was similar to ***Aztatlan***, which would mean "the place of herons," some spot where these birds would love to congregate, from ***aztatl***, the heron, and in after ages, this latter, as the plainer and more concrete signification, came to prevail, and was adopted by the myth-makers.

Polyonomy is another procedure often seen in these myths. A divinity has several or many titles; one or another of these becomes prominent, and at last obscures in a particular myth or locality the original personality of the hero of the tale. In America this is most obvious in Peru.

Akin to this is what Prof. Max Mueller has termed ***henotheism***. In this mental process one god or one form of a god is exalted beyond all others, and even addressed as the one, only, absolute and supreme deity. Such expressions are not to be construed literally as evidences of a monotheism, but simply that at that particular time the worshiper's mind was so filled with the power and majesty of the divinity to whom he appealed, that he applied to him these superlatives, very much as he would to a great ruler. The next day he might apply them to another deity, without any hypocrisy or sense of logical contradiction. Instances of this are common in the Aztec prayers which have been preserved.

One difficulty encountered in Aryan mythology is extremely rare in America, and that is, the adoption of foreign names. A proper name without a definite concrete significance in the tongue of the people who used it is almost unexampled in the red race. A word without a meaning was something quite foreign to their mode of thought. One of our most eminent students[1] has justly said: "Every Indian synthesis--names of persons and places not excepted--must preserve the consciousness of its roots, and must not only have a meaning, but be so framed as to convey that meaning with precision, to all who speak the language to which it belongs." Hence, the names of their divinities can nearly always be interpreted, though for the reasons above given the most obvious and current interpretation is not in every case the correct one.

[1: J. Hammond Trumbull, ***On the Composition of Indian Geographical Names***, p. 3 (Hartford, 1870).]

As foreign names were not adopted, so the mythology of one tribe very rarely influenced that of another. As a rule, all the religions were tribal or national, and their votaries had no desire to extend them. There was little of the proselytizing spirit among the red race. Some exceptions can be pointed out to this statement, in the Aztec and Peruvian monarchies. Some borrowing seems to have been done either by or from the Mayas; and the hero-myth of the Iroquois has so many of the lineaments of that of the Algonkins that it is difficult to believe that it was wholly independent of it. But, on the whole, the identities often found in American myths are more justly attributable to a similarity of surroundings and impressions than to any other cause.

The diversity and intricacy of American mythology have been greatly fostered by the delight the more developed nations took in rhetorical figures, in metaphor and simile, and in expressions of amplification and hyperbole. Those who imagine that there was a poverty of resources in these languages, or that their concrete form hemmed in the mind from the study of the abstract, speak without knowledge. One has but to look at the inexhaustible synonymy of the Aztec, as it is set forth by Olmos or Sahagun, or at its power to render correctly the refinements of scholastic theology, to see how wide of the fact is any such opinion. And what is true of the Aztec, is not less so of the Qquichua and other tongues.

I will give an example, where the English language itself falls short of the nicety of the Qquichua in handling a metaphysical tenet. *Cay* in Qquichua expresses the real being of things, the *essentia*; as, *runap caynin*, the being of the human race, humanity in the abstract; but to convey the idea of actual being, the *existentia* as united to the *essentia*, we must add the prefix *cascan*, and thus have *runap-cascan-caynin*, which strictly means "the essence of being in general, as existent in humanity."[1] I doubt if the dialect of German metaphysics itself, after all its elaboration, could produce in equal compass a term for this conception. In Qquichua, moreover, there is nothing strained and nothing foreign in this example; it is perfectly pure, and in thorough accord with the genius of the tongue.

[1: "El ser existente de hombre, que es el modo de estar el primer ser que es la essentia que en Dios y los Angeles y el hombre es modo personal." Diego Gonzalez Holguin, *Vocabvlario de la Lengva Qqichua, o del Inca; sub voce, Cay*. (Ciudad de los Reyes, 1608.)]

I take some pains to impress this fact, for it is an important one in estimating the religious ideas of the race. We must not think we have grounds for skepticism if we occasionally come across some that astonish us by their subtlety. Such are quite in keeping with the psychology and languages of the race we are studying.

Yet, throughout America, as in most other parts of the world, the teaching of religious tenets was twofold, the one popular, the other for the initiated, an esoteric and an exoteric doctrine. A difference in dialect was assiduously cultivated, a sort of "sacred language" being employed to conceal while it conveyed the mysteries of faith. Some linguists think that these dialects are archaic forms of the language, the memory of which was retained in ceremonial observances; others maintain that they were simply affectations of expression, and form a sort of slang, based on the every day language, and current among the initiated. I am inclined to the latter as the correct opinion, in many cases.

Whichever it was, such a sacred dialect is found in almost all tribes. There are fragments of it from the cultivated races of Mexico, Yucatan and Peru; and at the other end of the scale we may instance the Guaymis, of Darien, naked savages, but whose "chiefs of the law," we are told, taught "the doctrines of their religion in a peculiar idiom, invented for the purpose, and very different from the common language."[1]

[1: Franco, *Noticia de los Indios Guaymies y de sus Costumbres*, p. 20, in Pinart, *Coleccion de Linguistica y Etnografia Americana*. Tom. iv.]

This becomes an added difficulty in the analysis of myths, as not only were the names of the divinities and of localities expressed in terms in the highest degree metaphorical, but they were at times obscured by an affected pronunciation, devised to conceal their exact derivation.

The native tribes of this Continent had many myths, and among them there was one which was so prominent, and recurred with such strangely similar features in localities widely asunder, that it has for years attracted my attention, and I have been led to present it as it occurs among several nations far apart, both geographically and in point of culture. This myth is that of the national hero, their mythical civilizer and teacher of the tribe, who, at the same time, was often identified with the supreme deity and the creator of the world. It is the fundamental myth of a very large number of American tribes, and on its recognition and interpretation depends the correct understanding of most of their mythology and religious life.

The outlines of this legend are to the effect that in some exceedingly remote time this divinity took an active part in creating the world and in fitting it to be the abode of man, and may himself have formed or called forth the race. At any rate, his interest in its advancement was such that he personally appeared among the ancestors of the nation, and taught them the useful arts, gave them the maize or other food plants, initiated them into the mysteries of their religious rites, framed the laws which governed their social relations, and having thus started them on the road to self development, he left them, not suffering death, but disappearing in some way from their view. Hence it was nigh universally expected that at some time he would return.

The circumstances attending the birth of these hero-gods have great similarity. As a rule, each is a twin or one of four brothers born at one birth; very generally at the cost of their mother's life, who is a virgin, or at least had never been impregnated by mortal man. The hero is apt to come into conflict with his brother, or one of his brothers, and the long and desperate struggle resulting, which often involved the universe in repeated destructions, constitutes one of the leading topics of the myth-makers. The duel is not generally--not at all, I believe, when we can get at the genuine native form of the myth--between a morally good and an evil spirit, though, undoubtedly, the one is more friendly and favorable to the welfare of man than the other.

The better of the two, the true hero-god, is in the end triumphant, though the national temperament represented this variously. At any rate, his people are not deserted by him, and though absent, and perhaps for a while driven away by his potent adversary, he is sure to come back some time or other.

The place of his birth is nearly always located in the East; from that quarter he first came when he appeared as a man among men; toward that point he returned when he disappeared; and there he still lives, awaiting the appointed time for his reappearance.

Whenever the personal appearance of this hero-god is described, it is, strangely enough, represented to be that of one of the white race, a man of fair complexion, with long, flowing beard, with abundant hair, and clothed in ample and loose robes. This extraordinary fact naturally suggests the gravest suspicion that these stories were made up after the whites had reached the American shores, and nearly all historians have summarily rejected their authenticity, on this account. But a most careful scrutiny of their sources positively refutes this opinion. There is irrefragable evidence that these myths and this ideal of the hero-god, were intimately known and widely current in America long before any one of its millions of inhabitants had ever seen a white man. Nor is there any difficulty in explaining this, when we divest these figures of the fanciful garbs in which they have been clothed by the religious imagination, and recognize what are the phenomena on which they are based, and the physical processes whose histories they embody. To show this I will offer, in the most concise terms, my interpretation of their main details.

The most important of all things to life is ***Light***. This the primitive savage felt, and, personifying it, he made Light his chief god. The beginning of the day served, by analogy, for the beginning of the world. Light comes before the sun, brings it forth, creates it, as it were. Hence the Light-God is not the Sun-God, but his Antecedent and Creator.

The light appears in the East, and thus defines that cardinal point, and by it the others are located. These points, as indispensable guides to the wandering hordes, became, from earliest times, personified as important deities, and were identified with the winds that blew from them, as wind and rain gods. This explains the four brothers, who were nothing else than the four cardinal points, and their mother, who dies in producing them, is the eastern light, which is soon lost in the growing day. The East, as their leader, was also the supposed ruler of the winds, and thus god of the air and rain. As more immediately connected with the advent and departure of light, the East and West are twins, the one of which sends forth the glorious day-orb, which the other lies in wait to conquer. Yet the light-god is not slain. The sun shall rise again in undiminished glory, and he lives, though absent.

By sight and light we see and learn. Nothing, therefore, is more natural than to attribute to the light-god the early progress in the arts of domestic and social life. Thus light came to be personified as the embodiment of culture and knowledge, of wisdom, and of the peace and prosperity which are necessary for the growth of learning.

The fair complexion of these heroes is nothing but a reference to the white light of the dawn. Their ample hair and beard are the rays of the sun that flow from his radiant visage. Their loose and large robes typify the enfolding of the firmament by the light and the winds.

This interpretation is nowise strained, but is simply that which, in Aryan mythology, is now universally accepted for similar mythological creations. Thus, in the Greek Phoebus and Perseus, in the Teutonic Lif, and in the Norse Baldur, we have also beneficent hero-gods, distinguished by their fair complexion and ample golden locks. "Amongst the dark as well as amongst the fair races, amongst those who are marked by black hair and dark eyes, they exhibit the same unfailing type of blue-eyed heroes whose golden locks flow over their shoulders, and whose faces gleam as with the light of the new risen sun."[1]

[1: Sir George W. Cox, *An Introduction to the Science of Comparative Mythology and Folk-Lore*, p. 17.]

Everywhere, too, the history of these heroes is that of a struggle against some potent enemy, some dark demon or dragon, but as often against some member of their own household, a brother or a father.

The identification of the Light-God with the deity of the winds is also seen in Aryan mythology. Hermes, to the Greek, was the inventor of the alphabet, music, the cultivation of the olive, weights and measures, and such humane arts. He was also the messenger of the gods, in other words, the breezes, the winds, the air in motion. His name Hermes, Hermeias, is but a transliteration of the Sanscrit Sarameyas, under which he appears in the Vedic songs, as the son of Sarama, the Dawn. Even his character as the master thief and patron saint of the light-fingered gentry, drawn from the way the winds and breezes penetrate every crack and cranny of the house, is absolutely repeated in the Mexican hero-god Quetzalcoatl, who was also the patron of thieves. I might carry the comparison yet further, for as Sarameyas is derived from the root *sar*, to creep, whence *serpo*, serpent, the creeper, so the name Quetzalcoatl can be accurately translated, "the wonderful serpent." In name, history and functions the parallelism is maintained throughout.

Or we can find another familiar myth, partly Aryan, partly Semitic, where many of the same outlines present themselves. The Argive Thebans attributed the founding of their city and state to Cadmus. He collected their ancestors into a community, gave them laws, invented the alphabet of sixteen letters, taught them the art of smelting metals, established oracles, and introduced the Dyonisiac worship, or that of the reproductive principle. He subsequently left them and lived for a time with other nations, and at last did not die, but was changed into a dragon and carried by Zeus to Elysion.

The birthplace of this culture hero was somewhere far to the eastward of Greece, somewhere in "the purple land" (Phoenicia); his mother was "the far gleaming one" (Telephassa); he was one of four children, and his sister was Europe, the Dawn, who was seized and carried westward by Zeus, in the shape of a white bull. Cadmus seeks to recover her, and sets out, following the westward course of the sun. "There can be no rest until the lost one is found again. The sun must journey westward until he sees again the beautiful tints which greeted his eyes in the morning."[1] Therefore Cadmus leaves the purple land to pursue his quest. It is one of toil and struggle. He has to fight the dragon offspring of Ares and the bands of armed men who spring from the dragon's teeth which were sown, that is, the clouds and gloom of the overcast sky. He conquers, and is rewarded, but does not recover his sister.

[1: Sir George W. Cox, *Ibid.*, p. 76.]

When we find that the name Cadmus is simply the Semitic word ***kedem***, the east, and notice all this mythical entourage, we see that this legend is but a lightly veiled account of the local source and progress of the light of day, and of the advantages men derive from it. Cadmus brings the letters of the alphabet from the east to Greece, for the same reason that in ancient Maya myth Itzamna, "son of the mother of the morning," brought the hieroglyphs of the Maya script also from the east to Yucatan--because both represent the light by which we see and learn.

Egyptian mythology offers quite as many analogies to support this interpretation of American myths as do the Aryan god-stories.

The heavenly light impregnates the virgin from whom is born the sun-god, whose life is a long contest with his twin brother. The latter wins, but his victory is transient, for the light, though conquered and banished by the darkness, cannot be slain, and is sure to return with the dawn, to the great joy of the sons of men. This story the Egyptians delighted to repeat under numberless disguises. The groundwork and meaning are the same, whether the actors are Osiris, Isis and Set, Ptah, Hapi and the Virgin Cow, or the many other actors of this drama. There, too, among a brown race of men, the light-god was deemed to be not of their own hue, but "light colored, white or yellow," of comely countenance, bright eyes and golden hair. Again, he is the one who invented the calendar, taught the arts, established the rituals, revealed the medical virtues of plants, recommended peace, and again was identified as one of the brothers of the cardinal points.[1]

[1: See Dr. C.P. Tiele, **History of the Egyptian Religion**, pp. 93, 95, 99, et al.]

The story of the virgin-mother points, in America as it did in the old world, to the notion of the dawn bringing forth the sun. It was one of the commonest myths in both continents, and in a period of human thought when miracles were supposed to be part of the order of things had in it nothing difficult of credence. The Peruvians, for instance, had large establishments where were kept in rigid seclusion the "virgins of the sun." Did one of these violate her vow of chastity, she and her fellow criminal were at once put to death; but did she claim that the child she bore was of divine parentage, and the contrary could not be shown, then she was feted as a queen, and the product of her womb was classed among princes, as a son of the sun. So, in the inscription at Thebes, in the temple of the virgin goddess Mat, we read where she says of herself: "My garment no man has lifted up; the fruit that I have borne was begotten of the sun."[1]

[1: "[Greek: Ton emon chitona oudeis apechaluphen on ego charpon etechan, aelios egeneto.]" Proclus, quoted by Tiele, ubi supra, p. 204, note.]

I do not venture too much in saying that it were easy to parallel every event in these American hero-myths, every phase of character of the personages they represent, with others drawn from Aryan and Egyptian legends long familiar to students, and which now are fully recognized as having in them nothing of the substance of history, but as pure creations of the religious imagination working on the processes of nature brought into relation to the hopes and fears of men.

If this is so, is it not time that we dismiss, once for all, these American myths from the domain of historical traditions? Why should we try to make a king of Itzamna, an enlightened ruler of Quetzalcoatl, a cultured nation of the Toltecs, when the proof is of the strongest, that every one of these is an absolutely baseless fiction of mythology? Let it be understood, hereafter, that whoever uses these names in an historical sense betrays an ignorance of the subject he handles, which, were it in the better known field of Aryan or Egyptian lore, would at once convict him of not meriting the name of scholar.

In European history the day has passed when it was allowable to construct primitive chronicles out of fairy tales and nature myths. The science of comparative mythology has assigned to these venerable stories a different, though not less noble, interpretation. How much longer must we wait to see the same canons of criticism applied to the products of the religious fancy of the red race?

Furthermore, if the myths of the American nations are shown to be capable of a consistent interpretation by the principles of comparative mythology, let it be recognized that they are neither to be discarded because they resemble some familiar to their European conquerors, nor does that similarity mean that they are historically derived, the one from the other. Each is an independent growth, but as each is the reflex in a common psychical nature of the same phenomena, the same forms of expression were adopted to convey them.

CHAPTER II.
THE HERO-GODS OF THE ALGONKINS AND IROQUOIS.

Sec.1. *The Algonkin Myth of Michabo.*

THE MYTH OF THE GIANT RABBIT--THE RABBIT CREATES THE WORLD--HE MARRIES THE MUSKRAT--BECOMES THE ALL-FA-THER--DERIVATION OF MICHABO--OF WAJASHK, THE MUSKRAT--THE MYTH EXPLAINED--THE LIGHT-GOD AS GOD OF THE EAST--THE FOUR DIVINE BROTHERS--MYTH OF THE HUAROCHIRIS--THE DAY-MAKERS--MICHABO'S CONTESTS WITH HIS FATHER AND BROTHER--EXPLANATION OF THESE--THE SYMBOLIC FLINT STONE--MICHABO DESTROYS THE SERPENT KING--MEANING OF THIS MYTH--RELATIONS OF THE LIGHT-GOD AND WIND-GOD--MICHABO AS GOD OF WATERS AND FERTILITY--REPRESENTED AS A BEARDED MAN.

Sec.2. *The Iroquois Myth of Ioskeha.*

THE CREATION OF THE EARTH--THE MIRACULOUS BIRTH OF IO-SKEHA--HE OVERCOMES HIS BROTHER, TAWISCARA--CREATES AND TEACHES MANKIND--VISITS HIS PEOPLE--HIS GRANDMOTH-ER, ATAENSIC--IOSKEHA AS FATHER OF HIS MOTHER--SIMILAR CONCEPTIONS IN EGYPTIAN MYTHS--DERIVATION OF IOSKEHA AND ATAENSIC--IOSKEHA AS THARONHIAWAKON, THE SKY SUPPORTER--HIS BROTHER TAWISCARA OR TEHOTENNHIARON IDENTIFIED--SIMILARITY TO ALGONKIN MYTHS.

Nearly all that vast area which lies between Hudson Bay and the Savannah river, and the Mississippi river and the Atlantic coast, was peopled at the epoch of the discovery by the members of two linguistic families--the Algonkins and the Iroquois. They were on about the same plane of culture, but differed much in temperament and radically in language. Yet their religious notions were not dissimilar.

Sec.1. *The Algonkin Myth of Michabo.*

Among all the Algonkin tribes whose myths have been preserved we find much is said about a certain Giant Rabbit, to whom all sorts of powers were attributed. He was the master of all animals; he was the teacher who first instructed men in the arts of fishing and hunting; he imparted to the Algonkins the mysteries of their religious rites; he taught them picture writing and the interpretation of dreams; nay, far more than that, he was the original ancestor, not only of their nation, but of the whole race of man, and, in fact, was none other than the primal Creator himself, who fashioned the earth and gave life to all that thereon is.

Hearing all this said about such an ignoble and weak animal as the rabbit, no wonder that the early missionaries and travelers spoke of such fables with undisguised contempt, and never mentioned them without excuses for putting on record trivialities so utter.

Yet it appears to me that under these seemingly weak stories lay a profound truth, the appreciation of which was lost in great measure to the natives themselves, but which can be shown to have been in its origin a noble myth, setting forth in not unworthy images the ceaseless and mighty rhythm of nature in the alternations of day and night, summer and winter, storm and sunshine.

I shall quote a few of these stories as told by early authorities, not adding anything to relieve their crude simplicity, and then I will see whether, when submitted to the test of linguistic analysis, this unpromising ore does not yield the pure gold of genuine mythology.

The beginning of things, according to the Ottawas and other northern Algonkins, was at a period when boundless waters covered the face of the earth. On this infinite ocean floated a raft, upon which were many species of animals, the captain and chief of whom was Michabo, the Giant Rabbit. They ardently desired land on which to live, so this mighty rabbit ordered the beaver to dive and bring him up ever so little a piece of mud. The beaver obeyed, and remained down long, even so that he came up utterly exhausted, but reported that he had not reached bottom. Then the Rabbit sent down the otter, but he also returned nearly dead and without success. Great was the disappointment of the company on the raft, for what better divers had they than the beaver and the otter?

In the midst of their distress the (female) muskrat came forward and announced her willingness to make the attempt. Her proposal was received with derision, but as poor help is better than none in an emergency, the Rabbit gave her permission, and down she dived. She too remained long, very long, a whole day and night, and they gave her up for lost. But at length she floated to the surface, unconscious, her belly up, as if dead. They hastily hauled her on the raft and examined her paws one by one. In the last one of the four they found a small speck of mud. Victory! That was all that was needed. The muskrat was soon restored, and the Giant Rabbit, exerting his creative power, moulded the little fragment of soil, and as he moulded it, it grew and grew, into an island, into a mountain, into a country, into this great earth that we all dwell upon. As it grew the Rabbit walked round and round it, to see how big it was; and the story added that he is not yet satisfied; still he continues his journey and his labor, walking forever around and around the earth and ever increasing it more and more.

The animals on the raft soon found homes on the new earth. But it had yet to be covered with forests, and men were not born. The Giant Rabbit formed the trees by shooting his arrows into the soil, which became tree trunks, and, transfixing them with other arrows, these became branches; and as for men, some said he formed them from the dead bodies of certain animals, which in time became the "totems" of the Algonkin tribes; but another and probably an older and truer story was that he married the muskrat which had been of such service to him, and from this union were born the ancestors of the various races of mankind which people the earth.

Nor did he neglect the children he had thus brought into the world of his creation. Having closely studied how the spider spreads her web to catch flies, he invented the art of knitting nets for fish, and taught it to his descendants; the pieces of native copper found along the shores of Lake Superior he took from his treasure house inside the earth, where he sometimes lives. It is he who is the Master of Life, and if he appears in a dream to a person in danger, it is a certain sign of a lucky escape. He confers fortune in the chase, and therefore the hunters invoke him, and offer him tobacco and other dainties, placing them in the clefts of rocks or on isolated boulders. Though called the Giant Rabbit, he is always referred to as a man, a giant or demigod perhaps, but distinctly as of human nature, the mighty father or elder brother of the race.[1]

[1: The writers from whom I have taken this myth are Nicolas Perrot, *Memoire sur les Meurs, Coustumes et Relligion des Sauvages de l'Amerique Septentrionale*, written by an intelligent layman who lived among the natives from 1665 to 1699; and the various *Relations des Jesuites*, especially for the years 1667 and 1670.]

Such is the national myth of creation of the Algonkin tribes, as it has been handed down to us in fragments by those who first heard it. Has it any meaning? Is it more than the puerile fable of savages?

Let us see whether some of those unconscious tricks of speech to which I referred in the introductory chapter have not disfigured a true nature myth. Perhaps those common processes of language, personification and otosis, duly taken into account, will enable us to restore this narrative to its original sense.

In the Algonkin tongue the word for Giant Rabbit is *Missabos*, compounded from *mitchi* or *missi*, great, large, and *wabos*, a rabbit. But there is a whole class of related words, referring to widely different perceptions, which sound very much like *wabos*. They are from a general root *wab*, which goes to form such words of related signification as *wabi*, he sees, *waban*, the east, the Orient, *wabish*, white, *bidaban* (*bid-waban*), the dawn, *waban*, daylight, *wasseia*, the light, and many others. Here is where we are to look for the real meaning of the name *Missabos*. It originally meant the Great Light, the Mighty Seer, the Orient, the Dawn-- which you please, as all distinctly refer to the one original idea, the Bringer of Light and Sight, of knowledge and life. In time this meaning became obscured, and the idea of the rabbit, whose name was drawn probably from the same root, as in the northern winters its fur becomes white, was substituted, and so the myth of light degenerated into an animal fable.

I believe that a similar analysis will explain the part which the muskrat plays in the story. She it is who brings up the speck of mud from the bottom of the primal ocean, and from this speck the world is formed by him whom we now see was the Lord of the Light and the Day, and subsequently she becomes the mother of his sons. The word for muskrat in Algonkin is ***wajashk***, the first letter of which often suffers elision, as in ***nin nod-ajashkwe***, I hunt muskrats. But this is almost the word for mud, wet earth, soil, ***ajishki***. There is no reasonable doubt but that here again otosis and personification came in and gave the form and name of an animal to the original simple statement.

That statement was that from wet mud dried by the sunlight, the solid earth was formed; and again, that this damp soil was warmed and fertilized by the sunlight, so that from it sprang organic life, even man himself, who in so many mythologies is "the earth born," ***homo ab humo, homo chamaigenes***.[1]

[1: Mr. J. Hammond Trumbull has pointed out that in Algonkin the words for father, ***osh***, mother, ***okas***, and earth, ***ohke*** (Narraganset dialect), can all be derived, according to the regular rules of Algonkin grammar, from the same verbal root, signifying "to come out of, or from." (Note to Roger Williams' ***Key into the Language of America***, p. 56). Thus the earth was, in their language, the parent of the race, and what more natural than that it should become so in the myth also?]

This, then, is the interpretation I have to offer of the cosmogonical myth of the Algonkins. Does some one object that it is too refined for those rude savages, or that it smacks too much of reminiscences of old-world teachings? My answer is that neither the early travelers who wrote it down, nor probably the natives who told them, understood its meaning, and that not until it is here approached by modern methods of analysis, has it ever been explained. Therefore it is impossible to assign to it other than an indigenous and spontaneous origin in some remote period of Algonkin tribal history.

After the darkness of the night, man first learns his whereabouts by the light kindling in the Orient; wandering, as did the primitive man, through pathless forests, without a guide, the East became to him the first and most important of the fixed points in space; by it were located the West, the North, the South; from it spread the welcome dawn; in it was born the glorious sun; it was full of promise and of instruction; hence it became to him the home of the gods of life and light and wisdom.

As the four cardinal points are determined by fixed physical relations, common to man everywhere, and are closely associated with his daily motions and well being, they became prominent figures in almost all early myths, and were personified as divinities. The winds were classified as coming from them, and in many tongues the names of the cardinal points are the same as those of the winds that blow from them. The East, however, has, in regard to the others, a pre-eminence, for it is not merely the home of the east wind, but of the light and the dawn as well. Hence it attained a marked preponderance in the myths; it was either the greatest, wisest and oldest of the four brothers, who, by personification, represented the cardinal points and the four winds, or else the Light-God was separated from the quadruplet and appears as a fifth personage governing the other four, and being, in fact, the supreme ruler of both the spiritual and human worlds.

Such was the mental processes which took place in the Algonkin mind, and gave rise to two cycles of myths, the one representing Wabun or Michabo as one of four brothers, whose names are those of the cardinal points, the second placing him above them all.

The four brothers are prominent characters in Algonkin legend, and we shall find that they recur with extraordinary frequency in the mythology of all American nations. Indeed, I could easily point them out also in the early religious conceptions of Egypt and India, Greece and China, and many other old-world lands, but I leave these comparisons to those who wish to treat of the principles of general mythology.

According to the most generally received legend these four brothers were quadruplets--born at one birth--and their mother died in bringing them into life. Their names are given differently by the various tribes, but are usually identical with the four points of the compass, or something relating to them. Wabun the East, Kabun the West, Kabibonokka the North, and Shawano the South, are, in the ordinary language of the interpreters, the names applied to them. Wabun was the chief and leader, and assigned to his brothers their various duties, especially to blow the winds.

These were the primitive and chief divinities of the Algonkin race in all parts of the territory they inhabited. When, as early as 1610, Captain Argoll visited the tribes who then possessed the banks of the river Potomac, and inquired concerning their religion, they replied, "We have five gods in all; our chief god often appears to us in the form of a mighty great hare; the other four have no visible shape, but are indeed the four winds, which keep the four corners of the earth."[1]

[1: William Strachey, ***Historie of Travaile into Virginia***, p. 98.]

Here we see that Wabun, the East, was distinguished from Michabo (***missi-wabun***), and by a natural and transparent process, the eastern light being separated from the eastern wind, the original number four was increased to five. Precisely the same differentiation occurred, as I shall show, in Mexico, in the case of Quetzalcoatl, as shown in his ***Yoel***, or Wheel of the Winds, which was his sacred pentagram.

Or I will further illustrate this development by a myth of the Huarochiri Indians, of the coast of Peru. They related that in the beginning of things there were five eggs on the mountain Condorcoto. In due course of time these eggs opened and from them came forth five falcons, who were none other than the Creator of all things, Pariacaca, and his brothers, the four winds. By their magic power they transformed themselves into men and went about the world performing miracles, and in time became the gods of that people.[1]

[1: Doctor Francisco de Avila, ***Narrative of the Errors and False Gods of the Indians of Huarochiri*** (1608). This interesting document has been partly translated by Mr. C.B. Markham, and published in one of the volumes of the Hackluyt Society's series.]

These striking similarities show with what singular uniformity the religious sense develops itself in localities the furthest asunder.

Returning to Michabo, the duplicate nature thus assigned him as the Light-God, and also the God of the Winds and the storms and rains they bring, led to the production of two cycles of myths which present him in these two different aspects. In the one he is, as the god of light, the power that conquers the darkness, who brings warmth and sunlight to the earth and knowledge to men. He was the patron of hunters, as these require the light to guide them on their way, and must always direct their course by the cardinal points.

The morning star, which at certain seasons heralds the dawn, was sacred to him, and its name in Ojibway is ***Wabanang***, from ***Waban***, the east. The rays of light are his servants and messengers. Seated at the extreme east, "at the place where the earth is cut off," watching in his medicine lodge, or passing his time fishing in the endless ocean which on every side surrounds the land, Michabo sends forth these messengers, who, in the myth, are called *Gijigouai*, which means "those who make the day," and they light the world. He is never identified with the sun, nor was he supposed to dwell in it, but he is distinctly the impersonation of light.[1]

[1: See H.R. Schoolcraft, *Indian Tribes*, Vol. v, pp. 418, 419. *Relations des Jesuites*, 1634, p. 14, 1637, p. 46.]

In one form of the myth he is the grandson of the Moon, his father is the West Wind, and his mother, a maiden who has been fecundated miraculously by the passing breeze, dies at the moment of giving him birth. But he did not need the fostering care of a parent, for he was born mighty of limb and with all knowledge that it is possible to attain.[1] Immediately he attacked his father, and a long and desperate struggle took place. "It began on the mountains. The West was forced to give ground. His son drove him across rivers and over mountains and lakes, and at last, he came to the brink of the world. 'Hold!' cried he, 'my son, you know my power, and that it is impossible to kill me.'" The combat ceased, the West acknowledging the Supremacy of his mighty son.[2]

[1: In the Ojibway dialect of the Algonkins, the word for day, sky or heaven, is *gijig*. This same word as a verb means to be an adult, to be ripe (of fruits), to be finished, complete. Rev. Frederick Baraga, *A Dictionary of the Olchipwe Language*, Cincinnati, 1853. This seems to correspond with the statement in the myth.]

[2: H.E. Schoolcraft, *Algic Researches*, vol. i, pp. 135, et seq.]

It is scarcely possible to err in recognizing under this thin veil of imagery a description of the daily struggle between light and darkness, day and night. The maiden is the dawn from whose virgin womb rises the sun in the fullness of his glory and might, but with his advent the dawn itself disappears and dies. The battle lasts all day, beginning when the earliest rays gild the mountain tops, and continues until the West is driven to the edge of the world. As the evening precedes the morning, so the West, by a figure of speech, may be said to fertilize the Dawn.

In another form of the story the West was typified as a flint stone, and the twin brother of Michabo. The feud between them was bitter, and the contest long and dreadful. The face of the land was seamed and torn by the wrestling of the mighty combatants, and the Indians pointed out the huge boulders on the prairies as the weapons hurled at each other by the enraged brothers. At length Michabo mastered his fellow twin and broke him into pieces. He scattered the fragments over the earth, and from them grew fruitful vines.

A myth which, like this, introduces the flint stone as in some way connected with the early creative forces of nature, recurs at other localities on the American continent very remote from the home of the Algonkins. In the calendar of the Aztecs the day and god Tecpatl, the Flint-Stone, held a prominent position. According to their myths such a stone fell from heaven at the beginning of things and broke into sixteen hundred pieces, each of which became a god. The Hun-pic-tok, Eight Thousand Flints, of the Mayas, and the Toh of the Kiches, point to the same association.[1]

[1: Brasseur de Bourbourg, ***Dissertation sur les Mythes de l'Antiquite Americaine***, Sec.vii.]

Probably the association of ideas was not with the flint as a fire-stone, though the fact that a piece of flint struck with a nodule of pyrites will emit a spark was not unknown. But the flint was everywhere employed for arrow and lance heads. The flashes of light, the lightning, anything that darted swiftly and struck violently, was compared to the hurtling arrow or the whizzing lance. Especially did this apply to the phenomenon of the lightning. The belief that a stone is shot from the sky with each thunderclap is shown in our word "thunderbolt," and even yet the vulgar in many countries point out certain forms of stones as derived from this source. As the refreshing rain which accompanies the thunder gust instills new life into vegetation, and covers the ground parched by summer droughts with leaves and grass, so the statement in the myth that the fragments of the flint-stone grew into fruitful vines is an obvious figure of speech which at first expressed the fertilizing effects of the summer showers.

In this myth Michabo, the Light-God, was represented to the native mind as still fighting with the powers of Darkness, not now the darkness of night, but that of the heavy and gloomy clouds which roll up the sky and blind the eye of day. His weapons are the lightning and the thunderbolt, and the victory he achieves is turned to the good of the world he has created.

This is still more clearly set forth in an Ojibway myth. It relates that in early days there was a mighty serpent, king of all serpents, whose home was in the Great Lakes. Increasing the waters by his magic powers, he began to flood the land, and threatened its total submergence. Then Michabo rose from his couch at the sun-rising, attacked the huge reptile and slew it by a cast of his dart. He stripped it of its skin, and clothing himself in this trophy of conquest, drove all the other serpents to the south.[1] As it is in the south that, in the country of the Ojibways, the lightning is last seen in the autumn, and as the Algonkins, both in their language and pictography, were accustomed to assimilate the lightning in its zigzag course to the sinuous motion of the serpent,[2] the meteorological character of this myth is very manifest.

[1: H.R. Schoolcraft, *Algic Researches*, Vol. i, p. 179, Vol. ii, p. 117. The word *animikig* in Ojibway means "it thunders and lightnings;" in their myths this tribe says that the West Wind is created by Animiki, the Thunder. (Ibid. *Indian Tribes*, Vol. v, p. 420.)]

[2: When Father Buteux was among the Algonkins, in 1637, they explained to him the lightning as "a great serpent which the Manito vomits up." (*Relation de la Nouvelle France*, An. 1637, p. 53.) According to John Tanner, the symbol for the lightning in Ojibway pictography was a rattlesnake. (*Narrative*, p. 351.)]

Thus we see that Michabo, the hero-god of the Algonkins, was both the god of light and day, of the winds and rains, and the creator, instructor and teacher of mankind. The derivation of his name shows unmistakably that the earliest form under which he was a mythological existence was as the light-god. Later he became more familiar as god of the winds and storms, the hero of the celestial warfare of the air-currents.

This is precisely the same change which we are enabled to trace in the early transformations of Aryan religion. There, also, the older god of the sky and light, Dyaus, once common to all members of the Indo-European family, gave way to the more active deities, Indra, Zeus and Odin, divinities of the storm and the wind, but which, after all, are merely other aspects of the ancient deity, and occupied his place to the religious sense.[1] It is essential, for the comprehension of early mythology, to understand this twofold character, and to appreciate how naturally the one merges into and springs out of the other.

[1: This transformation is well set forth in Mr. Charles Francis Keary's *Outlines of Primitive Belief Among the Indo-European Races* (London, 1882), chaps, iv, vii. He observes: "The wind is a far more physical and less abstract conception than the sky or heaven; it is also a more variable phenomenon; and by reason of both these recommendations the wind-god superseded the older Dyaus. * * * Just as the chief god of Greece, having descended to be a divinity of storm, was not content to remain only that, but grew again to some likeness of the older Dyaus, so Odhinn came to absorb almost all the qualities which belong of right to a higher god. Yet he did this without putting off his proper nature. He was the heaven as well as the wind; he was the All-father, embracing all the earth and looking down upon mankind."]

In almost every known religion the *bird* is taken as a symbol of the sky, the clouds and the winds. It is not surprising, therefore, to find that by the Algonkins birds were considered, especially singing birds, as peculiarly sacred to Michabo. He was their father and protector. He himself sent forth the east wind from his home at the sun-rising; but he appointed an owl to create the north wind, which blows from the realms of darkness and cold; while that which is wafted from the sunny south is sent by the butterfly.[1]

[1: H.R. Schoolcraft, *Algic Researches*, Vol. i, p. 216. *Indian Tribes*, Vol. v, p. 420.]

Michabo was thus at times the god of light, at others of the winds, and as these are the rain-bringers, he was also at times spoken of as the god of waters. He was said to have scooped out the basins of the lakes and to have built the cataracts in the rivers, so that there should be fish preserves and beaver dams.[1]

[1: "Michabou, le Dieu des Eaux," etc. Charlevoix, *Journal Historique*, p. 281 (Paris, 1721).]

In his capacity as teacher and instructor, it was he who had pointed out to the ancestors of the Indians the roots and plants which are fit for food, and which are of value as medicine; he gave them fire, and recommended them never to allow it to become wholly extinguished in their villages; the sacred rites of what is called the *meday* or ordinary religious ceremonial were defined and taught by him; the maize was his gift, and the pleasant art of smoking was his invention.[1]

[1: John Tanner, *Narrative of Captivity and Adventure*, p. 351. Schoolcraft, *Indian Tribes*, Vol. v, p. 420, etc.]

A curious addition to the story was told the early Swedish settlers on the river Delaware by the Algonkin tribe which inhabited its shores. These related that their various arts of domestic life and the chase were taught them long ago by a venerable and eloquent man who came to them from a distance, and having instructed them in what was desirable for them to know, he departed, not to another region or by the natural course of death, but by ascending into the sky. They added that this ancient and beneficent teacher **wore a long beard**.[1] We might suspect that this last trait was thought of after the bearded Europeans had been seen, did it not occur so often in myths elsewhere on the continent, and in relics of art finished long before the discovery, that another explanation must be found for it. What this is I shall discuss when I come to speak of the more Southern myths, whose heroes were often "white and bearded men from the East."

[1: Thomas Campanius (Holm), **Description of the Province of New Sweden**, book iii, ch. xi. Campanius does not give the name of the hero-god, but there can be no doubt that it was the "Great Hare."]

Sec.2. *The Iroquois Myth of Ioskeha.*[1]

[1: The sources from which I draw the elements of the Iroquois hero-myth of Ioskeha are mainly the following: **Relations de la Nouvelle France**, 1636, 1640, 1671, etc. Sagard, **Histoire du Canada**, pp. 451, 452 (Paris, 1636); David Cusick, **Ancient History of the Six Nations**, and manuscript material kindly furnished me by Horatio Hale, Esq., who has made a thorough study of the Iroquois history and dialects.]

The most ancient myth of the Iroquois represents this earth as covered with water, in which dwelt aquatic animals and monsters of the deep. Far above it were the heavens, peopled by supernatural beings. At a certain time one of these, a woman, by name Ataensic, threw herself through a rift in the sky and fell toward the earth. What led her to this act was variously recorded. Some said that it was to recover her dog which had fallen through while chasing a bear. Others related that those who dwelt in the world above lived off the fruit of a certain tree; that the husband of Ataensic, being sick, dreamed that to restore him this tree must be cut down; and that when Ataensic dealt it a blow with her stone axe, the tree suddenly sank through the floor of the sky, and she precipitated herself after it.

However the event occurred, she fell from heaven down to the primeval waters. There a turtle offered her his broad back as a resting-place until, from a little mud which was brought her, either by a frog, a beaver or some other animal, she, by magic power, formed dry land on which to reside.

At the time she fell from the sky she was pregnant, and in due time was delivered of a daughter, whose name, unfortunately, the legend does not record. This daughter grew to womanhood and conceived without having seen a man, for none was as yet created. The product of her womb was twins, and even before birth one of them betrayed his restless and evil nature, by refusing to be born in the usual manner, but insisting on breaking through his parent's side (or armpit). He did so, but it cost his mother her life. Her body was buried, and from it sprang the various vegetable productions which the new earth required to fit it for the habitation of man. From her head grew the pumpkin vine; from her breast, the maize; from her limbs, the bean and other useful esculents.

Meanwhile the two brothers grew up. The one was named Ioskeha. He went about the earth, which at that time was arid and waterless, and called forth the springs and lakes, and formed the sparkling brooks and broad rivers. But his brother, the troublesome Tawiscara, he whose obstinacy had caused their mother's death, created an immense frog which swallowed all the water and left the earth as dry as before. Ioskeha was informed of this by the partridge, and immediately set out for his brother's country, for they had divided the earth between them.

Soon he came to the gigantic frog, and piercing it in the side (or armpit), the waters flowed out once more in their accustomed ways. Then it was revealed to Ioskeha by his mother's spirit that Tawiscara intended to slay him by treachery. Therefore, when the brothers met, as they soon did, it was evident that a mortal combat was to begin.

Now, they were not men, but gods, whom it was impossible really to kill, nor even could either be seemingly slain, except by one particular substance, a secret which each had in his own keeping. As therefore a contest with ordinary weapons would have been vain and unavailing, they agreed to tell each other what to each was the fatal implement of war. Ioskeha acknowledged that to him a branch of the wild rose (or, according to another version, a bag filled with maize) was more dangerous than anything else; and Tawiscara disclosed that the horn of a deer could alone reach his vital part.

They laid off the lists, and Tawiscara, having the first chance, attacked his brother violently with a branch of the wild rose, and beat him till he lay as one dead; but quickly reviving, Ioskeha assaulted Tawiscara with the antler of a deer, and dealing him a blow in the side, the blood flowed from the wound in streams.

The unlucky combatant fled from the field, hastening toward the west, and as he ran the drops of his blood which fell upon the earth turned into flint stones. Ioskeha did not spare him, but hastening after, finally slew him. He did not, however, actually kill him, for, as I have said, these were beings who could not die; and, in fact, Tawiscara was merely driven from the earth and forced to reside in the far west, where he became ruler of the spirits of the dead. These go there to dwell when they leave the bodies behind them here.

Ioskeha, returning, peaceably devoted himself to peopling the land. He opened a cave which existed in the earth and allowed to come forth from it all the varieties of animals with which the woods and prairies are peopled. In order that they might be more easily caught by men, he wounded every one in the foot except the wolf, which dodged his blow; for that reason this beast is one of the most difficult to catch. He then formed men and gave them life, and instructed them in the art of making fire, which he himself had learned from the great tortoise. Furthermore he taught them how to raise maize, and it is, in fact, Ioskeha himself who imparts fertility to the soil, and through his bounty and kindness the grain returns a hundred fold.

Nor did they suppose that he was a distant, invisible, unapproachable god. No, he was ever at hand with instruction and assistance. Was there to be a failure in the harvest, he would be seen early in the season, thin with anxiety about his people, holding in his hand a blighted ear of corn. Did a hunter go out after game, he asked the aid of Ioskeha, who would put fat animals in the way, were he so minded. At their village festivals he was present and partook of the cheer.

Once, in 1640, when the smallpox was desolating the villages of the Hurons, we are told by Father Lalemant that an Indian said there had appeared to him a beautiful youth, of imposing stature, and addressed him with these words: "Have no fear; I am the master of the earth, whom you Hurons adore under the name *Ioskeha*. The French wrongly call me Jesus, because they do not know me. It grieves me to see the pestilence that is destroying my people, and I come to teach you its cause and its remedy. Its cause is the presence of these strangers; and its remedy is to drive out these black robes (the missionaries), to drink of a certain water which I shall tell you of, and to hold a festival in my honor, which must be kept up all night, until the dawn of day."

The home of Ioskeha is in the far East, at that part of the horizon where the sun rises. There he has his cabin, and there he dwells with his grandmother, the wise Ataensic. She is a woman of marvelous magical power, and is capable of assuming any shape she pleases. In her hands is the fate of all men's lives, and while Ioskeha looks after the things of life, it is she who appoints the time of death, and concerns herself with all that relates to the close of existence. Hence she was feared, not exactly as a maleficent deity, but as one whose business is with what is most dreaded and gloomy.

It was said that on a certain occasion four bold young men determined to journey to the sun-rising and visit the great Ioskeha. They reached his cabin and found him there alone. He received them affably and they conversed pleasantly, but at a certain moment he bade them hide themselves for their life, as his grandmother was coming. They hastily concealed themselves, and immediately Ataensic entered. Her magic insight had warned her of the presence of guests, and she had assumed the form of a beautiful girl, dressed in gay raiment, her neck and arms resplendent with collars and bracelets of wampum. She inquired for the guests, but Ioskeha, anxious to save them, dissembled, and replied that he knew not what she meant. She went forth to search for them, when he called them forth from their hiding place and bade them flee, and thus they escaped.

It was said of Ioskeha that he acted the part of husband to his grandmother. In other words, the myth presents the germ of that conception which the priests of ancient Egypt endeavored to express when they taught that Osiris was "his own father and his own son," that he was the "self-generating one," even that he was "the father of his own mother." These are grossly materialistic expressions, but they are perfectly clear to the student of mythology. They are meant to convey to the mind the self-renewing power of life in nature, which is exemplified in the sowing and the seeding, the winter and the summer, the dry and the rainy seasons, and especially the sunset and sunrise. They are echoes in the soul of man of the ceaseless rhythm in the operations of nature, and they become the only guarantors of his hopes for immortal life.[1]

[1: Such epithets were common, in the Egyptian religion, to most of the gods of fertility. Amun, called in some of the inscriptions "the soul of Osiris," derives his name from the root *men*, to impregnate, to beget. In the Karnak inscriptions he is also termed "the husband of his mother." This, too, was the favorite appellation of Chem, who was a form of Horos. See Dr. C.P. Tiele, ***History of the Egyptian Religion***, pp. 124, 146. 149, 150, etc.]

Let us look at the names in the myth before us, for confirmation of this. ***Ioskeha*** is in the Oneida dialect of the Iroquois an impersonal verbal form of the third person singular, and means literally, "it is about to grow white," that is, to become light, to dawn. ***Ataensic*** is from the root ***aouen***, water, and means literally, "she who is in the water."[1] Plainly expressed, the sense of the story is that the orb of light rises daily out of the boundless waters which are supposed to surround the land, preceded by the dawn, which fades away as soon as the sun has risen. Each day the sun disappears in these waters, to rise again from them the succeeding morning. As the approach of the sun causes the dawn, it was merely a gross way of stating this to say that the solar god was the father of his own mother, the husband of his grandmother.

[1: I have analyzed these words in a note to another work, and need not repeat the matter here, the less so, as I am not aware that the etymology has been questioned. See ***Myths of the New World***, 2d Ed., p. 183, note.]

The position of Ioskeha in mythology is also shown by the other name under which he was, perhaps, even more familiar to most of the Iroquois. This is ***Tharonhiawakon***, which is also a verbal form of the third person, with the dual sign, and literally means, "He holds (or holds up) the sky with his two arms."[1] In other words, he is nearly allied to the ancient Aryan Dyaus, the Sky, the Heavens, especially the Sky in the daytime.

[1: A careful analysis of this name is given by Father J.A. Cuoq, probably the best living authority on the Iroquois, in his ***Lexique de la Langue Iroquoise***, p. 180 (Montreal, 1882). Here also the Iroquois followed precisely the line of thought of the ancient Egyptians. Shu, in the religion of Heliopolis, represented the cosmic light and warmth, the quickening, creative principle. It is he who, as it is stated in the inscriptions, "holds up the heavens," and he is depicted on the monuments as a man with uplifted arms who supports the vault of heaven, because it is the intermediate light that separates the earth from the sky. Shu was also god of the winds; in a passage of the Book of the Dead, he is made to say: "I am Shu, who drives the winds onward to the confines of heaven, to the confines of the earth, even to the confines of space." Again, like Ioskeha, Shu is said to have begotten himself in the womb of his mother, Nu or Nun, who was, like Ataensic, the goddess of water, the heavenly ocean, the primal sea. Tiele, *History of the Egyptian Religion*, pp. 84-86.]

The signification of the conflict with his twin brother is also clearly seen in the two names which the latter likewise bears in the legends. One of these is that which I have given, *Tawiscara*, which, there is little doubt, is allied to the root, *tiokaras*, it grows dark. The other is *Tehotennhiaron*, the root word of which is *kannhia*, the flint stone. This name he received because, in his battle with his brother, the drops of blood which fell from his wounds were changed into flints.[1] Here the flint had the same meaning which I have already pointed out in Algonkin myth, and we find, therefore, an absolute identity of mythological conception and symbolism between the two nations.

[1: Cuoq, *Lexique de la Langue Iroquoise*, p. 180, who gives a full analysis of the name.]

Could these myths have been historically identical? It is hard to disbelieve it. Yet the nations were bitter enemies. Their languages are totally unlike. These same similarities present themselves over such wide areas and between nations so remote and of such different culture, that the theory of a parallelism of development is after all the more credible explanation.

The impressions which natural occurrences make on minds of equal stages of culture are very much alike. The same thoughts are evoked, and the same expressions suggest themselves as appropriate to convey these thoughts in spoken language. This is often exhibited in the identity of expression between master-poets of the same generation, and between cotemporaneous thinkers in all branches of knowledge. Still more likely is it to occur in primitive and uncultivated conditions, where the most obvious forms of expression are at once adopted, and the resources of the mind are necessarily limited. This is a simple and reasonable explanation for the remarkable sameness which prevails in the mental products of the lower stages of civilization, and does away with the necessity of supposing a historic derivation one from the other or both from a common stock.

CHAPTER III.
THE HERO-GOD OF THE AZTEC TRIBES.

THE WINDS, THE PENTAGON AND THE CROSS--CLOSE RELATION TO THE GODS OF RAIN AND WATERS--INVENTOR OF THE CALENDAR--GOD OF FERTILITY AND CONCEPTION--RECOMMENDS SEXUAL AUSTERITY--PHALLIC SYMBOLS--GOD OF MERCHANTS--THE PATRON OF THIEVES--HIS PICTOGRAPHIC REPRESENTATIONS.

Sec.5. *The Return of Quetzalcoatl.*
HIS EXPECTED RE-APPEARANCE--THE ANXIETY OF MONTEZUMA--HIS ADDRESS TO CORTES--THE GENERAL EXPECTATION--EXPLANATION OF HIS PREDICTED RETURN.

I now turn from the wild hunting tribes who peopled the shores of the Great Lakes and the fastnesses of the northern forests to that cultivated race whose capital city was in the Valley of Mexico, and whose scattered colonies were found on the shores of both oceans from the mouths of the Rio Grande and the Gila, south, almost to the Isthmus of Panama. They are familiarly known as Aztecs or Mexicans, and the language common to them all was the *Nahuatl*, a word of their own, meaning "the pleasant sounding."

Their mythology has been preserved in greater fullness than that of any other American people, and for this reason I am enabled to set forth in ampler detail the elements of their hero-myth, which, indeed, may be taken as the most perfect type of those I have collected in this volume.

Sec.1. *The Two Antagonists.*
The culture hero of the Aztecs was Quetzalcoatl, and the leading drama, the central myth, in all the extensive and intricate theology of the Nahuatl speaking tribes was his long contest with Tezcatlipoca, "a contest," observes an eminent Mexican antiquary, "which came to be the main element in the Nahuatl religion and the cause of its modifications, and which materially influenced the destinies of that race from its earliest epochs to the time of its destruction."[1]

[1: Alfredo Chavero, *La Piedra del Sol*, in the *Anales del Museo Nacional de Mexico*, Tom. II, p. 247.]

The explanations which have been offered of this struggle have varied with the theories of the writers propounding them. It has been regarded as a simple historical fact; as a figure of speech to represent the struggle for supremacy between two races; as an astronomical statement referring to the relative positions of the planet Venus and the Moon; as a conflict between Christianity, introduced by Saint Thomas, and the native heathenism; and as having other meanings not less unsatisfactory or absurd.

Placing it side by side with other American hero-myths, we shall see that it presents essentially the same traits, and undoubtedly must be explained in the same manner. All of them are the transparent stories of a simple people, to express in intelligible terms the daily struggle that is ever going on between Day and Night, between Light and Darkness, between Storm and Sunshine.

Like all the heroes of light, Quetzalcoatl is identified with the East. He is born there, and arrives from there, and hence Las Casas and others speak of him as from Yucatan, or as landing on the shores of the Mexican Gulf from some unknown land. His day of birth was that called Ce Acatl, One Reed, and by this name he is often known. But this sign is that of the East in Aztec symbolism.[1] In a myth of the formation of the sun and moon, presented by Sahagun,[2] a voluntary victim springs into the sacrificial fire that the gods have built. They know that he will rise as the sun, but they do not know in what part of the horizon that will be. Some look one way, some another, but Quetzalcoatl watches steadily the East, and is the first to see and welcome the Orb of Light. He is fair in complexion, with abundant hair and a full beard, bordering on the red,[3] as are all the dawn heroes, and like them he was an instructor in the arts, and favored peace and mild laws.

[1: Chavero, ***Anales del Museo Nacional de Mexico***, Tom. II, p. 14, 243.]

[2: ***Historia de las Cosas de Nueva Espana***, Lib. VII, cap. II.]

[3: "La barba longa entre cana y roja; el cabello largo, muy llano." Diego Duran, ***Historia***, in Kingsborough, Vol. viii, p. 260.]

His name is symbolic, and is capable of several equally fair renderings. The first part of it, ***quetzalli***, means literally a large, handsome green feather, such as were very highly prized by the natives. Hence it came to mean, in an adjective sense, precious, beautiful, beloved, admirable. The bird from which these feathers were obtained was the ***quetzal-tototl*** (***tototl***, bird) and is called by ornithologists ***Trogon splendens***.

The latter part of the name, ***coatl***, has in Aztec three entirely different meanings. It means a guest, also twins, and lastly, as a syncopated form of ***cohuatl***, a serpent. Metaphorically, *cohuatl* meant something mysterious, and hence a supernatural being, a god. Thus Montezuma, when he built a temple in the city of Mexico dedicated to the whole body of divinities, a regular Pantheon, named it *Coatecalli*, the House of the Serpent.[1]

[1: "Coatecalli, que quiere decir el *templo de la culebra*, que sin metafora quiere decir *templo de diversos dioses*." Duran, *Historia de las Indias de Nueva Espana*, cap. LVIII.]

Through these various meanings a good defence can be made of several different translations of the name, and probably it bore even to the natives different meanings at different times. I am inclined to believe that the original sense was that advocated by Becerra in the seventeenth century, and adopted by Veitia in the eighteenth, both competent Aztec scholars.[1] They translate Quetzalcoatl as "the admirable twin," and though their notion that this refers to Thomas Didymus, the Apostle, does not meet my views, I believe they were right in their etymology. The reference is to the duplicate nature of the Light-God as seen in the setting and rising sun, the sun of to-day and yesterday, the same yet different. This has its parallels in many other mythologies.[2]

[1: Becerra, *Felicidad de Mejico*, 1685, quoted in Veitia, *Historia del Origen de las Gentes que poblaron la America Septentrional*, cap. XIX.]

[2: In the Egyptian "Book of the Dead," Ra, the Sun-God, says, "I am a soul and its twins," or, "My soul is becoming two twins." "This means that the soul of the sun-god is one, but, now that it is born again, it divides into two principal forms. Ra was worshipped at An, under his two prominent manifestations, as Tum the primal god, or more definitely, god of the sun at evening, and as Harmachis, god of the new sun, the sun at dawn." Tiele, *History of the Egyptian Religion*, p. 80.]

The correctness of this supposition seems to be shown by a prevailing superstition among the Aztecs about twins, and which strikingly illustrates the uniformity of mythological conceptions throughout the world. All readers are familiar with the twins Romulus and Remus in Roman story, one of whom was fated to destroy their grandfather Amulius; with Edipus and Telephos, whose father Laios, was warned that his death would be by one of his children; with Theseus and Peirithoos, the former destined to cause the suicide of his father Aigeus; and with many more such myths. They can be traced, without room for doubt, back to simple expressions of the fact that the morning and the evening of the one day can only come when the previous day is past and gone; expressed figuratively by the statement that any one day must destroy its predecessor. This led to the stories of "the fatal children," which we find so frequent in Aryan mythology.[1]

[1: Sir George W. Cox, *The Science of Comparative Mythology and Folk Lore*, pp. 14, 83, 130, etc.]

The Aztecs were a coarse and bloody race, and carried out their superstitions without remorse. Based, no doubt, on this mythical expression of a natural occurrence, they had the belief that if twins were allowed to live, one or the other of them would kill and eat his father or mother; therefore, it was their custom when such were brought into the world to destroy one of them.[1]

[1: Geronimo de Mendieta, *Historia Eclesiastica Indiana*. Lib. II, cap. XIX.]

We shall see that, as in Algonkin story Michabo strove to slay his father, the West Wind, so Quetzalcoatl was in constant warfare with his father, Tezcatlipoca-Camaxtli, the Spirit of Darkness. The effect of this oft-repeated myth on the minds of the superstitious natives was to lead them to the brutal child murder I have mentioned.

It was, however, natural that the more ordinary meaning, "the feathered or bird-serpent," should become popular, and in the picture writing some combination of the serpent with feathers or other part of a bird was often employed as the rebus of the name Quetzalcoatl.

He was also known by other names, as, like all the prominent gods in early mythologies, he had various titles according to the special attribute or function which was uppermost in the mind of the worshipper. One of these was *Papachtic*, He of the Flowing Locks, a word which the Spaniards shortened to Papa, and thought was akin to their title of the Pope. It is, however, a pure Nahuatl word,[1] and refers to the abundant hair with which he was always credited, and which, like his ample beard, was, in fact, the symbol of the sun's rays, the aureole or glory of light which surrounded his face.

[1: "*Papachtic*, guedejudo; *Papachtli*, guedeja o vedija de capellos, o de otra cosa assi." Molina, *Vocabulario de la Lengua Mexicana*. sub voce. Juan de Tobar, in Kingsborough, Vol. viii, p. 259, note.]

His fair complexion was, as usual, significant of light. This association of ideas was so familiar among the Mexicans that at the time of an eclipse of the sun they sought out the whitest men and women they could find, and sacrificed them, in order to pacify the sun.[1]

[1: Mendieta, *Historia Eclesiastica Indiana*, Lib. ii, cap. xvi.]

His opponent, Tezcatlipoca, was the most sublime figure in the Aztec Pantheon. He towered above all other gods, as did Jove in Olympus. He was appealed to as the creator of heaven and earth, as present in every place, as the sole ruler of the world, as invisible and omniscient.

The numerous titles by which he was addressed illustrate the veneration in which he was held. His most common name in prayers was *Titlacauan*, We are his Slaves. As believed to be eternally young, he was Telpochtli, the Youth; as potent and unpersuadable, he was *Moyocoyatzin*, the Determined Doer;[1] as exacting in worship, *Monenegui*, He who Demands Prayers; as the master of the race, *Teyocoyani*, Creator of Men, and *Teimatini*, Disposer of Men. As he was jealous and terrible, the god who visited on men plagues, and famines, and loathsome diseases, the dreadful deity who incited wars and fomented discord, he was named *Yaotzin*, the Arch Enemy, *Yaotl necoc*, the Enemy of both Sides, *Moquequeloa*, the Mocker, *Nezaualpilli*, the Lord who Fasts, *Tlamatzincatl*, He who Enforces Penitence; and as dark, invisible and inscrutable, he was *Yoalli ehecatl*, the Night Wind.[2]

[1: *Moyocoyatzin*, is the third person singular of *yocoya*, to do, to make, with the reverential termination *tzin*. Sahagun says this title was given him because he could do what he pleased, on earth or in heaven, and no one could prevent him. (Historia de Nueva Espana, Lib. III. cap. II.) It seems to me that it would rather refer to his demiurgic, creative power.]

[2: All these titles are to be found in Sahagun, *Historia de Nueva Espana*.]

He was said to be formed of thin air and darkness; and when he was seen of men it was as a shadow without substance. He alone of all the gods defied the assaults of time, was ever young and strong, and grew not old with years.[1] Against such an enemy who could hope for victory?

[1: The description of Clavigero is worth quoting: "TEZCATLIPOCA: Questo era il maggior Dio, che in que paesi si adorava, dopo il Dio invisible, o Supremo Essere. Era il Dio della Providenza, l' anima del Mondo, il Creator del Cielo e della

Terra, ed il Signor di tutle le cose. Rappresentavanlo tuttora giovane per significare, che non s' invecchiava mai, ne s' indeboliva cogli anni." **Storia Antica di Messico**, Lib. vi, p. 7.]

The name "Tezcatlipoca" is one of odd significance. It means The Smoking Mirror. This strange metaphor has received various explanations. The mirrors in use among the Aztecs were polished plates of obsidian, trimmed to a circular form. There was a variety of this black stone called ***tezcapoctli***, smoky mirror stone, and from this his images were at times made.[1] This, however, seems too trivial an explanation.

[1: Sahagun, **Historia**, Lib. ii, cap. xxxvii.]

Others have contended that Tezcatlipoca, as undoubtedly the spirit of darkness and the night, refers, in its meaning, to the moon, which hangs like a bright round mirror in the sky, though partly dulled by what the natives thought a smoke.[1]

[1: **Anales del Museo Nacional**, Tom. ii, p. 257.]

I am inclined to believe, however, that the mirror referred to is that first and most familiar of all, the surface of water: and that the smoke is the mist which at night rises from lake and river, as actual smoke does in the still air.

As presiding over the darkness and the night, dreams and the phantoms of the gloom were supposed to be sent by Tezcatlipoca, and to him were sacred those animals which prowl about at night, as the skunk and the coyote.[1]

[1: Sahagun, **Historia**. Lib. vi, caps. ix, xi, xii.]

Thus his names, his various attributes, his sacred animals and his myths unite in identifying this deity as a primitive personification of the Darkness, whether that of the storm or of the night.[1]

[1: Senor Alfredo Chavero believes Tezcatlipoca to have been originally the moon, and there is little doubt at times this was one of his symbols, as the ruler of the darkness. M. Girard de Rialle, on the other hand, claims him as a solar deity. "Il est la personnification du soleil sous son aspect corrupteur et destructeur, ennemi des hommes et de la nature." **La Mythologie Comparee**, p. 334 (Paris, 1878). A closer study of the original authorities would, I am sure, have led M. de Rialle to change this opinion. He is singularly far from the conclusion reached by M. Ternaux-Compans, who says: "Tezcatlipoca fut la personnification du bon principe." **Essai sur la Theogonie Mexicaine**, p. 23 (Paris, 1840). Both opinions are equally incomplete.

Dr. Schultz-Sellack considers him the "Wassergott," and assigns him to the North, in his essay, ***Die Amerikanischen Goetter der Vier Weltgegenden, Zeitschrift fuer Ethnologie***, Bd. xi, 1879. This approaches more closely to his true character.]

This is further shown by the beliefs current as to his occasional appearance on earth. This was always at night and in the gloom of the forest. The hunter would hear a sound like the crash of falling trees, which would be nothing else than the mighty breathings of the giant form of the god on his nocturnal rambles. Were the hunter timorous he would die outright on seeing the terrific presence of the god; but were he of undaunted heart, and should rush upon him and seize him around the waist, the god was helpless and would grant him anything he wished. "Ask what you please," the captive deity would say, "and it is yours. Only fail not to release me before the sun rises. For I must leave before it appears."[1]

[1: Torquemada, ***Monarquia Indiana***, Lib. XIV, cap. XXII.]

Sec.2. ***Quetzalcoatl the God.***

In the ancient and purely mythical narrative, Quetzalcoatl is one of four divine brothers, gods like himself, born in the uttermost or thirteenth heaven to the infinite and uncreated deity, which, in its male manifestations, was known as ***Tonaca tecutli***, Lord of our Existence, and ***Tzin teotl***, God of the Beginning, and in its female expressions as ***Tonaca cihuatl***, Queen of our Existence, ***Xochiquetzal***, Beautiful Rose, ***Citlallicue***, the Star-skirted or the Milky Way, ***Citlalatonac***, the Star that warms, or The Morning, and ***Chicome coatl***, the Seven Serpents.[1]

[1: The chief authorities on the birth of the god Quetzalcoatl, are Ramirez de Fuen-leal ***Historia de los Mexicanos por sus Pinturas***, Cap. i, printed in the ***Anales del Museo Nacional***; the ***Codex Telleriano-Remensis***, and the ***Codex Vaticanus***, both of which are in Kingsborough's ***Mexican Antiquities***.

The usual translation of ***Tonaca tecutli*** is "God of our Subsistence," ***to***, our, ***naca***, flesh, ***tecutli***, chief or lord. It really has a more subtle meaning. ***Naca*** is not applied to edible flesh--that is expressed by the word ***nonoac***--but is the flesh of our own bodies, our life, existence. See ***Anales de Cuauhtitlan***, p. 18, note.]

Of these four brothers, two were the black and the red Tezcatlipoca, and the fourth was Huitzilopochtli, the Left handed, the deity adored beyond all others in the city of Mexico. Tezcatlipoca--for the two of the name blend rapidly into one as the myth progresses--was wise beyond compute; he knew all thoughts and hearts, could see to all places, and was distinguished for power and forethought.

At a certain time the four brothers gathered together and consulted concerning the creation of things. The work was left to Quetzalcoatl and Huitzilopochtli. First they made fire, then half a sun, the heavens, the waters and a certain great fish therein, called Cipactli, and from its flesh the solid earth. The first mortals were the man, Cipactonal, and the woman, Oxomuco,[1] and that the son born to them might have a wife, the four gods made one for him out of a hair taken from the head of their divine mother, Xochiquetzal.

[1: The names Cipactli and Cipactonal have not been satisfactorily analyzed. The derivation offered by Senor Chavero (***Anales del Museo Nacional***, Tom. ii, p.116), is merely fanciful; ***tonal*** is no doubt from ***tona***, to shine, to warn; and I think ***cipactli*** is a softened form with the personal ending from ***chipauac***, something beautiful or clear. Hence the meaning of the compound is The Beautiful Shining One. Oxomuco, which Chavero derives from ***xomitl***, foot, is perhaps the same as ***Xmukane***, the mother of the human race, according to the ***Popol Vuh***, a name which, I have elsewhere shown, appears to be from a Maya root, meaning to conceal or bury in the ground. The hint is of the fertilizing action of the warm light on the seed hidden in the soil. See ***The Names of the Gods in the Kiche Myths, Trans. of the Amer. Phil. Soc.*** 1881.]

Now began the struggle between the two brothers, Tezcatlipoca and Quetzalcoatl, which was destined to destroy time after time the world, with all its inhabitants, and to plunge even the heavenly luminaries into a common ruin.

The half sun created by Quetzalcoatl lighted the world but poorly, and the four gods came together to consult about adding another half to it. Not waiting for their decision, Tezcatlipoca transformed himself into a sun, whereupon the other gods filled the world with great giants, who could tear up trees with their hands. When an epoch of thirteen times fifty-two years had passed, Quetzalcoatl seized a great stick, and with a blow of it knocked Tezcatlipoca from the sky into the waters, and himself became sun. The fallen god transformed himself into a tiger, and emerged from the waves to attack and devour the giants with which his brothers had enviously filled the world which he had been lighting from the sky. After this, he passed to the nocturnal heavens, and became the constellation of the Great Bear.

For an epoch the earth flourished under Quetzalcoatl as sun, but Tezcatlipoca was merely biding his time, and the epoch ended, he appeared as a tiger and gave Quetzalcoatl such a blow with his paw that it hurled him from the skies. The overthrown god revenged himself by sweeping the earth with so violent a tornado that it destroyed all the inhabitants but a few, and these were changed into monkeys. His victorious brother then placed in the heavens, as sun, Tlaloc, the god of darkness, water and rains, but after half an epoch, Quetzalcoatl poured a flood of fire upon the earth, drove Tlaloc from the sky, and placed in his stead, as sun, the goddess Chalchiutlicue, the Emerald Skirted, wife of Tlaloc. In her time the rains poured so upon the earth that all human beings were drowned or changed into fishes, and at last the heavens themselves fell, and sun and stars were alike quenched.

Then the two brothers whose strife had brought this ruin, united their efforts and raised again the sky, resting it on two mighty trees, the Tree of the Mirror (*tezcaquahuitl*) and the Beautiful Great Rose Tree (*quetzalveixochitl*), on which the concave heavens have ever since securely rested; though we know them better, perhaps, if we drop the metaphor and call them the "mirroring sea" and the "flowery earth," on one of which reposes the horizon, in whichever direction we may look.

Again the four brothers met together to provide a sun for the now darkened earth. They decided to make one, indeed, but such a one as would eat the hearts and drink the blood of victims, and there must be wars upon the earth, that these victims could be obtained for the sacrifice. Then Quetzalcoatl builded a great fire and took his son--his son born of his own flesh, without the aid of woman--and cast him into the flames, whence he rose into the sky as the sun which lights the world. When the Light-God kindles the flames of the dawn in the orient sky, shortly the sun emerges from below the horizon and ascends the heavens. Tlaloc, god of waters, followed, and into the glowing ashes of the pyre threw his son, who rose as the moon.

Tezcatlipoca had it now in mind to people the earth, and he, therefore, smote a certain rock with a stick, and from it issued four hundred barbarians (*chichimeca*). [1] Certain five goddesses, however, whom he had already created in the eighth heaven, descended and slew these four hundred, all but three. These goddesses likewise died before the sun appeared, but came into being again from the garments they had left behind. So also did the four hundred Chichimecs, and these set about to burn one of the five goddesses, by name Coatlicue, the Serpent Skirted, because it was discovered that she was with child, though yet unmarried. But, in fact, she was a spotless virgin, and had known no man. She had placed some white plumes in her bosom, and through these the god Huitzilopochtli entered her body to be born again. When, therefore, the four hundred had gathered together to burn her, the god came forth fully armed and slew them every one.

[1: The name Chichimeca has been a puzzle. The derivation appears to be from *chichi*, a dog, *mecatl*, a rope. According to general tradition the Chichimecs were a barbarous people who inhabited Mexico before the Aztecs came. Yet Sahagun says the Toltecs were the real Chichimecs (Lib. x, cap. xxix). In the myth we are now considering, they were plainly the stars.]

It is not hard to guess who are these four hundred youths slain before the sun rises, destined to be restored to life and yet again destroyed. The veil of metaphor is thin which thus conceals to our mind the picture of the myriad stars quenched every morning by the growing light, but returning every evening to their appointed places. And did any doubt remain, it is removed by the direct statement in the echo of this tradition preserved by the Kiches of Guatemala, wherein it is plainly said that the four hundred youths who were put to death by Zipacna, and restored to life by Hunhun Ahpu, "rose into the sky and became the stars of heaven."[1]

[1: *Popol Vuh, Le Livre Sacre des Quiches*, p. 193.]

Indeed, these same ancient men whose explanations I have been following added that the four hundred men whom Tezcatlipoca created continued yet to live in the third heaven, and were its guards and watchmen. They were of five colors, yellow, black, white, blue and red, which in the symbolism of their tongue meant that they were distributed around the zenith and to each of the four cardinal points. [1]

[1: See H. de Charencey, *Des Couleurs Considerees comme Symboles des Points de l'Horizon chez les Peuples du Nouveau Monde*, in the *Actes de la Societe Philologiques*, Tome vi. No. 3.]

Nor did these sages suppose that the struggle of the dark Tezcatlipoca to master the Light-God had ceased; no, they knew he was biding his time, with set purpose and a fixed certainty of success. They knew that in the second heaven there were certain frightful women, without flesh or bones, whose names were the Terrible, or the Thin Dart-Throwers, who were waiting there until this world should end, when they would descend and eat up all mankind.[1] Asked concerning the time of this destruction, they replied that as to the day or season they knew it not, but it would be "when Tezcatlipoca should steal the sun from heaven for himself"; in other words, when eternal night should close in upon the Universe.[2]

[1: These frightful beings were called the *Tzitzimime*, a word which Molina in his Vocabulary renders "cosa espantosa o cosa de aguero." For a thorough discussion of their place in Mexican mythology, see *Anales del Museo Nacional*, Tom. ii, pp. 358-372.]

[2: The whole of this version of the myth is from the work of Ramirez de Fuenleal, which I consider in some respects the most valuable authority we possess. It was taken directly from the sacred books of the Aztecs, as explained by the most competent survivors of the Conquest.]

The myth which I have here given in brief is a prominent one in Aztec cosmogony, and is known as that of the Ages of the World or the Suns. The opinion was widely accepted that the present is the fifth age or period of the world's history; that it has already undergone four destructions by various causes, and that the present period is also to terminate in another such catastrophe. The agents of such universal ruin have been a great flood, a world-wide conflagration, frightful tornadoes and famine, earthquakes and wild beasts, and hence the Ages, Suns or Periods were called respectively, from their terminations, those of Water, Fire, Air and Earth. As we do not know the destiny of the fifth, the present one, it has as yet no name.

I shall not attempt to go into the details of this myth, the less so as it has recently been analyzed with much minuteness by the Mexican antiquary Chavero.[1] I will merely point out that it is too closely identified with a great many similar myths for us to be allowed to seek an origin for it peculiar to Mexican or even American soil. We can turn to the Tualati who live in Oregon, and they will tell us of the four creations and destructions of mankind; how at the end of the first Age all human beings were changed into stars; at the end of the second they became stones; at the end of the third into fishes; and at the close of the fourth they disappeared, to give place to the tribes that now inhabit the world.[2] Or we can read from the cuneiform inscriptions of ancient Babylon, and find the four destructions of the race there specified, as by a flood, by wild beasts, by famine and by pestilence.[3]

[1: Alfredo Chavero, *La Piedra del Sol*, in the *Anales del Museo Nacional*, Tom. i, p. 353, et seq.]

[2: A.S. Gatschet, *The Four Creations of Mankind*, a Tualati myth, in *Transactions of the Anthropological Society of Washington*, Vol. i, p. 60 (1881).]

[3: Paul Haupt, *Der Keilinschriftliche Sintfluthbericht*, p. 17 (Leipzig, 1881).]

The explanation which I have to give of these coincidences--which could easily be increased--is that the number four was chosen as that of the four cardinal points, and that the fifth or present age, that in which we live, is that which is ruled by the ruler of the four points, by the Spirit of Light, who was believed to govern them, as, in fact, the early dawn does, by defining the relations of space, act as guide and governor of the motions of men.

All through Aztec mythology, traditions and customs, we can discover this ancient myth of the four brothers, the four ancestors of their race, or the four chieftains who led their progenitors to their respective habitations. The rude mountaineers of Meztitlan, who worshiped with particular zeal Tezcatlipoca and Quetzalcoatl, and had inscribed, in gigantic figures, the sacred five points, symbol of the latter, on the side of a vast precipice in their land, gave the symbolic titles to the primeval quadruplet;--

Ixcuin, He who has four faces.

Hueytecpatl, the ancient Flint-stone.

Tentetemic, the Lip-stone that slays.

Nanacatltzatzi, He who speaks when intoxicated with the poisonous mushroom, called *nanacatl*.

These four brothers, according to the myth, were born of the goddess, Hueytonantzin, which means "our great, ancient mother," and, with unfilial hands, turned against her and slew her, sacrificing her to the Sun and offering her heart to that divinity.[1] In other words, it is the old story of the cardinal points, defined at daybreak by the Dawn, the eastern Aurora, which is lost in or sacrificed to the Sun on its appearance.

[1: Gabriel de Chaves, *Relacion de la Provincia de Meztitlan*, 1556, in the *Colecion de Documentos Ineditos del Archivo de Indias*, Tom. iv, pp. 535 and 536.

The translations of the names are not given by Chaves, but I think they are correct, except, possibly, the third, which may be a compound of *tentetl*, lipstone, *temictli*, dream, instead of with *temicti*, slayer.]

Of these four brothers I suspect the first, Ixcuin, "he who looks four ways," or "has four faces," is none other than Quetzalcoatl,[1] while the Ancient Flint is probably Tezcatlipoca, thus bringing the myth into singularly close relationship with that of the Iroquois, given on a previous page.

[1: *Ixcuina* was also the name of the goddess of pleasure. The derivation is from *ixtli*, face, *cui*, to take, and *na*, four. See the note of MM. Jourdanet and Simeon to their translation of Sahagun, *Historia* p. 22.]

Another myth of the Aztecs gave these four brothers or primitive heroes, as:--
Huitzilopochtli. Huitznahua. Itztlacoliuhqui. Pantecatl.

Of these Dr. Schultz-Sellack advances plausible reasons for believing that Itztlacoliuhqui, which was the name of a certain form of head-dress, was another title of Quetzalcoatl; and that Pantecatl was one of the names of Tezcatlipoca.[1] If this is the case we have here another version of the same myth.

[1: Dr. Schultz Sellack, *Die Amerikanischen Goetter der Vier Weltgegenden und ihre Tempel in Palenque*, in the *Zeitschrift fuer Ethnologie*, Bd. xi, (1879).]

Sec.3. *Quetzalcoatl, the Hero of Tula.*

But it was not Quetzalcoatl the god, the mysterious creator of the visible world, on whom the thoughts of the Aztec race delighted to dwell, but on Quetzalcoatl, high priest in the glorious city of Tollan (Tula), the teacher of the arts, the wise lawgiver, the virtuous prince, the master builder and the merciful judge.

Here, again, though the scene is transferred from heaven to earth and from the cycles of other worlds to a date not extremely remote, the story continues to be of his contest with Tezcatlipoca, and of the wiles of this enemy, now diminished to a potent magician and jealous rival, to dispossess and drive him from famous Tollan.

No one versed in the metaphors of mythology can be deceived by the thin veil of local color which surrounds the myth in this its terrestrial and historic form. Apart from its being but a repetition or continuation of the genuine ancient account of the conflict of day and night, light and darkness, which I have already given, the name Tollan is enough to point out the place and the powers with which the story deals. For this Tollan, where Quetzalcoatl reigned, is not by any means, as some have supposed, the little town of Tula, still alive, a dozen leagues or so northwest from the city of Mexico; nor was it, as the legend usually stated, in some undefined locality from six hundred to a thousand leagues northwest of that city; nor yet in Asia, as some antiquaries have maintained; nor, indeed, anywhere upon this weary world; but it was, as the name denotes, and as the native historian Tezozomoc long since translated it, where the bright sun lives, and where the god of light forever rules so long as that orb is in the sky. Tollan is but a syncopated form of *Tonatlan*, the Place of the Sun.[1]

[1: "Tonalan, o lugar del sol," says Tezozomoc (***Cronica Mexicana***, chap. i). The full form is *Tonatlan*, from *tona*, "hacer sol," and the place ending *tlan*. The derivation from *tollin*, a rush, is of no value, and it is nothing to the point that in the picture writing Tollan was represented by a bundle of rushes (Kingsborough, vol. vi, p. 177, note), as that was merely in accordance with the rules of the picture writing, which represented names by rebuses. Still more worthless is the derivation given by Herrera (***Historia de las Indias Occidentals***, Dec. iii, Lib. i, cap. xi), that it means "Lugar de Tuna" or the place where the tuna (the fruit of the Opuntia) is found; inasmuch as the word *tuna* is not from the Aztec at all, but belongs to that dialect of the Arawack spoken by the natives of Cuba and Haiti.]

It is worth while to examine the whereabouts and character of this marvelous city of Tollan somewhat closely, for it is a place that we hear of in the oldest myths and legends of many and different races. Not only the Aztecs, but the Mayas of Yucatan and the Kiches and Cakchiquels of Guatemala bewailed, in woful songs, the loss to them of that beautiful land, and counted its destruction as a common starting point in their annals.[1] Well might they regret it, for not again would they find its like. In that land the crop of maize never failed, and the ears grew as long as a man's arm; the cotton burst its pods, not white only, but naturally of all beautiful colors, scarlet, green, blue, orange, what you would; the gourds could not be clasped in the arms; birds of beauteous plumage filled the air with melodious song. There was never any want nor poverty. All the riches of the world were there, houses built of silver and precious jade, of rosy mother of pearl and of azure turquoises. The servants of the great king Quetzalcoatl were skilled in all manner of arts; when he sent them forth they flew to any part of the world with infinite speed; and his edicts were proclaimed from the summit of the mountain Tzatzitepec, the Hill of

Shouting, by criers of such mighty voice that they could be heard a hundred leagues away.[2] His servants and disciples were called "Sons of the Sun" and "Sons of the Clouds."[3]

[1: The **Books of Chilan Balam**, of the Mayas, the **Record from Tecpan Atitlan**, of the Cakchiquels, and the **Popol vuh**, National Book, of the Kiches, have much to say about Tulan. These works were all written at a very early date, by natives, and they have all been preserved in the original tongues, though unfortunately only the last mentioned has been published.]

[2: Sahagun, **Historia**, Lib. iii, cap. iii.]

[3: Duran, **Historia de los Indios**, in Kingsborough, vol. viii, p. 267.]

Where, then, was this marvelous land and wondrous city? Where could it be but where the Light-God is on his throne, where the life-giving sun is ever present, where are the mansions of the day, and where all nature rejoices in the splendor of its rays?

But this is more than in one spot. It may be in the uppermost heavens, where light is born and the fleecy clouds swim easily; or in the west, where the sun descends to his couch in sanguine glory; or in the east, beyond the purple rim of the sea, whence he rises refreshed as a giant to run his course; or in the underworld, where he passes the night.

Therefore, in ancient Cakchiquel legend it is said: "Where the sun rises, there is one Tulan; another is in the underworld; yet another where the sun sets; and there is still another, and there dwells the God. Thus, O my children, there are four Tulans, as the ancient men have told us."[1]

[1: Francisco Ernantez Arana Xahila, **Memorial de Tecpan Atitlan**. MS. in Cakchiquel, in my possession.]

The most venerable traditions of the Maya race claimed for them a migration from "Tollan in Zuyva." "Thence came we forth together," says the Kiche myth, "there was the common parent of our race, thence came we, from among the Yaqui men, whose god is Yolcuat Quetzalcoat."[1] This Tollan is certainly none other than the abode of Quetzalcoatl, named in an Aztec manuscript as **Zivena vitzcatl**, a word of uncertain derivation, but applied to the highest heaven.

[1: **Le Popol Vuh**, p. 247. The name **Yaqui** means in Kiche civilized or polished, and was applied to the Aztecs, but it is, in its origin, from an Aztec root **yauh**, whence *yaque*, travelers, and especially merchants. The Kiches recognizing in the Aztec merchants a superior and cultivated class of men, adopted into their tongue the name which the merchants gave themselves, and used the word in the above sense. Compare Sahagun, *Historia de Nueva Espana*, Lib. ix, cap. xii.]

Where Quetzalcoatl finally retired, and whence he was expected back, was still a Tollan--Tollan Tlapallan--and Montezuma, when he heard of the arrival of the Spaniards, exclaimed, "It is Quetzalcoatl, returned from Tula."

The cities which selected him as their tutelary deity were named for that which he was supposed to have ruled over. Thus we have Tollan and Tollantzinco ("behind Tollan") in the Valley of Mexico, and the pyramid Cholula was called "Tollan-Cholollan," as well as many other Tollans and Tulas among the Nahuatl colonies.

The natives of the city of Tula were called, from its name, the *Tolteca*, which simply means "those who dwell in Tollan." And who, let us ask, were these Toltecs?

They have hovered about the dawn of American history long enough. To them have been attributed not only the primitive culture of Central America and Mexico, but of lands far to the north, and even the earthworks of the Ohio Valley. It is time they were assigned their proper place, and that is among the purely fabulous creations of the imagination, among the giants and fairies, the gnomes and sylphs, and other such fancied beings which in all ages and nations the popular mind has loved to create.

Toltec, Toltecatl,[1] which in later days came to mean a skilled craftsman or artificer, signifies, as I have said, an inhabitant of Tollan--of the City of the Sun--in other words, a Child of Light. Without a metaphor, it meant at first one of the far darting, bright shining rays of the sun. Not only does the tenor of the whole myth show this, but specifically and clearly the powers attributed to the ancient Toltecs. As the immediate subjects of the God of Light they were called "Those who fly the whole day without resting,"[2] and it was said of them that they had the power of reaching instantly even a very distant place. When the Light-God himself departs, they too disappear, and their city is left uninhabited and desolate.

[1: Toltecatl, according to Molina, is "oficial de arte mecanica o maestro," (*Vocabulario de la Lengua Mexicana*, s.v.). This is a secondary meaning. Veitia justly says, "Toltecatl quiere decir artifice, porque en Thollan comenzaron a ensenar, aunque a Thollan llamaron Tula, y por decir Toltecatl dicen Tuloteca" (*Historia*, cap. xv).]

[2: Their title was ***Tlanqua cemilhuique***, compounded of ***tlanqua***, to set the teeth, as with strong determination, and ***cemilhuitia***, to run during a whole day. Sahagun, ***Historia***, Lib. iii, cap. iii, and Lib. x, cap. xxix; compare also the myth of Tezcatlipoca disguised as an old woman parching corn, the odor of which instantly attracted the Toltecs, no matter how far off they were. When they came she killed them. Id. Lib. iii, cap. xi.]

In some, and these I consider the original versions of the myth, they do not constitute a nation at all, but are merely the disciples or servants of Quetzalcoatl.[1] They have all the traits of beings of supernatural powers. They were astrologers and necromancers, marvelous poets and philosophers, painters as were not to be found elsewhere in the world, and such builders that for a thousand leagues the remains of their cities, temples and fortresses strewed the land. "When it has happened to me," says Father Duran, "to ask an Indian who cut this pass through the mountains, or who opened that spring of water, or who built that old ruin, the answer was, 'The Toltecs, the disciples of Papa.'"[2]

[1: "Discipulos," Duran, ***Historia***, in Kingsborough, vol. vii, p. 260.]
[2: Ibid.]

They were tall in stature, beyond the common race of men, and it was nothing uncommon for them to live hundreds of years. Such was their energy that they allowed no lazy person to live among them, and like their master they were skilled in every art of life and virtuous beyond the power of mortals. In complexion they are described as light in hue, as was their leader, and as are usually the personifications of light, and not the less so among the dark races of men.[1]

[1: For the character of the Toltecs as here portrayed, see Ixtlilxochitl, ***Relaciones Historicas***, and Veitia, ***Historia, passion***.]

When Quetzalcoatl left Tollan most of the Toltecs had already perished by the stratagems of Tezcatlipoca, and those that survived were said to have disappeared on his departure. The city was left desolate, and what became of its remaining inhabitants no one knew. But this very uncertainty offered a favorable opportunity for various nations, some speaking Nahuatl and some other tongues, to claim descent from this mysterious, ancient and wondrous race.

The question seems, indeed, a difficult one. When the Light-God disappears from the sky, shorn of his beams and bereft of his glory, where are the bright rays, the darting gleams of light which erewhile bathed the earth in refulgence? Gone, gone, we know not whither.

The original home of the Toltecs was said to have been in Tlapallan--the very same Red Land to which Quetzalcoatl was fabled to have returned; only the former was distinguished as Old Tlapallan--Hue Tlapallan--as being that from which he and they had emerged. Other myths called it the Place of Sand, Xalac, an evident reference to the sandy sea strand, the same spot where it was said that Quetzalcoatl was last seen, beyond which the sun rises and below which he sinks. Thither he returned when driven from Tollan, and reigned over his vassals many years in peace. [1]

[1: "Se metio (Quetzalcoatl) la tierra adentro hasta Tlapallan o segun otros Huey Xalac, antigua patria de sus antepasados, en donde vivio muchos anos." Ixtlilxochitl, **Relaciones Historicas**, p. 394, in Kingsborough, vol. ix. Xalac, is from **xalli**, sand, with the locative termination. In Nahuatl **xalli aquia**, to enter the sand, means to die.]

We cannot mistake this Tlapallan, new or old. Whether it is bathed in the purple and gold of the rising sun or in the crimson and carnation of his setting, it always was, as Sahagun tells us, with all needed distinctness, "the city of the Sun," the home of light and color, whence their leader, Quetzalcoatl had come, and whither he was summoned to return.[1]

[1: "Dicen que camino acia el Oriente, y que se fue a la ciudad del Sol, llamada Tlapallan, y fue llamado del sol." Libro. viii, Prologo.]

The origin of the earthly Quetzalcoatl is variously given; one cycle of legends narrates his birth in Tollan in some extraordinary manner; a second cycle claims that he was not born in any country known to the Aztecs, but came to them as a stranger.

Of the former cycle probably one of the oldest versions is that he was a son or descendant of Tezcatlipoca himself, under his name Camaxtli. This was the account given to the chancellor Ramirez,[1] and it is said by Torquemada to have been the canonical doctrine taught in the holy city of Cholollan, the centre of the worship of Quetzalcoatl.[2] It is a transparent metaphor, and could be paralleled by a hundred similar expressions in the myths of other nations. The Night brings forth the Day, the darkness leads on to the light, and though thus standing in the relation of father and son, the struggle between them is forever continued.

[1: Ramirez de Fuen-leal, *Hist. de los Mexicanos*, cap. viii.]

[2: *Monarquia Indiana*, Lib. vi, cap. xxiv. *Camaxtli* is also found in the form *Yoamaxtli*; this shows that it is a compound of *maxtli*, covering, clothing, and *ca*, the substantive verb, or in the latter instance, *yoalli*, night; hence it is, "the Mantle," or, "the garb of night" ("la faja nocturna," *Anales del Museo Nacional*, Tom. ii, p. 363).]

Another myth represents him as the immediate son of the All-Father Tonaca tecutli, under his title Citlallatonac, the Morning, by an earth-born maiden in Tollan. In that city dwelt three sisters, one of whom, an unspotted virgin, was named Chimalman. One day, as they were together, the god appeared to them. Chimalman's two sisters were struck to death by fright at his awful presence, but upon her he breathed the breath of life, and straightway she conceived. The son she bore cost her life, but it was the divine Quetzalcoatl, surnamed *Topiltcin*, Our Son, and, from the year of his birth, *Ce Acatl*, One Reed. As soon as he was born he was possessed of speech and reason and wisdom. As for his mother, having perished on earth, she was transferred to the heavens, where she was given the honored name Chalchihuitzli, the Precious Stone of Sacrifice.[1]

[1: *Codex Vaticanus*, Tab. x; *Codex Telleriano-Remensis*, Pt. ii, Lam. ii. The name is from *chalchihuitl*, jade, and *vitztli*, the thorn used to pierce the tongue, ears and penis, in sacrifice. *Chimalman*, more correctly, *Chimalmatl*, is from *chimalli*, shield, and probably, *matlalin*, green.]

This, also, is evidently an ancient and simple figure of speech to express that the breath of Morning announces the dawn which brings forth the sun and disappears in the act.

The virgin mother Chimalman, in another legend, is said to have been brought with child by swallowing a jade or precious green stone (*chalchihuitl*);[1] while another averred that she was not a virgin, but the wife of Camaxtli (Tezcatlipoca);[2] or again, that she was the second wife of that venerable old man who was the father of the seven sons from whom all tribes speaking the Nahuatl language, and several who did not speak it (Otomies, Tarascos), were descended.[3] This latter will repay analysis.

[1: Mendieta, *Historia Eclesiastica Indiana*, Lib. ii, cap. vi.]

[2: Ibid.]

[3: Motolinia, *Historia de los Indios de Nueva Espana, Epistola Proemial*, p. 10. The first wife was Ilancueitl, from *ilantli*, old woman, and *cueitl*, skirt. Gomara, *Conquista de Mejico*, p. 432.]

All through Mexico and Central America this legend of the Seven Sons, Seven Tribes, the Seven Caves whence they issued, or the Seven Cities where they dwelt, constantly crops out. To that land the Aztecs referred as their former dwelling place. It was located at some indefinite distance to the north or northwest--in the same direction as Tollan. The name of that land was significant. It was called the White or Bright Land, *Aztlan*.[1] In its midst was situated the mountain or hill Colhuacan the Divine, *Teoculhuacan*.[2] In the base of this hill were the Seven Caverns, *Chicomoztoc*, whence the seven tribes with their respective gods had issued, those gods including Quetzalcoatl, Huitzilopochtli and the Tezcatlipocas. There continued to live their mother, awaiting their return.

[1: The derivation of Aztlan from *aztatl*, a heron, has been rejected by Buschmann and the best Aztec scholars. It is from the same root as *izlac*, white, with the local ending *tlan*, and means the White or Bright Land. See the subject discussed in Buschmann, *Ueber die Atzekischen Ortsnamen*. p. 612, and recently by Senor Orozco y Berra, in *Anales del Museo Nacional*, Tom. ii, p. 56.]

[2: Colhuacan, is a locative form. It is usually derived from *coloa*, to curve, to round. Father Duran says it is another name for Aztlan: "Estas cuevas son en Teoculacan, *que por otro nombre* se llama Aztlan." *Historia de los Indios de Nueva Espana*, Lib. i, cap. i.]

Teo is from *teotl*, god, deity. The description in the text of the relations of land and water in this mythical land, is also from Duran's work.

The lord of this land and the father of the seven sons is variously and indistinctly named. One legend calls him the White Serpent of the Clouds, or the White Cloud Twin, *Iztac Mixcoatl*.[1] Whoever he was we can hardly mistake the mountain in which or upon which he dwelt. *Colhuacan* means the bent or curved mountain. It is none other than the Hill of Heaven, curving down on all sides to the horizon;

upon it in all times have dwelt the gods, and from it they have come to aid the men they favor. Absolutely the same name was applied by the Choctaws to the mythical hill from which they say their ancestors first emerged into the light of day. They call it **Nane Waiyah**, the Bent or Curved Hill[2]. Such identity of metaphorical expression leaves little room for discussion.

[1: Mendieta, ***Historia Eclesiastica Indiana***, Lib. ii, cap. xxxiii.]

[2: See my work, ***The Myths of the New World***, p. 242.]

If it did, the other myths which surround the mystic mountain would seem to clear up doubt. Colhuacan, we are informed, continued to be the residence of the great Mother of the Gods. On it she dwelt, awaiting their return from earth. No one can entirely climb the mountain, for from its middle distance to the summit it is of fine and slippery sand; but it has this magical virtue, that whoever ascends it, however old he is, grows young again, in proportion as he mounts, and is thus restored to pristine vigor. The happy dwellers around it have, however, no need of its youth restoring power; for in that land no one grows old, nor knows the outrage of years.[1]

[1: "En esta tierra nunca envejecen los hombres. * * * Este cerro tiene esta virtud, que el que ya viejo se quiere remozar, sube hasta donde le parece, y vuelve de la edad que quiere." Duran, in Kingsborough, Vol. viii, p. 201.]

When Quetzalcoatl, therefore, was alleged to be the son of the Lord of the Seven Caves, it was nothing more than a variation of the legend that gave him out as the son of the Lord of the High Heavens. They both mean the same thing. Chimalman, who appears in both myths as his mother, binds the two together, and stamps them as identical, while Mixcoatl is only another name for Tezcatlipoca.

Such an interpretation, if correct, would lead to the dismissal from history of the whole story of the Seven Cities or Caves, and the pretended migration from them. In fact, the repeated endeavors of the chroniclers to assign a location to these fabulous residences, have led to no result other than most admired disorder and confusion. It is as vain to seek their whereabouts, as it is that of the garden of Eden or the Isle of Avalon. They have not, and never had a place on this sublunary sphere, but belong in that ethereal world which the fancy creates and the imagination paints.

A more prosaic account than any of the above, is given by the historian, Alva

Ixtlilxochitl, so prosaic that it is possible that it has some grains of actual fact in it.[1] He tells us that a King of Tollan, Tecpancaltzin, fell in love with the daughter of one of his subjects, a maiden by name Xochitl, the Rose. Her father was the first to collect honey from the maguey plant, and on pretence of buying this delicacy the king often sent for Xochitl. He accomplished her seduction, and hid her in a rose garden on a mountain, where she gave birth to an infant son, to the great anger of the father. Casting the horoscope of the infant, the court astrologer found all the signs that he should be the last King of Tollan, and should witness the destruction of the Toltec monarchy. He was named *Meconetzin*, the Son of the Maguey, and in due time became king, and the prediction was accomplished.[2]

[1: Ixtlilxochitl, *Relaciones Historicas*, p. 330, in Kingsborough, Vol. ix.]

[2: In the work of Ramirez de Fuen-leal (cap. viii), Tezcatlipoca is said to have been the discoverer of pulque, the intoxicating wine of the Maguey. In Meztitlan he was associated with the gods of this beverage and of drunkenness. Hence it is probable that the name *Meconetzin* applied to Quetzalcoatl in this myth meant to convey that he was the son of Tezcatlipoca.]

In several points, however, this seemingly historic narrative has a suspicious resemblance to a genuine myth preserved to us in a certain Aztec manuscript known as the *Codex Telleriano-Remensis*. This document tells how Quetzalcoatl, Tezcatlipoca and their brethren were at first gods, and dwelt as stars in the heavens. They passed their time in Paradise, in a Rose Garden, *Xochitlycacan* ("where the roses are lifted up"); but on a time they began plucking the roses from the great Rose tree in the centre of the garden, and Tonaca-tecutli, in his anger at their action, hurled them to the earth, where they lived as mortals.

The significance of this myth, as applied to the daily descent of sun and stars from the zenith to the horizon, is too obvious to need special comment; and the coincidences of the rose garden on the mountain (in the one instance the Hill of Heaven, in the other a supposed terrestrial elevation) from which Quetzalcoatl issues, and the anger of the parent, seem to indicate that the supposed historical relation of Ixtlilxochitl is but a myth dressed in historic garb.

The second cycle of legends disclaimed any miraculous parentage for the hero of Tollan. Las Casas narrates his arrival from the East, from some part of Yucatan, he thinks, with a few followers,[1] a tradition which is also repeated with definitiveness by the native historian, Alva Ixtlilxochitl, but leaving the locality uncertain.[2] The historian, Veytia, on the other hand, describes him as arriving from the North, a full grown man, tall of stature, white of skin, and full-bearded, barefooted and bareheaded, clothed in a long white robe strewn with red crosses, and carrying a staff in his hand.[3]

[1: Torquemada, **Monarquia Indiana**, Lib. vi, cap. xxiv. This was apparently the canonical doctrine in Cholula. Mendieta says: "El dios o idolo de Cholula, llamado Quetzalcoatl, fue el mas celebrado y tenido por mejor y mas digno sobre los otro dioses, segun la reputacion de todos. Este, segun sus historias (aunque algunos digan que de Tula) vino de las partes de Yucatan a la ciudad de Cholula." **Historia Eclesiastica Indiana**, Lib. ii, cap. x.]

[2: **Historia Chichimeca**, cap. i.]

[3: **Historia**, cap. xv.]

Whatever the origin of Quetzalcoatl, whether the child of a miraculous conception, or whether as an adult stranger he came from some far-off land, all accounts agree as to the greatness and purity of his character, and the magnificence of Tollan under his reign. His temple was divided into four apartments, one toward the East, yellow with gold; one toward the West, blue with turquoise and jade; one toward the South, white with pearls and shells, and one toward the North, red with bloodstones; thus symbolizing the four cardinal points and four quarters of the world over which the light holds sway.[1]

[1: Sahagun, Lib. ix, cap. xxix.]

Through the midst of Tollan flowed a great river, and upon or over this river was the house of Quetzalcoatl. Every night at midnight he descended into this river to bathe, and the place of his bath was called, In the Painted Vase, or, In the Precious Waters.[1] For the Orb of Light dips nightly into the waters of the World Stream, and the painted clouds of the sun-setting surround the spot of his ablutions.

[1: The name of the bath of Quetzalcoatl is variously given as **Xicapoyan**, from **xicalli**, vases made from gourds, and **poyan**, to paint (Sahagun, Lib. iii, cap. iii); **Chalchiuhapan**, from **atl**, water **pan**, in, and **chalchiuitl**, precious, brilliant, the jade stone (**id.**, Lib. x, cap. xxix); and **Atecpanamochco**, from **atl**, water, **tecpan**, royal, **amochtli**, any shining white metal, as tin, and the locative **co**, hence,

In the Shining Royal Water (***Anales de Cuauhtitlan***, p. 21). These names are interesting as illustrating the halo of symbolism which surrounded the history of the Light-God.]

I have said that the history of Quetzalcoatl in Tollan is but a continuation of the conflict of the two primal brother gods. It is still the implacable Tezcatlipoca who pursues and finally conquers him. But there is this significant difference, that whereas in the elemental warfare portrayed in the older myth mutual violence and alternate destruction prevail, in all these later myths Quetzalcoatl makes no effort at defence, scarcely remonstrates, but accepts his defeat as a decree of Fate which it is vain to resist. He sees his people fall about him, and the beautiful city sink into destruction, but he knows it is the hand of Destiny, and prepares himself to meet the inevitable with what stoicism and dignity he may.

The one is the quenching of the light by the darkness of the tempest and the night, represented as a struggle; in the other it is the gradual and calm but certain and unavoidable extinction of the sun as it noiselessly sinks to the western horizon.

The story of the subtlety of Tezcatlipoca is variously told. In what may well be its oldest and simplest version it is said that in his form as Camaxtli he caught a deer with two heads, which, so long as he kept it, secured him luck in war; but falling in with one of five goddesses he had created, he begat a son, and through this act he lost his good fortune. The son was Quetzalcoatl, surnamed Ce Acatl, and he became Lord of Tollan, and a famous warrior. For many years he ruled the city, and at last began to build a very great temple. While engaged in its construction Tezcatlipoca came to him one day and told him that toward Honduras, in a place called Tlapallan, a house was ready for him, and he must quit Tollan and go there to live and die. Quetzalcoatl replied that the heavens and stars had already warned him that after four years he must go hence, and that he would obey. The time past, he took with him all the inhabitants of Tula, and some he left in Cholula, from whom its inhabitants are descended, and some he placed in the province of Cuzcatan, and others in Cempoal, and at last he reached Tlapallan, and on the very day he arrived there, he fell sick and died. As for Tula, it remained without an inhabitant for nine years.[1]

[1: Ramirez de Fuen-leal, ***Historia de los Mexicanos por sus Pinturas***, cap. viii.]

A more minute account is given by the author of the ***Annals of Cuauhtitlan***, a work written at an early date, in the Aztec tongue. He assures his readers that his narrative of these particular events is minutely and accurately recorded from the oldest and most authentic traditions. It is this:--

When those opposed to Quetzalcoatl did not succeed in their designs, they summoned to their aid a demon or sorcerer, by name Tezcatlipoca, and his assistants. He said: "We will give him a drink to dull his reason, and will show him his own face in a mirror, and surely he will be lost." Then Tezcatlipoca brewed an intoxicating beverage, the *pulque*, from the maguey, and taking a mirror he wrapped it in a rabbit skin, and went to the house of Quetzalcoatl.

"Go tell your master," he said to the servants, "that I have come to show him his own flesh."

"What is this?" said Quetzalcoatl, when the message was delivered. "What does he call my own flesh? Go and ask him."

But Tezcatlipoca refused. "I have not come to see you, but your master," he said to the servants. Then he was admitted, and Quetzalcoatl said:--

"Welcome, youth, you have troubled yourself much. Whence come you? What is this, my flesh, that you would show me?"

"My Lord and Priest," replied the youth, "I come from the mountain-side of Nonoalco. Look, now, at your flesh; know yourself; see yourself as you are seen of others;" and with that he handed him the mirror.

As soon as Quetzalcoatl saw his face in the mirror he exclaimed:--

"How is it possible my subjects can look on me without affright? Well might they flee from me. How can a man remain among them filled as I am with foul sores, his face wrinkled and his aspect loathsome? I shall be seen no more; I shall no longer frighten my people."

Then Tezcatlipoca went away to take counsel, and returning, said:--

"My lord and master, use the skill of your servant. I have come to console you. Go forth to your people. I will conceal your defects by art."

"Do what you please," replied Quetzalcoatl. "I will see what my fate is to be."

Tezcatlipoca painted his cheeks green and dyed his lips red. The forehead he colored yellow, and taking feathers of the *quechol* bird, he arranged them as a beard. Quetzalcoatl surveyed himself in the mirror, and rejoiced at his appearance, and forthwith sallied forth to see his people.

Tezcatlipoca withdrew to concoct another scheme of disgrace. With his attendants he took of the strong *pulque* which he had brewed, and came again to the palace of the Lord of Tollan. They were refused admittance and asked their country. They replied that they were from the Mountain of the Holy Priest, from the Hill of Tollan. When Quetzalcoatl heard this, he ordered them to be admitted, and asked their business. They offered him the *pulque*, but he refused, saying that he was sick, and, moreover, that it would weaken his judgment and might cause his death. They urged him to dip but the tip of his finger in it to taste it; he complied, but even so little of the magic liquor overthrew his self control, and taking the bowl he quaffed a full draught and was drunk. Then these perverse men ridiculed him, and cried out:--

"You feel finely now, my son; sing us a song; sing, worthy priest."

Thereupon Quetzalcoatl began to sing, as follows:--

"My pretty house, my coral house,

I call it Zacuan by name; And must I leave it, do you say?

Oh my, oh me, and ah for shame."[1]

[1: The original is--

Quetzal, quetzal, no calli,

Zacuan, no callin tapach No callin nic yacahuaz

An ya, an ya, an quilmach.

Literally--

Beautiful, beautiful (is) my house

Zacuan, my house of coral; My house, I must leave it.

Alas, alas, they say.

Zacuan, instead of being a proper name, may mean a rich yellow leather from the bird called *zacuantototl*.]

As the fumes of the liquor still further disordered his reason, he called his attendants and bade them hasten to his sister Quetzalpetlatl, who dwelt on the Mountain Nonoalco, and bring her, that she too might taste the divine liquor. The attendants hurried off and said to his sister:--

"Noble lady, we have come for you. The high priest Quetzalcoatl awaits you. It is his wish that you come and live with him."

She instantly obeyed and went with them. On her arrival Quetzalcoatl seated her beside him and gave her to drink of the magical pulque. Immediately she felt its influence, and Quetzalcoatl began to sing, in drunken fashion--

"Sister mine, beloved mine,

Quetzal--petlatl--tzin, Come with me, drink with me,

'Tis no sin, sin, sin."

Soon they were so drunken that all reason was forgotten; they said no prayers, they went not to the bath, and they sank asleep on the floor.[1]

[1: It is not clear, at least in the translations, whether the myth intimates an incestuous relation between Quetzalcoatl and his sister. In the song he calls her "Nohueltiuh," which means, strictly, "My elder sister;" but Mendoza translates it "Querida esposa mia." ***Quetzalpetlatl*** means "the Beautiful Carpet," ***petlatl*** being the rug or mat used on floors, etc. This would be a most appropriate figure of speech to describe a rich tropical landscape, "carpeted with flowers," as we say; and as the earth is, in primitive cosmogony, older than the sun, I suspect that this story of Quetzalcoatl and his sister refers to the sun sinking from heaven, seemingly, into the earth. "Los Nahoas," remarks Chavero, "figuraban la tierra en forma de un cuadrilatero dividido en pequenos quatros, lo que semijaba una estera, ***petlatl***" (***Anales del Museo Nacional***, Tom. ii, p. 248).]

Sad, indeed, was Quetzalcoatl the next morning.

"I have sinned," he said; "the stain on my name can never be erased. I am not fit to rule this people. Let them build for me a habitation deep under ground; let them bury my bright treasures in the earth; let them throw the gleaming gold and shining stones into the holy fountain where I take my daily bath."

All this was done, and Quetzalcoatl spent four days in his underground tomb. When he came forth he wept and told his followers that the time had come for him to depart for Tlapallan, the Red Land, Tlillan, the Dark Land, and Tlatlallan, the Fire Land, all names of one locality.

He journeyed eastward until he came to a place where the sky, and land, and water meet together.[1] There his attendants built a funeral pile, and he threw himself into the flames. As his body burned his heart rose to heaven, and after four days became the planet Venus.[2]

[1: Designated in the Aztec original by the name ***Teoapan Ilhuicaatenco***, from ***teotl***, divine, ***atl***, water, ***pan***, in or near, ***ilhuicac***, heaven, ***atenco***, the waterside: "Near the divine water, where the sky meets the strand."]

[2: The whole of this account is from the *Anales de Cuauhtitlan*, pp. 16-22.]

That there is a profound moral significance in this fiction all will see; but I am of opinion that it is accidental and adventitious. The means that Tezcatlipoca employs to remove Quetzalcoatl refer to the two events that mark the decline of day. The sun is reflected by a long lane of beams in the surface waters of lake or sea; it loses the strength of its rays and fails in vigor; while the evening mists, the dampness of approaching dewfall, and the gathering clouds obscure its power and foretell the extinction which will soon engulf the bright luminary. As Quetzalcoatl cast his shining gold and precious stones into the water where he took his nightly bath, or buried them in underground hiding places, so the sun conceals his glories under the waters, or in the distant hills, into which he seems to sink. As he disappears at certain seasons, the Star of Evening shines brightly forth amid the lingering and fading rays, rising, as it were, from the dying fires of the sunset.

To this it may be objected that the legend makes Quetzalcoatl journey toward the East, and not toward the sunset. The explanation of this apparent contradiction is easy. The Aztec sages had at some time propounded to themselves the question of how the sun, which seems to set in the West, can rise the next morning in the East? Mungo Parke tells us that when he asked the desert Arabs this conundrum, they replied that the inquiry was frivolous and childish, as being wholly beyond the capacities of the human mind. The Aztecs did not think so, and had framed a definite theory which overcame the difficulty. It was that, in fact, the sun only advances to the zenith, and then returns to the East, from whence it started. What we seem to see as the sun between the zenith and the western horizon is, in reality, not the orb itself, but only its *brightness*, one of its accidents, not its substance, to use the terms of metaphysics. Hence to the Aztec astronomer and sage, the house of the sun is always toward the East.[1]

[1: Ramirez de Fuen-leal, *Historia*, cap. xx, p. 102.]

We need not have recourse even to this explanation. The sun, indeed, disappears in the West; but his journey must necessarily be to the East, for it is from that point that he always comes forth each morning. The Light-God must necessarily daily return to the place whence he started.

The symbols of the mirror and the mystic drink are perfectly familiar in Aryan sun-myths. The best known of the stories referring to the former is the transparent tale of Narcissus forced by Nemesis to fall in love with his own image reflected in the waters, and to pine away through unsatisfied longing; or, as Pausanias tells the story, having lost his twin sister (the morning twilight), he wasted his life in noting the likeness of his own features to those of his beloved who had passed away. "The sun, as he looks down upon his own face reflected in a lake or sea, sinks or dies at last, still gazing on it."[1]

[1: Sir George A. Cox, *The Science of Mythology and Folk Lore*, p. 96.]

Some later writers say that the drink which Quetzalcoatl quaffed was to confer immortality. This is not stated in the earliest versions of the myth. The beverage is health-giving and intoxicating, and excites the desire to seek Tlapallan, but not more. It does not, as the Soma of the Vedas, endow with unending life.

Nevertheless, there is another myth which countenances this view and explains it. It was told in the province of Meztitlan, a mountainous country to the northwest of the province of Vera Cruz. Its inhabitants spoke the Nahuatl tongue, but were never subject to the Montezumas. Their chief god was Tezcatlipoca, and it was said of him that on one occasion he slew Ometochtli (Two Rabbits), the god of wine, at the latter's own request, he believing that he thus would be rendered immortal, and that all others who drank of the beverage he presided over would die. His death, they added, was indeed like the stupor of a drunkard, who, after his lethargy has passed, rises healthy and well. In this sense of renewing life after death, he presided over the native calendar, the count of years beginning with Tochtli, the Rabbit.[1] Thus we see that this is a myth of the returning seasons, and of nature waking to life again after the cold months ushered in by the chill rains of the late autumn. The principle of fertility is alone perennial, while each individual must perish and die. The God of Wine in Mexico, as in Greece, is one with the mysterious force of reproduction.

[1: Gabriel de Chaves, *Relacion de la Provincia de Meztitlan*, 1556, in the *Colecion de Documentos Ineditos del Archivo de Indias*, Tom. iv, p. 536.]

No writer has preserved such numerous traditions about the tricks of Tezcatlipoca in Tollan, as Father Sahagun. They are, no doubt, almost verbally reported as he was told them, and as he wrote his history first in the Aztec tongue, they preserve all the quaintness of the original tales. Some of them appear to be idle amplifications of story tellers, while others are transparent myths. I shall translate a few of them quite literally, beginning with that of the mystic beverage.

The time came for the luck of Quetzalcoatl and the Toltecs to end; for there appeared against them three sorcerers, named Vitzilopochtli, Titlacauan and Tlacauepan,[1] who practiced many villanies in the city of Tullan. Titlacauan began them, assuming the disguise of an old man of small stature and white hairs. With this figure he approached the palace of Quetzalcoatl and said to the servants:--

[1: Titlacauan was the common name of Tezcatlipoca. The three sorcerers were really Quetzalcoatl's three brothers, representing the three other cardinal points.]

"I wish to see the King and speak to him."

"Away with you, old man;" said the servants. "You cannot see him. He is sick. You would only annoy him."

"I must see him," answered the old man.

The servants said, "Wait," and going in, they told Quetzalcoatl that an old man wished to see him, adding, "Sire, we put him out in vain; he refuses to leave, and says that he absolutely must see you." Quetzalcoatl answered:--

"Let him in. I have been waiting his coming for a long time."

They admitted the old man and he entered the apartment of Quetzalcoatl, and said to him:--

"My lord and son, how are you? I have with me a medicine for you to drink."

"You are welcome, old man," replied Quetzalcoatl. "I have been looking for your arrival for many days."

"Tell me how you are," asked the old man. "How is your body and your health?"

"I am very ill," answered Quetzalcoatl. "My whole body pains me, and I cannot move my hands or feet."

Then the old man said:--

"Sire, look at this medicine which I bring you. It is good and healthful, and intoxicates him who drinks it. If you will drink it, it will intoxicate you, it will heal you, it will soothe your heart, it will prepare you for the labors and fatigues of death, or of your departure."

"Whither, oh ancient man," asked Quetzalcoatl, "Whither must I go?"

The old man answered:--

"You must without fail go to Tullan Tlapallan, where there is another old man

awaiting you; you and he will talk together, and at your return you will be transformed into a youth, and you will regain the vigor of your boyhood."

When Quetzalcoatl heard these words, his heart was shaken with strong emo-
tion, and the old man added:--

"My lord, drink this medicine."

"Oh ancient man," answered the king, "I do not want to drink it."

"Drink it, my lord," insisted the old man, "for if you do not drink it now, later
you will long for it; at least, lift it to your mouth and taste a single drop."

Quetzalcoatl took the drop and tasted it, and then quaffed the liquor, exclaim-
ing:--

"What is this? It seems something very healthful and well-flavored. I am no
longer sick. It has cured me. I am well."

"Drink again," said the old man. "It is a good medicine, and you will be health-
ier than ever."

Again did Quetzalcoatl drink, and soon he was intoxicated. He began to weep;
his heart was stirred, and his mind turned toward the suggestion of his departure,
nor did the deceit of the old sorcerer permit him to abandon the thought of it. The
medicine which Quetzalcoatl drank was the white wine of the country, made of
those magueys call *teometl*.[1]

[1: From *teotl*, deity, divine, and *metl*, the maguey. Of the twenty-nine varieties of the maguey, now described in Mexico, none bears this name; but Hernandez
speaks of it, and says it was so called because there was a superstition that a person
soon to die could not hold a branch of it; but if he was to recover, or escape an
impending danger, he could hold it with ease and feel the better for it. See Nieremberg, *Historia Naturae*, Lib. xiv, cap. xxxii. "Teomatl, vitae et mortis Index."]

This was but the beginning of the guiles and juggleries of Tezcatlipoca.
Transforming himself into the likeness of one of those Indians of the Maya race,
called *Toveyome*,[1] he appeared, completely nude, in the market place of Tollan,
having green peppers to sell. Now Huemac, who was associated with Quetzalcoatl
in the sovereignty of Tollan (although other myths apply this name directly to
Quetzalcoatl, and this seems the correct version),[2] had an only daughter of sur-
passing beauty, whom many of the Toltecs had vainly sought in marriage. This
damsel looked forth on the market where Tezcatlipoca stood in his nakedness, and

her virginal eyes fell upon the sign of his manhood. Straightway an unconquerable longing seized her, a love so violent that she fell ill and seemed like to die. Her women told her father the reason, and he sent forth and had the false Toveyo brought before him. Huemac addressed him:--

[1: **Toveyome** is the plural of **toveyo**, which Molina, in his dictionary, translates "foreigner, stranger." Sahagun says that it was applied particularly to the Huastecs, a Maya tribe living in the province of Panuco. *Historia*, etc., Lib. x, cap. xxix, Sec.8.]

[2: **Huemac** is a compound of **uey**, great, and **maitl**, hand. Tezozomoc, Duran, and various other writers assign this name to Quetzalcoatl.]

"Whence come you?"

"My lord," replied the Toveyo, "I am a stranger, and I have come to sell green peppers."

"Why," asked the king "do you not wear a **maxtli** (breech-cloth), and cover your nakedness with a garment?"

"My lord," answered the stranger, "I follow the custom of my country."

Then the king added:--

"You have inspired in my daughter a longing; she is sick with desire; you must cure her."

"Nay, my lord," said the stranger, "this may not be. Rather slay me here; I wish to die; for I am not worthy to hear such words, poor as I am, and seeking only to gain my bread by selling green peppers."

But the king insisted, and said:--

"Have no fear; you alone can restore my daughter; you must do so."

Thereupon the attendants cut the sham Toveyo's hair; they led him to the bath, and colored his body black; they placed a **maxtli** and a robe upon him, and the king said:--

"Go in unto my daughter."

Tezcatlipoca went in unto her, and she was healed from that hour.

Thus did the naked stranger become the son-in-law of the great king of Tula. But the Toltecs were deeply angered that the maiden had given his black body the preference over their bright forms, and they plotted to have him slain. He was placed in the front of battle, and then they left him alone to fight the enemy. But he destroyed the opposing hosts and returned to Tula with a victory all the more brilliant for their desertion of him.

Then he requited their treachery with another, and pursued his intended destruction of their race. He sent a herald to the top of the Hill of Shouting, and through him announced a magnificent festival to celebrate his victory and his marriage. The Toltecs swarmed in crowds, men, women and children, to share in the joyous scene. Tezcatlipoca received them with simulated friendship. Taking his drum, he began to beat upon it, accompanying the music with a song. As his listeners heard the magic music, they became intoxicated with the strains, and yielding themselves to its seductive influence, they lost all thought for the future or care for the present. The locality to which the crafty Tezcatlipoca had invited them was called, The Rock upon the Water.[1] It was the summit of a lofty rock at the base of which flowed the river called, By the Rock of Light.[2] When the day had departed and midnight approached, the magician, still singing and dancing, led the intoxicated crowd to the brink of the river, over which was a stone bridge. This he had secretly destroyed, and as they came to the spot where it should have been and sought to cross, the innumerable crowd pressing one upon the other, they all fell into the water far below, where they sank out of sight and were changed into stones.

[1: *Texcalapan*, from *texcalli*, rock, and *apan*, upon or over the water.]

[2: *Texcaltlauhco*, from *texcalli*, rock, *tlaulli*, light, and the locative ending *co*, by, in or at.]

Is it pushing symbolism too far to attempt an interpretation of this fable, recounted with all the simplicity of the antique world, with greater directness, indeed, than I have thought wise to follow?

I am strongly inclined to regard it as a true myth, which, in materialistic language, sets forth the close of the day and the extinction of the light. May we not construe the maiden as the Evening Twilight, the child of the Day at the close of its life? The black lover with whom she is fatally enamored, is he not the Darkness, in which the twilight fades away? The countless crowds of Toltecs that come to the wedding festivities, and are drowned before midnight in the waters of the strangely named river, are they not the infinitely numerous light-rays which are quenched in the world-stream, when the sun has sunk, and the gloaming is lost in the night?

May we not go farther, and in this Rock of Light which stands hard by the river, recognize the Heavenly Hill which rises beside the World Stream? The bright light of one day cannot extend to the next. The bridge is broken by the intervening night, and the rays are lost in the dark waters.

But whether this interpretation is too venturesome or not, we cannot deny the deep human interest in the story, and its poetic capacities. The overmastering passion of love was evidently as present to the Indian mind as to that of the mediaeval Italian. In New as well as in Old Spain it could break the barriers of rank and overcome the hesitations of maidenly modesty. Love clouding the soul, as night obscures the day, is a figure of speech, used, I remember, by the most pathetic of Ireland's modern bards:--

"Love, the tyrant, evinces,

Alas! an omnipotent might; He treads on the necks of princes,

He darkens the mind, like night."[1]

[1: Clarence Mangan, *Poems*, "The Mariner's Bride."]

I shall not detail the many other wiles with which Tezcatlipoca led the Toltecs to their destruction. A mere reference to them must suffice. He summoned thousands to come to labor in the rose-garden of Quetzalcoatl, and when they had gathered together, he fell upon them and slew them with a hoe. Disguised with Huitzilopochtli, he irritated the people until they stoned the brother gods to death, and from the corrupting bodies spread a pestilential odor, to which crowds of the Toltecs fell victims. He turned the thought of thousands into madness, so that they voluntarily offered themselves to be sacrificed. By his spells all articles of food soured, and many perished of famine.

At length Quetzalcoatl, wearied with misfortune, gave orders to burn the beautiful houses of Tollan, to bury his treasures, and to begin the journey to Tlapallan. He transformed the cacao trees into plants of no value, and ordered the birds of rich plumage to leave the land before him.

The first station he arrived at was Quauhtitlan, where there was a lofty and spreading tree. Here he asked of his servants a mirror, and looking in it said: "I am already old." Gathering some stones, he cast them at the tree. They entered the wood and remained there.

As he journeyed, he was preceded by boys playing the flute. Thus he reached a certain spot, where he sat upon a stone by the wayside, and wept for the loss of Tollan. The marks of his hands remained upon the stone, and the tears he dropped pierced it through. To the day of the Conquest these impressions on the solid rock were pointed out.

At the fountain of Cozcapan, sorcerers met him, minded to prevent his departure:--

"Where are you going?" they asked. "Why have you left your capital? In whose care is it? Who will perform the sacred rites?"

But Quetzalcoatl answered:--

"You can in no manner hinder my departure. I have no choice but to go."

The sorcerers asked again: "Whither are you going?"

"I am going," replied Quetzalcoatl, "to Tlapallan. I have been sent for. The Sun calls me."

"Go, then, with good luck," said they. "But leave with us the art of smelting silver, of working stone and wood, of painting, of weaving feathers and other such arts."

Thus they robbed him, and taking the rich jewels he carried with him he cast them into the fountain, whence it received its name *Cozcapan*, Jewels in the Water.

Again, as he journeyed, a sorcerer met him, who asked him his destination:--

"I go," said Quetzalcoatl, "to Tlallapan."

"And luck go with you," replied the sorcerer, "but first take a drink of this wine."

"No," replied Quetzalcoatl, "not so much as a sip."

"You must taste a little of it," said the sorcerer, "even if it is by force. To no living person would I give to drink freely of it. I intoxicate them all. Come and drink of it."

Quetzalcoatl took the wine and drank of it through a reed, and as he drank he grew drunken and fell in the road, where he slept and snored.

Thus he passed from place to place, with various adventures. His servants were all dwarfs or hunchbacks, and in crossing the Sierra Nevada they mostly froze to death. By drawing a line across the Sierra he split it in two and thus made a passage. He plucked up a mighty tree and hurling it through another, thus formed a cross. At another spot he caused underground houses to be built, which were called Mictlancalco, At the House of Darkness.

At length he arrived at the sea coast where he constructed a raft of serpents, and seating himself on it as in a canoe, he moved out to sea. No one knows how or in what manner he reached Tlapallan.[1]

[1: These myths are from the third book of Sahagun's ***Historia de las Cosas de Nueva Espana***. They were taken down in the original Nahuatl, by him, from the mouth of the natives, and he gives them word for word, as they were recounted.]

The legend which appears to have been prevalent in Cholula was somewhat different. According to that, Quetzalcoatl was for many years Lord of Tollan, ruling over a happy people. At length, Tezcatlipoca let himself down from heaven by a cord made of spider's web, and, coming to Tollan, challenged its ruler to play a game of ball. The challenge was accepted, and the people of the city gathered in thousands to witness the sport. Suddenly Tezcatlipoca changed himself into a tiger, which so frightened the populace that they fled in such confusion and panic that they rushed over the precipice and into the river, where nearly all were killed by the fall or drowned in the waters.

Quetzalcoatl then forsook Tollan, and journeyed from city to city till he reached Cholula, where he lived twenty years. He was at that time of light complexion, noble stature, his eyes large, his hair abundant, his beard ample and cut rounding. In life he was most chaste and honest. They worshiped his memory, especially for three things: first, because he taught them the art of working in metals, which previous to his coming was unknown in that land; secondly, because he forbade the sacrifice either of human beings or the lower animals, teaching that bread, and roses, and flowers, incense and perfumes, were all that the gods demanded; and lastly, because he forbade, and did his best to put a stop to, wars, fighting, robbery, and all deeds of violence. For these reasons he was held in high esteem and affectionate veneration, not only by those of Cholula, but by the neighboring tribes as well, for many leagues around. Distant nations maintained temples in his honor in that city, and made pilgrimages to it, on which journeys they passed in safety through their enemy's countries.

The twenty years past, Quetzalcoatl resumed his journey, taking with him four of the principal youths of the city. When he had reached a point in the province of Guazacoalco, which is situated to the southeast of Cholula, he called the four youths to him, and told them they should return to their city; that he had to go further; but that they should go back and say that at some future day white and bearded men like himself would come from the east, who would possess the land.[1]

[1: For this version of the myth, see Mendieta, *Historia Eclesiastica Indiana*, Lib. ii, caps, v and x.]

Thus he disappeared, no one knew whither. But another legend said that he died there, by the seashore, and they burned his body. Of this event some particulars are given by Ixtlilxochitl, as follows:[1]--

[1: Ixtlilxochitl, *Relaciones Historicas*, p. 388, in Kingsborough, vol. ix.]

Quetzalcoatl, surnamed Topiltzin, was lord of Tula. At a certain time he warned his subjects that he was obliged to go "to the place whence comes the Sun," but that after a term he would return to them, in that year of their calendar of the name *Ce Acatl*, One Reed, which returns every fifty-two years. He went forth with many followers, some of whom he left in each city he visited. At length he reached the town of Ma Tlapallan. Here he announced that he should soon die, and directed his followers to burn his body and all his treasures with him. They obeyed his orders, and for four days burned his corpse, after which they gathered its ashes and placed them in a sack made of the skin of a tiger.

The introduction of the game of ball and the tiger into the story is not so childish as it seems. The game of ball was as important an amusement among the natives of Mexico and Central America as were the jousts and tournaments in Europe in the Middle Ages.[1] Towns, nations and kings were often pitted against each other. In the great temple of Mexico two courts were assigned to this game, over which a special deity was supposed to preside.[2] In or near the market place of each town there were walls erected for the sport. In the centre of these walls was an orifice a little larger than the ball. The players were divided into two parties, and the ball having been thrown, each party tried to drive it through or over the wall. The hand was not used, but only the hip or shoulders.

[1: Torquemada gives a long but obscure description of it. *Monarquia Indiana*, Lib. xiv, cap. xii.]

[2: Nieremberg, "De septuaginta et octo partibus maximi templi Mexicani," in his *Historia Naturae*, Lib. viii, cap. xxii (Antwerpt, 1635). One of these was called "The Ball Court of the Mirror," perhaps with special reference to this legend. "Trigesima secunda Tezcatlacho, locus erat ubi ludebatur pila ex gumi olli, inter templa." The name is from *tezcatl*, mirror, *tlachtli*, the game of ball, and locative ending *co*.]

From the earth the game was transferred to the heavens. As a ball, hit by a player, strikes the wall and then bounds back again, describing a curve, so the stars in the northern sky circle around the pole star and return to the place they left. Hence their movement was called The Ball-play of the Stars.[1]

[1: "*Citlaltlachtli*," from *citlalin*, star, and *tlachtli*, the game of ball. Alvarado Tezozomoc, *Cronica Mexicana*, cap. lxxxii. The obscure passage in which Tezozomoc refers to this is ingeniously analyzed in the *Anales del Museo Nacional*, Tom. ii, p. 388.]

A recent writer asserts that the popular belief of the Aztecs extended the figure to a greater game than this.[1] The Sun and Moon were huge balls with which the gods played an unceasing game, now one, now the other, having the better of it. If this is so, then the game between Tezcatlipoca and Quetzalcoatl is again a transparent figure of speech for the contest between night and day.

[1: *Anales del Museo Nacional*, Tom. ii, p. 367.]

The Mexican tiger, the *ocelotl*, was a well recognized figure of speech, in the Aztec tongue, for the nocturnal heavens, dotted with stars, as is the tiger skin with spots.[1] The tiger, therefore, which destroyed the subjects of Quetzalcoatl--the swift-footed, happy inhabitants of Tula--was none other than the night extinguishing the rays of the orb of light. In the picture writings Tezcatlipoca appears dressed in a tiger's skin, the spots on which represent the stars, and thus symbolize him in his character as the god of the sky at night.

[1: "Segun los Anales de Cuauhtitlan el *ocelotl* es el cielo manchado de estrellas, como piel de tigre." *Anales del Mus. Nac.*, ii, p. 254.]

The apotheosis of Quetzalcoatl from the embers of his funeral pyre to the planet Venus has led several distinguished students of Mexican mythology to identify his whole history with the astronomical relations of this bright star. Such an interpretation is, however, not only contrary to results obtained by the general science of mythology, but it is specifically in contradiction to the uniform statements of the old writers. All these agree that it was not till *after* he had finished his career, *after* he had run his course and disappeared from the sight and knowledge of men, that he was translated and became the evening or morning star.[1] This clearly signifies that he was represented by the planet in only one, and that a subordinate, phase of his activity. We can readily see that the relation of Venus to the sun, and the evening and morning twilights, suggested the pleasing tale that as the light dies in the west, it is, in a certain way, preserved by the star which hangs so bright above the horizon.

[1: *Codex Telleriano-Remensis*, plate xiv.]

Sec.4. *Quetzalcoatl as Lord of the Winds.*

As I have shown in the introductory chapter, the Light-God, the Lord of the East, is also master of the cardinal points and of the winds which blow from them, and therefore of the Air.

This was conspicuously so with Quetzalcoatl. As a divinity he is most generally mentioned as the God of the Air and Winds. He was said to sweep the roads before Tlaloc; god of the rains, because in that climate heavy down-pours are preceded by violent gusts. Torquemada names him as "God of the Air," and states that in Cholula this function was looked upon as his chief attribute,[1] and the term was distinctly applied to him *Nanihe-hecatli*, Lord of the four Winds.

[1: Sahagun, *Historia*, Lib. i, cap. v. Torquemada, *Monarquia Indiana*, Lib. vi, cap. xxiv.]

In one of the earliest myths he is called *Yahualli ehecatl*, meaning "the Wheel of the Winds,"[1] the winds being portrayed in the picture writing as a circle or wheel, with a figure with five angles inscribed upon it, the sacred pentagram. His image carried in the left hand this wheel, and in the right a sceptre with the end recurved.

[1: "Quecalcoatl y por otro nombre yagualiecatl." Ramirez de Fuen-leal, *Historia*, cap. i. *Yahualli* is from the root *yaual* or *youal*, circular, rounding, and was applied to various objects of a circular form. The sign of Quetzalcoatl is called by Sahagun, using the native word, "el *Yoel* de los Vientos" (*Historia*, ubi supra).]

Another reference to this wheel, or mariner's box, was in the shape of the temples which were built in his honor as god of the winds. These, we are informed, were completely circular, without an angle anywhere.[1]

[1: "Se llaman (a Quetzalcoatl) Senor de el Viento * * * A este le hacian las yglesias redondas, sin esquina ninguna." *Codex Telleriano-Remensis*. Parte ii, Lam. ii. Describing the sacred edifices of Mexico, Motolinia says: "Habio en todos los mas de estos grandes patios un otro templo que despues de levantada aquella capa quadrada, hecho su altar, cubrianlo con una pared redonda, alta y cubierta con su chapital. Este era del dios del aire, cual dijimos tener su principal sella en Cholollan, y en toda esta provincia habia mucho de estos. A este dios del aire llamaban en su lengua Quetzal-coatl," *Historia de los Indios*, Epistola Proemial. Compare also Herrera, *Historia de las Indias Occidentals*, Dec. ii, Lib. vii, cap. xvii, who describes the temple of Quetzalcoatl, in the city of Mexico, and adds that it was circular, "porque asi como el Aire anda al rededor del Cielo, asi le hacian el Templo redondo."]

Still another symbol which was sacred to him as lord of the four winds was the Cross. It was not the Latin but the Greek cross, with four short arms of equal length. Several of these were painted on the mantle which he wore in the picture writings, and they are occasionally found on the sacred jades, which bear other of his symbols.

This has often been made use of by one set of writers to prove that Quetzalcoatl was some Christian teacher; and by others as evidence that these native tales were of a date subsequent to the Conquest. But a moment's consideration of the meaning of this cruciform symbol as revealed in its native names shows where it belongs and what it refers to. These names are three, and their significations are, "The Rain-God," "The Tree of our Life," "The God of Strength."[1] As the rains fertilize the fields and ripen the food crops, so he who sends them is indeed the prop or tree of our subsistence, and thus becomes the giver of health and strength. No other explanation is needed, or is, in fact, allowable.

[1: The Aztec words are *Quiahuitl teotl, quiahuitl*, rain, *teotl*, god; *Tonacaquahuitl*, from *to*, our, *naca*, flesh or life, *quahuitl*, tree; *Chicahual-izteotl*, from *chicahualiztli*, strength or courage, and *teotl*, god. These names are given by Ixtlilxochitl, *Historia chichimeca*, cap. i.]

The winds and rains come from the four cardinal points. This fact was figuratively represented by a cruciform figure, the ends directed toward each of these. The God of the Four Winds bore these crosses as one of his emblems. The sign came to be connected with fertility, reproduction and life, through its associations as a symbol of the rains which restore the parched fields and aid in the germination of seeds. Their influence in this respect is most striking in those southern countries where a long dry season is followed by heavy tropical showers, which in a few days change the whole face of nature, from one of parched sterility to one of a wealth of vegetable growth.

As there is a close connection, in meteorology, between the winds and the rains, so in Aztec mythology, there was an equally near one between Quetzalcoatl, as the god of the winds, and the gods of rain, Tlaloc and his sister, or wife, or mother, Chalchihuitlicue. According to one myth, these were created by the four primeval brother-gods, and placed in the heavens, where they occupy a large mansion divided into four apartments, with a court in the middle. In this court stand four enormous vases of water, and an infinite number of very small slaves (the rain drops) stand ready to dip out the water from one or the other vase and pour it on the earth in showers.[1]

[1: Ramirez de Fuen-leal, *Historia de los Mexicanos*, cap. ii.]

Tlaloc means, literally, "The wine of the Earth,"[1] the figure being that as man's heart is made glad, and his strength revived by the joyous spirit of wine, so is the soil refreshed and restored by the rains. *Tlaloc tecutli*, the Lord of the Wine of the Earth, was the proper title of the male divinity, who sent the fertilizing showers, and thus caused the seed to grow in barren places. It was he who gave abundant crops and saved the parched and dying grain after times of drought. Therefore, he was appealed to as the giver of good things, of corn and wine; and the name of his home, Tlalocan, became synonymous with that of the terrestrial paradise.

[1: *Tlalli*, earth, *oc* from *octli*, the native wine made from the maguey, enormous quantities of which are consumed by the lower classes in Mexico at this day, and which was well known to the ancients. Another derivation of the name is from *tlalli*, and *onoc*, being, to be, hence, "resident on the earth." This does not seem appropriate.]

His wife or sister, Chalchihuitlicue, She of the Emerald Skirts, was goddess of flowing streams, brooks, lakes and rivers. Her name, probably, has reference to their limpid waters.[1] It is derived from *chalchihuitl*, a species of jade or precious green stone, very highly esteemed by the natives of Mexico and Central America, and worked by them into ornaments and talismans, often elaborately engraved and inscribed with symbols, by an art now altogether lost.[2] According to one myth, Quetzalcoatl's mother took the name of *chalchiuitl* "when she ascended to heaven;"[3] by another he was engendered by such a sacred stone;[4] and by all he was designated as the discoverer of the art of cutting and polishing them, and the patron deity of workers in this branch.[5]

[1: From *chalchihuitl*, jade, and *cueitl*, skirt or petticoat, with the possessive prefix, *i*, her.]

[2: See E.G. Squier, *Observations on a Collection of Chalchihuitls from Central America*, New York, 1869, and Heinrich Fischer, *Nephrit und Jadeit nach ihrer Urgeschichtlichen und Ethnographischen Bedeutung*, Stuttgart, 1880, for a full discussion of the subject.]

[3: *Codex Telleriano-Remensis*, Pt. ii, Lam. ii.]

[4: See above, chapter iii, Sec.3]

[5: Torquemada, *Monarquia Indiana*, Lib. vi, cap. xxiv.]

The association of this stone and its color, a bluish green of various shades, with the God of Light and the Air, may have reference to the blue sky where he has his home, or to the blue and green waters where he makes his bed. Whatever the connection was, it was so close that the festivals of all three, Tlaloc, Chalchihuitlicue and Quetzalcoatl, were celebrated together on the same day, which was the first of the first month of the Aztec calendar, in February.[1]

[1: Sahagun, *Hisioria*, Lib. ii, cap. i. A worthy but visionary Mexican antiquary, Don J.M. Melgar, has recognized in Aztec mythology the frequency of the symbolism which expresses the fertilizing action of the sky (the sun and rains) upon the earth. He thinks that in some of the manuscripts, as the *Codex Borgia*, it is represented by the rabbit fecundating the frog. See his *Examen Comparativo entre los Signos Simbolicos de las Teogonias y Cosmogonias antiguas y los que existen en los Manuscritos Mexicanos*, p. 21 (Vera Cruz, 1872).]

In his character as god of days, the deity who brings back the diurnal suns, and thus the seasons and years, Quetzalcoatl was the reputed inventor of the Mexican Calendar. He himself was said to have been born on Ce Acatl, One Cane, which was the first day of the first month, the beginning of the reckoning, and the name of the day was often added to his own.[1] As the count of the days really began with the beginning, it was added that Heaven itself was created on this same day, Ce Acatl. [2]

[1: *Codex Vaticanus*, Pl. xv.]

[2: *Codex Telleriano Remensis*, Pl. xxxiii.]

In some myths Quetzalcoatl was the sole framer of the Calendar; in others he was assisted by the first created pair, Cipactli and Oxomuco, who, as I have said, appear to represent the Sky and the Earth. A certain cave in the province of Cuernava (Quauhnauac) was pointed out as the scene of their deliberations. Cipactonal chose the first name, Oxomuco the second, and Quetzalcoatl the third, and so on in turn. [1]

[1: Mendieta, *Hist. Eclesiastia Indiana*, Lib. ii, cap. xiv. "Una tonta ficcion," comments the worthy chronicler upon the narrative, "como son las demas que creian cerca de sus dioses." This has been the universal opinion. My ambition in writing this book is, that it will be universal no longer.]

In many mythologies the gods of light and warmth are, by a natural analogy, held to be also the deities which preside over plenty, fertility and reproduction. This was quite markedly the case with Quetzalcoatl. His land and city were the homes of abundance; his people, the Toltecs, "were skilled in all arts, all of which they had been taught by Quetzalcoatl himself. They were, moreover, very rich; they lacked nothing; food was never scarce and crops never failed. They had no need to save the small ears of corn, so all the use they made of them was to burn them in heating their baths."[1]

[1: Sahagun, *Historia*, Lib. iii, cap. iii.]

As thus the promoter of fertility in the vegetable world, he was also the genius of reproduction in the human race. The ceremonies of marriage which were in use among the Aztecs were attributed to him,[1] and when the wife found she was with child it was to him that she was told to address her thanks. One of her relatives recited to her a formal exhortation, which began as follows:--

[1: Veitia, cap. xvii, in Kingsborough.]

"My beloved little daughter, precious as sapphire and jade, tender and generous! Our Lord, who dwells everywhere and rains his bounties on whom he pleases, has remembered you. The God now wishes to give you the fruit of marriage, and has placed within you a jewel, a rich feather. Perhaps you have watched, and swept, and offered incense; for such good works the kindness of the Lord has been made manifest, and it was decreed in Heaven and Hell, before the beginning of the World, that this grace should be accorded you. For these reasons our Lord, Quetzalcoatl,

who is the author and creator of things, has shown you this favor; thus has resolved
He in heaven, who is at once both man and woman, and is known under the names
Twice Master and Twice Mistress."[1]

[1: Sahagun, *Historia*, Lib. vi, cap. xxv. The bisexual nature of the Mexican
gods, referred to in this passage, is well marked in many features of their mythology. Quetzalcoatl is often addressed in the prayers as "father and mother," just as,
in the Egyptian ritual, Chnum was appealed to as "father of fathers and mother
of mothers" (Tiele, *Hist. of the Egyptian Religion*, p. 134). I have endeavored to
explain this widespread belief in hermaphroditic deities in my work entitled, *The
Religious Sentiment, Its Source and Aim*, pp. 65-68, (New York, 1876).]

It is recorded in the old histories that the priests dedicated to his service wore a
peculiar head-dress, imitating a snail shell, and for that reason were called *Quatec-
zizque*.[1] No one has explained this curiously shaped bonnet. But it was undoubtedly because Quetzalcoatl was the god of reproduction, for among the Aztecs the
snail was a well known symbol of the process of parturition.[2]

[1: Duran, in Kingsborough, vol. viii, p. 267. The word is from *quaitl*, head or
top, and *tecziztli*, a snail shell.]

[2: "Mettevanli in testa una lumaca marina per dimostrare que siccome il pis-
cato esce dalle pieghe di quell'osso, o conca. cosi va ed esce l'uomo *ab utero matris
suae*." *Codice Vaticana, Tavola XXVI.*]

Quetzalcoatl was that marvelous artist who fashions in the womb of the mother
the delicate limbs and tender organs of the unborn infant. Therefore, when a couple
of high rank were blessed with a child, an official orator visited them, and the baby
being placed naked before him, he addressed it beginning with these words:--

"My child and lord, precious gem, emerald, sapphire, beauteous feather, product of a noble union, you have been formed far above us, in the ninth heaven,
where dwell the two highest divinities. His Divine Majesty has fashioned you in a
mould, as one fashions a ball of gold; you have been chiseled as a precious stone, ar-
tistically dressed by your Father and Mother, the great God and the great Goddess,
assisted by their son, Quetzalcoatl."[1]

[1: Sahagun, *Historia*, Lib. vi, cap. xxxiv.]

As he was thus the god on whom depended the fertilization of the womb, sterile women made their vows to him, and invoked his aid to be relieved from the shame of barrenness.[1]

[1: Torquemada, *Monarquia Indiana*, Lib. xi, cap. xxiv.]

In still another direction is this function of his godship shown. The worship of the genesiac principle is as often characterized by an excessive austerity as by indulgence in sexual acts. Here we have an example. Nearly all the accounts tell us that Quetzalcoatl was never married, and that he held himself aloof from all women, in absolute chastity. We are told that on one occasion his subjects urged upon him the propriety of marriage, and to their importunities he returned the dark answer that, Yes, he had determined to take a wife; but that it would be when the oak tree shall cast chestnuts, when the sun shall rise in the west, when one can cross the sea dry-shod, and when nightingales grow beards.[1]

[1: Duran, in Kingsborough, vol. viii, p. 267. I believe Alva Ixtlilxochitl is the only author who specifically assigns a family to Quetzalcoatl. This author does not mention a wife, but names two sons, one, Xilotzin, who was killed in war, the other, Pochotl, who was educated by his nurse, Toxcueye, and who, after the destruction of Tollan, collected the scattered Toltecs and settled with them around the Lake of Tezcuco (*Relaciones Historicas*, p. 394, in Kingsborough, vol. ix). All this is in contradiction to the reports of earlier and better authorities. For instance, Motolinia says pointedly, "no fue casado, ni se le conocio mujer" (*Historia de los Indios, Epistola Proemial*).]

Following the example of their Master, many of the priests of his cult refrained from sexual relations, and as a mortification of the flesh they practiced a painful rite by transfixing the tongue and male member with the sharp thorns of the maguey plant, an austerity which, according to their traditions, he was the first to institute. [1] There were also in the cities where his special worship was in vogue, houses of nuns, the inmates of which had vowed perpetual virginity, and it was said that Quetzalcoatl himself had founded these institutions.[2]

[1: *Codex Vaticanus*, Tab. xxii.]

[2: Veitia, *Historia*, cap. XVII.]

His connection with the worship of the reproductive principle seems to be further indicated by his surname, *Ce acatl*. This means One Reed, and is the name of a day in the calendar. But in the Nahuatl language, the word *acatl*, reed, cornstalk, is also applied to the virile member; and it has been suggested that this is the real signification of the word when applied to the hero-god. The suggestion is plausible, but the word does not seem to have been so construed by the early writers. If such an understanding had been current, it could scarcely have escaped the inquiries of such a close student and thorough master of the Nahuatl tongue as Father Sahagun.

On the other hand, it must be said, in corroboration of this identification, that the same idea appears to be conveyed by the symbol of the serpent. One correct translation of the name Quetzalcoatl is "the beautiful serpent;" his temple in the city of Mexico, according to Torquemada, had a door in the form of a serpent's mouth; and in the **Codex Vaticanus**, No. 3738, published by Lord Kingsborough, of which we have an explanation by competent native authority, he is represented as a serpent; while in the same Codex, in the astrological signs which were supposed to control the different parts of the human body, the serpent is pictured as the sign of the male member.[1] This indicates the probability that in his function as god of reproduction Quetzalcoatl may have stood in some relation to phallic rites.

[1: Compare the **Codex Vaticanus**, No. 3738, plates 44 and 75, Kingsborough, **Mexican Antiquities**, vol. ii.]

This same sign, **Ce Coatl**, One Serpent, used in their astrology, was that of one of the gods of the merchants, and apparently for this reason, some writers have identified the chief god of traffic, Yacatecutli (God of Journeying), with Quetzalcoatl. This seems the more likely as another name of this divinity was **Yacacoliuhqui**, With the End Curved, a name which appears to refer to the curved rod or stick which was both his sign and one of those of Quetzalcoatl.[1] The merchants also constantly associated in their prayers this deity with Huitzilopochtli, which is another reason for supposing their patron was one of the four primeval brothers, and but another manifestation of Quetzalcoatl. His character, as patron of arts, the model of orators, and the cultivator of peaceful intercourse among men, would naturally lend itself to this position.

[1: Compare Torquemada, **Monarquia Indiana**, Lib. vi, cap. xxviii and Sahagun, **Historia de Nueva Espana**, Lib. ix, **passim**.

Yacatecutli, is from **tecutli**, lord, and either **yaqui**, traveler, or else **yacana**, to conduct.

Yacacoliuhqui, is translated by Torquemada, "el que tiene la nariz aquilena." It is from *yaque*, a point or end, and hence, also, the nose, and *coliuhqui*, bent or curved. The translation in the text is quite as allowable as that of Torquemada, and more appropriate. I have already mentioned that this divinity was suspected, by Dr. Schultz-Sellack, to be merely another form of Quetzalcoatl. See above, chapter iii, Sec.2]

But Quetzalcoatl, as god of the violent wind-storms, which destroy the houses and crops, and as one, who, in his own history, was driven from his kingdom and lost his all, was not considered a deity of invariably good augury. His day and sign, *ce acatl*, One Reed, was of bad omen. A person born on it would not succeed in life.[1] His plans and possessions would be lost, blown away, as it were, by the wind, and dissipated into thin air.

[1: Sahagun. *Historia*, Lib. iv, cap. viii.]

Through the association of his person with the prying winds he came, curiously enough, to be the patron saint of a certain class of thieves, who stupefied their victims before robbing them. They applied to him to exercise his maleficent power on those whom they planned to deprive of their goods. His image was borne at the head of the gang when they made their raids, and the preferred season was when his sign was in the ascendant.[1] This is a singular parallelism to the Aryan Hermes myth, as I have previously observed (Chap. I).

[1: Ibid. Lib. IV, cap. XXXI.]

The representation of Quetzalcoatl in the Aztec manuscripts, his images and the forms of his temples and altars, referred to his double functions as Lord of the Light and the Winds.

He was not represented with pleasing features. On the contrary, Sahagun tells us that his face, that is, that of his image, was "very ugly, with a large head and a full beard."[1] The beard, in this and similar instances, was to represent the rays of the sun. His hair at times was also shown rising straight from his forehead, for the same reason.[2]

[1: "La cara que tenia era muy fea y la cabeza larga y barbuda." *Historia*, Lib. III, cap. III. On the other hand Ixtlilxochitl speaks of him as "de bella figura." *Historia Chichimeca*, cap. viii. He was occasionally represented with his face painted black, probably expressing the sun in its absence.]

[2: He is so portrayed in the Codex Vaticanus. and Ixtlilxochitl says, "tubiese el cabello levantado desde la frente hasta la nuca como a manera de penacho." ***Historia Chichimeca***, cap. viii.]

At times he was painted with a large hat and flowing robe, and was then called "Father of the Sons of the Clouds," that is, of the rain drops.[1]

[1: Diego Duran, ***Historia***, in Kingsborough, viii, p. 267.]

These various representations doubtless referred to him at different parts of his chequered career, and as a god under different manifestations of his divine nature. The religious art of the Aztecs did not demand any uniformity in this respect.

Sec.5. *The Return of Quetzalcoatl.*

Quetzalcoatl was gone.

Whether he had removed to the palace prepared for him in Tlapallan, whether he had floated out to sea on his wizard raft of serpent skins, or whether his body had been burned on the sandy sea strand and his soul had mounted to the morning star, the wise men were not agreed. But on one point there was unanimity. Quetzalcoatl was gone; but ***he would return***.

In his own good time, in the sign of his year, when the ages were ripe, once more he would come from the east, surrounded by his fair-faced retinue, and resume the sway of his people and their descendants. Tezcatlipoca had conquered, but not for aye. The immutable laws which had fixed the destruction of Tollan assigned likewise its restoration. Such was the universal belief among the Aztec race.

For this reason Quetzalcoatl's statue, or one of them, was in a reclining position and covered with wrappings, signifying that he was absent, "as of one who lays him down to sleep, and that when he should awake from that dream of absence, he should rise to rule again the land."[1]

[1: Torquemada, ***Monarquia Indiana***, Lib. vi, cap. xxiv. So in Egyptian mythology Tum was called "the concealed or imprisoned god, in a physical sense the Sun-god in the darkness of night, not revealing himself, but alive, nevertheless." Tiele, ***History of the Egyptian Religion***, p. 77.]

He was not dead. He had indeed built mansions underground, to the Lord of Mictlan, the abode of the dead, the place of darkness, but he himself did not occupy them.[1] Where he passed his time was where the sun stays at night. As this, too, is somewhere beneath the level of the earth, it was occasionally spoken of as *Tlil-*

lapa, The Murky Land,[2] and allied therefore to Mictlan. Caverns led down to it, especially one south of Chapultepec, called **Cincalco**, "To the Abode of Abundance," through whose gloomy corridors one could reach the habitation of the sun and the happy land still governed by Quetzalcoatl and his lieutenant Totec.[3]

[1: Sahagun, *Historia*, Lib. iii. cap. ult.]

[2: Mendieta, *Hist. Eclesiast. Indiana*, Lib. ii, cap. v. The name is from *tlilli*, something dark, obscure.]

[3: Sahagun, *Historia*, Lib. xii, cap. ix; Duran, *Historia*, cap. lxviii; Tezozomoc, *Cron. Mexicana*, cap. ciii. Sahagun and Tezozomoc give the name *Cincalco*, To the House of Maize, *i.e.*, Fertility, Abundance, the Paradise. Duran gives *Cicalco*, and translates it "casa de la liebre," *citli*, hare, *calli*, house, *co* locative. But this is, no doubt, an error, mistaking *citli* for *cintli*, maize.]

But the real and proper names of that land were Tlapallan, the Red Land, and Tizapan, the White Land, for either of these colors is that of the sun-light.[1]

[1: *Tizapan* from *tizatl*, white earth or other substance, and *pan*, in. Mendicta, Lib. ii, cap. iv.]

It was generally understood to be the same land whence he and the Toltecs had come forth in ancient times; or if not actually the same, nevertheless, very similar to it. While the myth refers to the latter as Tlapallan, it speaks of the former as Huey Tlapallan, Old Tlapallan, or the first Tlapallan. But Old Tlapallan was usually located to the West, where the sun disappears at night;[1] while New Tlapallan, the goal of Quetzalcoatl's journey, was in the East, where the day-orb rises in the morning. The relationship is obvious, and is based on the similarity of the morning and the evening skies, the heavens at sunset and at sunrise.

[1: "Huitlapalan, que es la que al presente llaman de Cortes, que por parecer vermeja le pusieron el nombre referido." Alva Ixtlilxochitl, *Historia Chichimeca*, Cap. ii.]

In his capacity as master of arts, and, at the same time, ruler of the underground realm, in other words, as representing in his absence the Sun at night, he was supposed to preside over the schools where the youth were shut up and severely trained in ascetic lives, previous to coming forth into the world. In this function he was addressed as **Quetzalcoatl Tlilpotonqui**, the Dark or Black Plumed, and the child, on admittance, was painted this color, and blood drawn from his ears and offered to the god.[1] Probably for the same reason, in many picture writings, both his face and body were blackened.

[1: Sahagun, Lib. iii, Append, cap. vii. and cf. Lib. i, cap v. The surname is from *tlilli*, black, and *potonia*, "emplumar a otro."]

It is at first sight singular to find his character and symbols thus in a sense reversed, but it would not be difficult to quote similar instances from Aryan and Egyptian mythology. The sun at night was often considered to be the ruler of the realm of the dead, and became associated with its gloomy symbolism.

Wherever he was, Quetzalcoatl was expected to return and resume the sceptre of sovereignty, which he had laid down at the instigation of Tezcatlipoca. In what cycle he would appear the sages knew not, but the year of the cycle was predicted by himself of old.

Here appears an extraordinary coincidence. The sign of the year of Quetzalcoatl was, as I have said, One Reed, Ce Acatl. In the Mexican calendar this recurs only once in their cycle of fifty-two years. The myth ran that on some recurrence of this year his arrival was to take place. The year 1519 of the Christian era was the year One Reed, and in that year Hernan Cortes landed his army on Mexican soil!

The approach of the year had, as usual, revived the old superstition, and possibly some vague rumors from Yucatan or the Islands had intensified the dread with which the Mexican emperor contemplated the possible loss of his sovereignty. Omens were reported in the sky, on earth and in the waters. The sages and diviners were consulted, but their answers were darker than the ignorance they were asked to dispel. Yes, they agreed, a change is to come, the present order of things will be swept away, perhaps by Quetzalcoatl, perhaps by hideous beings with faces of serpents, who walk with one foot, whose heads are in their breasts, whose huge hands serve as sun shades, and who can fold themselves in their immense ears.[1]

[1: The names of these mysterious beings are given by Tezozomoc as *Tezocui-lyoxique, Zenteicxique* and *Coayxaques. Cronica Mexicana*, caps, cviii and civ.]

Little satisfied with these grotesque prophecies the monarch summoned his dwarfs and hunchbacks--a class of dependents he maintained in imitation of Quetzalcoatl--and ordered them to proceed to the sacred Cave of Cincalco.

"Enter its darknes," he said, "without fear. There you will find him who ages ago lived in Tula, who calls himself Huemac, the Great Hand.[1] If one enters, he dies indeed, but only to be born to an eternal life in a land where food and wine are in perennial plenty. It is shady with trees, filled with fruit, gay with flowers, and those who dwell there know nought but joy. Huemac is king of that land, and he who lives with him is ever happy."

[1: Huemac, as I have already said, is stated by Sahagun to have been the war chief of Tula, as Quetzalcoatl was the sacerdotal head (Lib. iii, cap. v). But Duran and most writers state that it was simply another name of Quetzalcoatl.]

The dwarfs and hunchbacks departed on their mission, under the guidance of the priests. After a time they returned and reported that they had entered the cave and reached a place where four roads met. They chose that which descended most rapidly, and soon were accosted by an old man with a staff in his hand. This was Totec, who led them to his lord Huemac, to whom they stated the wish of Montezuma for definite information. The reply was vague and threatening, and though twice afterwards the emperor sent other embassies, only ominous and obscure announcements were returned by the priests.[1]

Clearly they preferred to be prophets of evil, and quite possibly they themselves were the slaves of gloomy forebodings.

[1: Tezozomoc, *Cronica Mexicana*, caps. cviii, cix; Sahagun, *Historia*, Lib. xii, cap. ix. The four roads which met one on the journey to the Under World are also described in the *Popol Vuh*, p. 83. Each is of a different color, and only one is safe to follow.]

Dissatisfied with their reports, Montezuma determined to visit the underground realm himself, and by penetrating through the cave of Cincalco to reach the mysterious land where his attendants and priests professed to have been. For obvious reasons such a suggestion was not palatable to them, and they succeeded in persuading him to renounce the plan, and their deceptions remained undiscovered.

Their idle tales brought no relief to the anxious monarch, and at length, when his artists showed him pictures of the bearded Spaniards and strings of glittering beads from Cortes, the emperor could doubt no longer, and exclaimed: "Truly this is the Quetzalcoatl we expected, he who lived with us of old in Tula. Undoubtedly it is he, *Ce Acatl Inacuil*, the god of One Reed, who is journeying."[1]

[1: Tezozomoc, *Cronica Mexicana*, cap. cviii.]

On his very first interview with Cortes, he addressed him through the interpreter Marina in remarkable words which have been preserved to us by the Spanish conqueror himself. Cortes writes:--

"Having delivered me the presents, he seated himself next to me and spoke as follows:--

"'We have known for a long time, by the writings handed down by our forefathers, that neither I nor any who inhabit this land are natives of it, but foreigners who came here from remote parts. We also know that we were led here by a ruler, whose subjects we all were, who returned to his country, and after a long time came here again and wished to take his people away. But they had married wives and built houses, and they would neither go with him nor recognize him as their king; therefore he went back. We have ever believed that those who were of his lineage would some time come and claim this land as his, and us as his vassals. From the direction whence you come, which is where the sun rises, and from what you tell me of this great lord who sent you, we believe and think it certain that he is our natural ruler, especially since you say that for a long time he has known about us. Therefore you may feel certain that we shall obey you, and shall respect you as holding the place of that great lord; and in all the land I rule you may give what orders you wish, and they shall be obeyed, and everything we have shall be put at your service. And since you are thus in your own heritage and your own house, take your ease and rest from the fatigue of the journey and the wars you have had on the way.'"[1]

[1: Cortes, ***Carta Segunda***, October 30th, 1520. According to Bernal Diaz Montezuma referred to the prediction several times. ***Historia Verdadera de la Conquista de la Nueva Espana***, cap. lxxxix, xc. The words of Montezuma are also given by Father Sahagun, ***Historia de Nueva Espana***, Lib. xii, cap. xvi. The statement of Montezuma that Quetzalcoatl ***had already returned***, but had not been well received by the people, and had, therefore, left them again, is very interesting. It is a part of the Quetzalcoatl myth which I have not found in any other Aztec source. But it distinctly appears in the Kiche which I shall quote on a later page, and is also in close parallelism with the hero-myths of Yucatan, Peru and elsewhere. It is, to my mind, a strong evidence of the accuracy of Marina's translation of Montezuma's words, and the fidelity of Cortes' memory.]

Such was the extraordinary address with which the Spaniard, with his handful of men, was received by the most powerful war chief of the American continent. It confessed complete submission, without a struggle. But it was the expression of a general sentiment. When the Spanish ships for the first time reached the Mexican shores the natives kissed their sides and hailed the white and bearded strangers from the east as gods, sons and brothers of Quetzalcoatl, come back from their celestial home to claim their own on earth and bring again the days of Paradise; [1] a hope, dryly observes Father Mendieta, which the poor Indians soon gave up when they came to feel the acts of their visitors.[2]

[1: Sahagun, **Historia**, Lib. xii, cap. ii.]

[2: "Los Indios siempre esperaron que se habia de cumplir aquella profecia y cuando vieron venir a los cristianos luego los llamaron dioses, hijos, y hermanos de Quetzalcoatl, aunque despues que conocieron y experimentaron sus obras, no los tuvieron por celestiales." **Historia Eclesiastica Indiana**, Lib. ii, cap. x.]

Such presentiments were found scattered through America. They have excited the suspicion of historians and puzzled antiquaries to explain. But their interpretation is simple enough. The primitive myth of the sun which had sunk but should rise again, had in the lapse of time lost its peculiarly religious sense, and had been in part taken to refer to past historical events. The Light-God had become merged in the divine culture hero. He it was who was believed to have gone away, not to die, for he was immortal, but to dwell in the distant east, whence in the fullness of time he would return.

This was why Montezuma and his subjects received the whites as expected guests, and quoted to them prophecies of their coming. The Mayas of Yucatan, the Muyscas of Bogota, the Qquichuas of Peru, all did the same, and all on the same grounds--the confident hope of the return of the Light-God from the under world.

This hope is an integral part of this great Myth of Light, in whatever part of the world we find it. Osiris, though murdered, and his body cast into "the unclean sea," will come again from the eastern shores. Balder, slain by the wiles of Loki, is not dead forever, but at the appointed time will appear again in nobler majesty. So in her divine fury sings the prophetess of the Voeluspa:--

"Shall arise a second time, Earth from ocean, green and fair, The waters ebb, the eagles fly, Snatch the fish from out the flood.

"Once again the wondrous runes, Golden tablets, shall be found; Mystic runes by Aesir carved, Gods who ruled Fiolnir's line.

"Then shall fields unseeded bear, Ill shall flee, and Balder come, Dwell in Odin's highest hall, He and all the happy gods.

"Outshines the sun that mighty hall, Glitters gold on heaven's hill; There shall god-like princes dwell, And rule for aye a happy world."

CHAPTER IV.
THE HERO-GODS OF THE MAYAS.

The high-water mark of ancient American civilization was touched by the Mayas, the race who inhabited the peninsula of Yucatan and vicinity. Its members extended to the Pacific coast and included the tribes of Vera Paz, Guatemala, and parts of Chiapas and Honduras, and had an outlying branch in the hot lowlands watered by the River Panuco, north of Vera Cruz. In all, it has been estimated that they numbered at the time of the Conquest perhaps two million souls. To them are due the vast structures of Copan, Palenque and Uxmal, and they alone possessed a mode of writing which rested distinctly on a phonetic basis.

The zenith of their prosperity had, however, been passed a century before the Spanish conquerors invaded their soil. A large part of the peninsula of Yucatan had been for generations ruled in peace by a confederation of several tribes, whose capital city was Mayapan, ten leagues south of where Merida now stands, and whose ruins still cover many hundred acres of the plain. Somewhere about the year 1440 there was a general revolt of the eastern provinces; Mayapan itself was assaulted and destroyed, and the Peninsula was divided among a number of petty chieftains.

Such was its political condition at the time of the discovery. There were numerous populous cities, well built of stone and mortar, but their inhabitants were at war with each other and devoid of unity of purpose.[1] Hence they fell a comparatively easy prey to the conquistadors.

[1: Francisco de Montejo, who was the first to explore Yucatan (1528), has left strong testimony to the majesty of its cities and the agricultural industry of its inhabitants. He writes to the King, in the report of his expedition: "La tierra es muy poblada y de muy grandes ciudades y villas muy frescas. Todos los pueblos son una huerta de frutales." *Carta a su Magestad, 13 Abril, 1529*, in the *Coleccion de Documentos Ineditos del Archivo de Indias*, Tom. xiii.]

Whence came this civilization? Was it an offshoot of that of the Aztecs? Or did it produce the latter?

These interesting questions I cannot discuss in full at this time. All that concerns my present purpose is to treat of them so far as they are connected with the mythology of the race. Incidentally, however, this will throw some light on these obscure points, and at any rate enable us to dismiss certain prevalent assumptions as erroneous.

One of these is the notion that the Toltecs were the originators of Yucatan culture. I hope I have said enough in the previous chapter to exorcise permanently from ancient American history these purely imaginary beings. They have served long enough as the last refuge of ignorance.

Let us rather ask what accounts the Mayas themselves gave of the origin of their arts and their ancestors.

Most unfortunately very meagre sources of information are open to us. We have no Sahagun to report to us the traditions and prayers of this strange people.

Only fragments of their legends and hints of their history have been saved, almost by accident, from the general wreck of their civilization. From these, however, it is possible to piece together enough to give us a glimpse of their original form, and we shall find it not unlike those we have already reviewed.

There appear to have been two distinct cycles of myths in Yucatan, the most ancient and general that relating to Itzamna, the second, of later date and different origin, referring to Kukulcan. It is barely possible that these may be different versions of the same; but certainly they were regarded as distinct by the natives at and long before the time of the Conquest.

This is seen in the account they gave of their origin. They did not pretend to be autochthonous, but claimed that their ancestors came from distant regions, in two bands. The largest and most ancient immigration was from the East, across, or rather through, the ocean--for the gods had opened twelve paths through it--and this was conducted by the mythical civilizer Itzamna. The second band, less in number and later in time, came in from the West, and with them was Kukulcan. The former was called the Great Arrival; the latter, the Less Arrival[1].

[1: Cogolludo contradicts himself in describing these events; saying first that the greater band came from the West, but later in the same chapter corrects himself, and criticizes Father Lizana for having committed the same error. Cogolludo's authority was the original MSS. of Gaspar Antonio, an educated native, of royal lineage, who wrote in 1582. *Historia de Yucatan*, Lib. iv, caps, iii, iv. Lizana gives the names of these arrivals as *Nohnial* and *Cenial*. These words are badly mutilated. They should read *noh emel* (*noh*, great, *emel*, descent, arrival) and *cec, emel* (*cec*, small). Landa supports the position of Cogolludo. *Relacion de las Cosas de Yucatan*, p. 28. It is he who speaks of the "doce caminos por el mar."]

Sec.1. *The Culture Hero, Itzamna.*

To this ancient leader, Itzamna, the nation alluded as their guide, instructor and civilizer. It was he who gave names to all the rivers and divisions of land; he was their first priest, and taught them the proper rites wherewith to please the gods and appease their ill-will; he was the patron of the healers and diviners, and had disclosed to them the mysterious virtues of plants; in the month *Uo* they assembled and made new fire and burned to him incense, and having cleansed their books with water drawn from a fountain from which no woman had ever drunk, the most learned of the sages opened the volumes to forecast the character of the coming year.

It was Itzamna who first invented the characters or letters in which the Mayas wrote their numerous books, and which they carved in such profusion on the stone and wood of their edifices. He also devised their calendar, one more perfect even than that of the Mexicans, though in a general way similar to it[1].

[1: The authorities on this phase of Itzamna's character are Cogolludo, *Historia de Yucatan*, Lib. iv, cap. iii; Landa, ***Cosas de Yucatan***, pp. 285, 289, and Beltran de Santa Rosa Maria, ***Arte del Idioma Maya***, p. 16. The latter has a particularly valuable extract from the now lost Maya Dictionary of F. Gabriel de San Buenaventura. "El primero que hallo las letras de la lengua Maya e hizo el computo de los anos, meses y edades, y lo enseno todo a los Indios de esta Provincia, fue un Indio llamado Kinchahau, y por otro nombre Tzamna. Noticia que debemos a dicho R.F. Gabriel, y trae en su Calepino, lit. K. verb. Kinchahau, fol. 390, vuelt."]

As city-builder and king, his history is intimately associated with the noble edifices of Itzamal, which he laid out and constructed, and over which he ruled, enacting wise laws and extending the power and happiness of his people for an indefinite period.

Thus Itzamna, regarded as ruler, priest and teacher, was, no doubt, spoken of as an historical personage, and is so put down by various historians, even to the most recent[1]. But another form in which he appears proves him to have been an incarnation of deity, and carries his history from earth to heaven. This is shown in the very earliest account we have of the Maya mythology.

[1: Crescencio Carrillo, ***Historia Antigua de Yucatan***, p. 144, Merida, 1881. Though obliged to differ on many points with this indefatigable archaeologist, I must not omit to state my appreciation and respect for his earnest interest in the language and antiquities of his country. I know of no other Yucatecan who has equal enthusiasm or so just an estimate of the antiquarian riches of his native land.]

For this account we are indebted to the celebrated Las Casas, the "Apostle of the Indians." In 1545 he sent a certain priest, Francisco Hernandez by name, into the peninsula as a missionary. Hernandez had already traversed it as chaplain to Montejo's expedition, in 1528, and was to some degree familiar with the Maya tongue. After nearly a year spent among the natives he forwarded a report to Las

Casas, in which, among other matters, he noted a resemblance which seemed to exist between the myths recounted by the Maya priests and the Christian dogmas. They told him that the highest deity they worshiped was Izona, who had made men and all things. To him was born a son, named Bacab or Bacabab, by a virgin, Chibilias, whose mother was Ixchel. Bacab was slain by a certain Eopuco, on the day called *hemix*, but after three days rose from the dead and ascended into heaven. The Holy Ghost was represented by Echuac, who furnished the world with all things necessary to man's life and comfort. Asked what Bacab meant, they replied, "the Son of the Great Father," and Echuac they translated by "the merchant."[1]

[1: Las Casas, ***Historia Apologetica de las Indias Occidentales***, cap. cxxiii.]

This is the story that a modern writer says, "ought to be repudiated without question."[1] But I think not. It is not difficult to restore these names to their correct forms, and then the fancied resemblance to Christian theology disappears, while the character of the original myth becomes apparent.

[1: John T. Short, ***The North Americans of Antiquity***, p. 231.]

Cogolludo long since justly construed *Izona* as a misreading for *Izamna*. *Bacabab* is the plural form of *Bacab*, and shows that the sons were several. We are well acquainted with the Bacabab. Bishop Landa tells us all about them. They were four in number, four gigantic brothers, who supported the four corners of the heavens, who blew the four winds from the four cardinal points, and who presided over the four Dominical signs of the Calendar. As each year in the Calendar was supposed to be under the influence of one or the other of these brothers, one Bacab was said to die at the close of the year; and after the "nameless" or intercalary days had passed the next Bacab would live; and as each computation of the year began on the day *Imix*, which was the third before the close of the Maya week, this was said figuratively to be the day of death of the Bacab of that year. And whereas three (or four) days later a new year began, with another Bacab, the one was said to have died and risen again.

The myth further relates that the Bacabs were sons of Ix-chel. She was the Goddess of the Rainbow, which her name signifies. She was likewise believed to be the guardian of women in childbirth, and one of the patrons of the art of medicine. The early historians, Roman and Landa, also associate her with Itzamna[1], thus verifying the legend recorded by Hernandez.

[1: Fray Hieronimo Roman, *De la Republica de las Indias Occidentales*, Lib. ii, cap. xv; Diego de Landa, *Relacion de las Cosas de Yucatan*, p. 288. Cogolludo also mentions *Ix chel*, *Historia de Yucatan*, Lib. iv, cap. vi. The word in Maya for rainbow is *chel* or *cheel*; *ix* is the feminine prefix, which also changes the noun from the inanimate to the animate sense.]

That the Rainbow should be personified as wife of the Light-God and mother of the rain-gods, is an idea strictly in accordance with the course of mythological thought in the red race, and is founded on natural relations too evident to be mis-construed. The rainbow is never seen but during a shower, and while the sun is shining; hence it is always associated with these two meteorological phenomena.

I may quote in comparison the rainbow myth of the Moxos of South America. They held it to be the wife of Arama, their god of light, and her duty was to pour the refreshing rains on the soil parched by the glaring eye of her mighty spouse. Hence they looked upon her as goddess of waters, of trees and plants, and of fertility in general.[1]

[1: "Fabula, ridicula adspersam superstitione, habebant de iride. Ajebant illam esse Aramam feminam, solis conjugem, cujus officium sit terras a viro exustas im-brium beneficio recreare. Cum enim viderent arcum illum non nisi pluvio tempore in conspectu venire, et tunc arborum cacuminibus velut insidere, persuadebant sibi aquarum illum esse Praesidem, arboresque proceras omnes sua in tutela habere." Franc. Xav., Eder, *Descriptio Provinciae Moxitarum in Regno Peruano* p. 249 (Budae, 1791).]

Or we may take the Muyscas, a cultivated and interesting nation who dwelt on the lofty plateau where Bogota is situated. They worshiped the Rainbow under the name *Cuchaviva* and personified it as a goddess, who took particular care of those sick with fevers and of women in childbirth. She was also closely associated in their myth with their culture-hero Bochica, the story being that on one occa-sion, when an ill-natured divinity had inundated the plain of Bogota, Bochica ap-peared to the distressed inhabitants in company with Cuchaviva, and cleaving the mountains with a blow of his golden sceptre, opened a passage for the waters into the valley below.[1]

[1: E. Uricoechea, *Gramatica de la Lengua Chibcha*, Introd., p. xx. The simi-larity of these to the Biblical account is not to be attributed to borrowing from the latter, but simply that it, as they, are both the mythological expressions of the same natural phenomenon. In Norse mythology, Freya is the rainbow goddess. She wears the bow as a necklace or girdle. It was hammered out for her by four dwarfs, the four winds from the cardinal points, and Odin seeks to get it from her. Schwartz, *Ursprung der Mythologie*, S. 117.]

As goddess of the fertilizing showers, of growth and life, it is easily seen how Ixchel came to be the deity both of women in childbirth and of the medical art, a Juno Sospita as well as a Juno Lucina.

The statement is also significant, that the Bacabs were supposed to be the victims of Ah-puchah, the Despoiler or Destroyer,[1] though the precise import of that character in the mythical drama is left uncertain.[2]

[1: *Eopuco* I take to be from the verb *puch* or *puk*, to melt, to dissolve, to shell corn from the cob, to spoil; hence *puk*, spoiled, rotten, *podrida*, and possibly *ppuch*, to flog, to beat. The prefix *ah*, signifies one who practices or is skilled in the action which the verb denotes.]

[2: The mother of the Bacabs is given in the myth as *Chibilias* (or *Chibirias*, but there is no *r* in the Maya alphabet). Cogolludo mentions a goddess *Ix chebel yax*, one of whose functions was to preside over drawing and painting. The name is from *chebel*, the brush used in these arts. But the connection is obscure.]

The supposed Holy Ghost, Echuac, properly Ah-Kiuic, Master of the Market, was the god of the merchants and the cacao plantations. He formed a triad with two other gods, Chac, one of the rain gods, and Hobnel, also a god of the food supply. To this triad travelers, on stopping for the night, set on end three stones and placed in front of them three flat stones, on which incense was burned. At their festival in the month *Muan* precisely three cups of native wine (mead) were drained by each person present.[1]

[1: Landa, *Relacion de las Cosas de Yucatan*, pp. 156, 260.]

The description of some such rites as these is, no doubt, what led the worthy Hernandez to suppose that the Mayas had Trinitarian doctrines. When they said that the god of the merchants and planters supplied the wants of men and furnished the world with desirable things, it was but a slightly figurative way of stating a simple truth.

The four Bacabs are called by Cogolludo "the gods of the winds." Each was identified with a particular color and a certain cardinal point. The first was that of the South. He was called Hobnil, the Belly; his color was yellow, which, as that of the ripe ears, was regarded as a favorable and promising hue; the augury of his year was propitious, and it was said of him, referring to some myth now lost, that he had never sinned as had his brothers. He answered to the day **Kan**. which was the first of the Maya week of thirteen days.[1] The remaining Bacabs were the Red, assigned to the East, the White, to the North, and the Black, to the West, and the winds and rains from those directions were believed to be under the charge of these giant caryatides.

[1: Landa, **Relacion**, pp. 208,-211, etc. **Hobnil** is the ordinary word for belly, stomach, from **hobol**, hollow. Figuratively, in these dialects it meant subsistence, life, as we use in both these senses the word "vitals." Among the Kiches of Guatemala, a tribe of Maya stock, we find, as terms applied to their highest divinity, **u pam uleu, u pam cah**, literally Belly of the Earth, Belly of the Sky, meaning that by which earth and sky exist. **Popol Vuh**, p. 332.]

Their close relation with Itzamna is evidenced, not only in the fragmentary myth preserved by Hernandez, but quite amply in the descriptions of the rites at the close of each year and in the various festivals during the year, as narrated by Bishop Landa. Thus at the termination of the year, along with the sacrifices to the Bacab of the year were others to Itzamna, either under his surname **Canil**, which has various meanings,[1] or as **Kinich-ahau**, Lord of the Eye of the Day,[2] or **Yax-coc-ahmut**, the first to know and hear of events,[3] or finally as **Uac-metun-ahau**, Lord of the Wheel of the Months.[4]

[1: **Can**, of which the "determinative" form is **canil**, may mean a serpent, or the yellow one, or the strong one, or he who gives gifts, or the converser.]

[2: **Kin**, the day; **ich**, eye; **ahau**, lord.]

[3: **Yax**, first; **coc**, which means literally deaf, and hence to listen attentively (whence the name Cocomes, for the ancient royal family of Chichen Itza, an appellation correctly translated "escuchadores") and **ah-mut**, master of the news, **mut** meaning news, good or bad.]

[4: **Uac**, the months, is a rare and now obsolete form of the plural of **u**, month,

"*Uac*, i.e. *u*, por meses y habla de tiempo pasado." *Diccionario Maya-Espanol del Convento de Motul*, MS. *Metun* (Landa, *mitun*) is from *met*, a wheel. The calendars, both in Yucatan and Mexico, were represented as a wheel.]

The word *bacab* means "erected," "set up."[1] It was applied to the Bacabs because they were imagined to be enormous giants, standing like pillars at the four corners of the earth, supporting the heavens. In this sense they were also called *chac*, the giants, as the rain senders. They were also the gods of fertility and abundance, who watered the crops, and on whose favor depended the return of the harvests. They presided over the streams and wells, and were the divinities whose might is manifested in the thunder and lightning, gods of the storms, as well as of the gentle showers.[2] The festival to these gods of the harvest was in the month *Mac*, which occurred in the early spring. In this ceremony, Itzamna was also worshiped as the leader of the Bacabs, and an important rite called "the extinction of the fire" was performed. "The object of these sacrifices and this festival," writes Bishop Landa, "was to secure an abundance of water for their crops."[3]

[1: The *Diccionario Maya del Convento de Motul*, MS., the only dictionary in which I find the exact word, translates *bacab* by "representante, juglar, bufon." This is no doubt a late meaning taken from the scenic representations of the supposed doings of the gods in the ritual ceremonies. The proper form of the word is *uacab* or *vacab*, which the dictionary mentioned renders "cosa que esta en pie o enhiesta delante de otra." The change from the initial *v* to *b* is quite common, as may be seen by comparing the two letters in Pio Perez's *Diccionario de la Lengua Maya*, e.g. *balak*, the revolution of a wheel, from *ualak*, to turn, to revolve.]

[2: The entries in the *Diccionario Maya-Espanol del Convento de Motul*, MS., are as follows:--

"*Chaac*: gigante, hombre de grande estatura.

"*Chaac*: fue un hombre asi grande que enseno la agricultura, al cual tuvieron despues por Dios de los panes, del agua, de los truenos y relampagos. Y asi se dice, *hac chaac*, el rayo: *u lemba chaac* el relampago; *u pec chaac*, el trueno," etc.]

[3: *Relacion, etc.*, p. 255.]

These four Chac or Bacabab were worshiped under the symbol of the cross, the four arms of which represented the four cardinal points. Both in language and religious art, this was regarded as a tree. In the Maya tongue it was called "the tree of bread," or "the tree of life."[1] The celebrated cross of Palenque is one of its representations, as I believe I was the first to point out, and has now been generally acknowledged to be correct.[2] There was another such cross, about eight feet high, in a temple on the island of Cozumel. This was worshiped as "the god of rain," or more correctly, as the symbol of the four rain gods, the Bacabs. In periods of drought offerings were made to it of birds (symbols of the winds) and it was sprinkled with water. "When this had been done," adds the historian, "they felt certain that the rains would promptly fall."[3]

[1: The Maya word is *uahomche*, from *uah*, originally the tortilla or maize cake, now used for bread generally. It is also current in the sense of *life* ("la vida en cierta manera," *Diccionario Maya Espanol del Convento de Motul*, MS.). *Che* is the generic word for tree. I cannot find any particular tree called *Homche*. *Hom* was the name applied to a wind instrument, a sort of trumpet. In the *Codex Troano*, Plates xxv, xxvii, xxxiv, it is represented in use. The four Bacabs were probably imagined to blow the winds from the four corners of the earth through such instruments. A similar representation is given in the *Codex Borgianus*, Plate xiii, in Kingsborough. As the Chac was the god of bread, *Dios de los panes*, so the cross was the tree of bread.]

[2: See the *Myths of the New World*, p. 95 (1st ed., New York, 1868). This explanation has since been adopted by Dr. Carl Schultz-Sellack, although he omits to state whence he derived it. His article is entitled *Die Amerikanischen Goetter der Vier Weltgegenden und ihre Tempel in Palenque* in the *Zeitschrift fuer Ethnologie*, 1879. Compare also Charles Rau, *The Palenque Tablet*, p. 44 (Washington, 1879).]

[3: "Al pie de aquella misma torre estaba un cercado de piedra y cal, muy bien lucido y almenado, en medio del cual habia una cruz de cal tan alta como diez palmos, a la cual tenian y adoraban por dios de la lluvia, porque quando no llovia y habia falta de agua, iban a ella en procesion y muy devotos; ofrescianle codornices sacrificadas por aplacarle la ira y enojo con que ellos tenia o mostraba tener, con la sangre de aquella simple avezica." Francisco Lopez de Gomara, *Conquista de Mejico*, p. 305 (Ed. Paris, 1852).]

Each of the four Bacabs was also called **Acantun**, which means "a stone set up," such a stone being erected and painted of the color sacred to the cardinal point that the Bacab represented[1]. Some of these stones are still found among the ruins of Yucatecan cities, and are to this day connected by the natives with reproductive signs[2]. It is probable, however, that actual phallic worship was not customary in Yucatan. The Bacabs and Itzamna were closely related to ideas of fertility and reproduction, indeed, but it appears to have been especially as gods of the rains, the harvests, and the food supply generally. The Spanish writers were eager to discover all the depravity possible in the religion of the natives, and they certainly would not have missed such an opportunity for their tirades, had it existed. As it is, the references to it are not many, and not clear.

[1: The feasts of the Bacabs Acantun are described in Landa's work. The name he does not explain. I take it to be **acaan**, past participle of **actal**, to erect, and **tun**, stone. But it may have another meaning. The word **acan** meant wine, or rather, mead, the intoxicating hydromel the natives manufactured. The god of this drink also bore the name Acan ("ACAN; el Dios del vino que es Baco," **Diccionario del Convento de Motul**, MS.). It would be quite appropriate for the Bacabs to be gods of wine.]

[2: Stephens, **Travels in Yucatan**, Vol. i, p. 434.]

From what I have now presented we see that Itzamna came from the distant east, beyond the ocean marge; that he was the teacher of arts and agriculture; that he, moreover, as a divinity, ruled the winds and rains, and sent at his will harvests and prosperity. Can we identify him further with that personification of Light which, as we have already seen, was the dominant figure in other American mythologies?

This seems indicated by his names and titles. They were many, some of which I have already analyzed. That by which he was best known was **Itzamna**, a word of contested meaning but which contains the same radicals as the words for the morning and the dawn[1], and points to his identification with the grand central fact at the basis of all these mythologies, the welcome advent of the light in the eastern horizon after the gloom of the night.

[1: Some have derived Itzamua from *i*, grandson by a son, used only by a female; **zamal**, morning, morrow, from **zam**, before, early, related to **yam**, first, whence also *zamalzam*, the dawn, the aurora; and *na*, mother. Without the accent *na*, means house. Crescencio Carrillo prefers the derivation from *itz*, anything that trickles in drops, as gum from a tree, rain or dew from the sky, milk from teats, and semen ("leche de amor," *Dicc. de Motul*, MS.). He says: "*Itzamna*, esto es, rocio diario, o sustancia cuotidiana del cielo, es el mismo nombre del fundador (de Itzamal)." *Historia Antigua de Yucatan*, p. 145. (Merida, 1881.) This does not explain the last syllable, *na*, which is always strongly accented. It is said that Itzamna spoke of himself only in the words *Itz en caan*, "I am that which trickles from the sky;" *Itz en muyal*, "I am that which trickles from the clouds." This plainly refers to his character as a rain god. Lizana, *Historia de Yucatan*, Lib. i, cap. 4. If a compound of *itz, amal, na*, the name, could be translated, "the milk of the mother of the morning," or of the dawn, i. e., the dew; while *i, zamal, na* would be "son of the mother of the morning."]

His next most frequent title was *Kin-ich-ahau*, which may be translated either, "Lord of the Sun's Face," or, "The Lord, the Eye of the Day."[1] As such he was the deity who presided in the Sun's disk and shot forth his scorching rays. There was a temple at Itzamal consecrated to him as *Kin-ich-kak-mo*, "the Eye of the Day, the Bird of Fire."[2] In a time of pestilence the people resorted to this temple, and at high noon a sacrifice was spread upon the altar. The moment the sun reached the zenith, a bird of brilliant plumage, but which, in fact, was nothing else than a fiery flame shot from the sun, descended and consumed the offering in the sight of all. At Campeche he had a temple, as *Kin-ich-ahau-haban*, "the Lord of the Sun's face, the *Hunter*," where the rites were sanguinary.[3]

[1: Cogolludo, who makes a distinction between Kinich-ahau and Itzamna (*Hist. de Yucatan*, Lib. iv, cap. viii), may be corrected by Landa and Buenaventura, whom I have already quoted.]

[2: *Kin*, the sun, the day; *ich*, the face, but generally the eye or eyes; *kak*, fire; *mo*, the brilliant plumaged, sacred bird, the ara or guacamaya, the red macaw. This was adopted as the title of the ruler of Itzamal, as we learn from the Chronicle of Chichen Itza--"Ho ahau paxci u cah yahau ah Itzmal Kinich Kakmo"--"In the fifth Age the town (of Chichen Itza) was destroyed by King Kinich Kakmo, of Itzamal." *El Libro de Chilan Balam de Chumayel*, MS.]

[3: Cogolludo, *Historia de Yucatan*, Lib. iv, cap. viii.]

Another temple at Itzamal was consecrated to him, under one of his names, *Kabil*, He of the Lucky Hand,[1] and the sick were brought there, as it was said that he had cured many by merely touching them. This fane was extremely popular, and to it pilgrimages were made from even such remote regions as Tabasco, Guatemala and Chiapas. To accommodate the pilgrims four paved roads had been constructed, to the North, South, East and West, straight toward the quarters of the four winds.

[1: Lizana says: "Se llama y nombra *Kab-ul* que quiere decir mano obradora," and all writers have followed him, although no such meaning can be made out of the name thus written. The proper word is *kabil*, which is defined in the *Diccionario del Convento de Motul*, MS., "el que tiene buena mano para sembrar, o para poner colmenas, etc." Landa also gives this orthography, *Relacion*, p. 216.]

Sec.2. *The Culture Hero, Kukulcan.*

The second important hero-myth of the Mayas was that about Kukulcan. This is in no way connected with that of Itzamna, and is probably later in date, and less national in character. The first reference to it we also owe to Father Francisco Hernandez, whom I have already quoted, and who reported it to Bishop Las Casas in 1545. His words clearly indicate that we have here to do with a myth relating to the formation of the calendar, an opinion which can likewise be supported from other sources.

The natives affirmed, says Las Casas, that in ancient times there came to that land twenty men, the chief of whom was called "Cocolcan," and him they spoke of as the god of fevers or agues, two of the others as gods of fishing, another two as the gods of farms and fields, another was the thunder god, etc. They wore flowing robes and sandals on their feet, they had long beards, and their heads were bare. They ordered that the people should confess and fast, and some of the natives fasted on Fridays, because on that day the god Bacab died; and the name of that day in their language is *himix*, which they especially honor and hold in reverence as the day of the death of Bacab.[1]

[1: Las Casas, *Historia Apologetica de las Indias Occidentales*, cap. cxxii.]

In the manuscript of Hernandez, which Las Casas had before him when he was writing his *Apologetical History*, the names of all the twenty were given; but unfortunately for antiquarian research, the good bishop excuses himself from quoting them, on account of their barbarous appearance. I have little doubt, however, that had he done so, we should find them to be the names of the twenty days of the native calendar month. These are the visitors who come, one every morning, with flowing robes, full beard and hair, and bring with them our good or bad luck--whatever the day brings forth. Hernandez made the same mistake as did Father Francisco de Bobadilla, when he inquired of the Nicaraguans the names of their gods, and they gave him those of the twenty days of the month.[1] Each day was, indeed, personified by these nations, and supposed to be at once a deity and a date, favorable or unfavorable to fishing or hunting, planting or fighting, as the case might be.

[1: Oviedo, *Historia General de las Indias*, Lib. xlii, cap. iii.]

Kukulcan seems, therefore, to have stood in the same relation in Yucatan to the other divinities of the days as did Votan in Chiapa and Quetzalcoatl Ce Acatl in Cholula.

His name has usually been supposed to be a compound, meaning "a serpent adorned with feathers," but there are no words in the Maya language to justify such a rendering. There is some variation in its orthography, and its original pronunciation may possibly be lost; but if we adopt as correct the spelling which I have given above, of which, however, I have some doubts, then it means, "The God of the Mighty Speech."[1]

[1: Eligio Ancona, after giving the rendering, "serpiente adornada de plumas," adds, "ha sido repetido por tal numero de etimologistas que tendremos necesidad de aceptarla, aunque nos parece un poco violento," *Historia de Yucatan*, Vol. i, p. 44. The Abbe Brasseur, in his *Vocabulaire Maya*, boldly states that *kukul* means "emplumado o adornado con plumas." This rendering is absolutely without authority, either modern or ancient. The word for feathers in Maya is *kukum*; *kul*, in composition, means "very" or "much," as "*kulvinic*, muy hombre, hombre de respeto o hecho," *Diccionario de Motul*, MS. *Ku* is god, divinity. For *can* see chapter iv, Sec.1. *Can* was and still is a common surname in Yucatan. (Berendt, *Nombres Proprios en Lengua Maya*, MS.)

I should prefer to spell the name *Kukulkan*, and have it refer to the first day of the Maya week, *Kan*.]

The reference probably was to the fame of this divinity as an oracle, as connected with the calendar. But it is true that the name could with equal correctness be translated "The God, the Mighty Serpent," for can is a homonym with these and other meanings, and we are without positive proof which was intended.

To bring Kukulcan into closer relations with other American hero-gods we must turn to the locality where he was especially worshiped, to the traditions of the ancient and opulent city of Chichen Itza, whose ruins still rank among the most imposing on the peninsula. The fragments of its chronicles, as preserved to us in the Books of Chilan Balam and by Bishop Landa, tell us that its site was first settled by four bands who came from the four cardinal points and were ruled over by four brothers. These brothers chose no wives, but lived chastely and ruled righteously, until at a certain time one died or departed, and two began to act unjustly and were put to death. The one remaining was Kukulcan. He appeased the strife which his brothers' acts had aroused, directed the minds of the people to the arts of peace, and caused to be built various important structures. After he had completed his work in Chichen Itza, he founded and named the great city of Mayapan, destined to be the capital of the confederacy of the Mayas. In it was built a temple in his honor, and named for him, as there was one in Chichen Itza. These were unlike others in Yucatan, having circular walls and four doors, directed, presumably, toward the four cardinal points[1].

[1: *El Libro de Chilan Balam de Chumayel*, MS.; Landa, *Relacion*, pp. 34-38. and 299; Herrera, *Historia de las Indias*, Dec. iv, Lib. x, cap ii.]

In gratifying confirmation of the legend, travelers do actually find in Mayapan and Chichen Itza, and nowhere else in Yucatan, the ruins of two circular temples with doors opening toward the cardinal points[1].

[1: Stephens, *Incidents of Travel in Yucatan*, Vol. ii, p. 298.]

Under the beneficent rule of Kukulcan, the nation enjoyed its halcyon days of peace and prosperity. The harvests were abundant and the people turned cheerfully to their daily duties, to their families and their lords. They forgot the use of arms, even for the chase, and contented themselves with snares and traps.

At length the time drew near for Kukulcan to depart. He gathered the chiefs together and expounded to them his laws. From among them he chose as his successor a member of the ancient and wealthy family of the Cocoms. His arrangements completed, he is said, by some, to have journeyed westward, to Mexico, or to some other spot toward the sun-setting. But by the people at large he was confidently believed to have ascended into the heavens, and there, from his lofty house, he was supposed to watch over the interests of his faithful adherents.

Such was the tradition of their mythical hero told by the Itzas. No wonder that the early missionaries, many of whom, like Landa, had lived in Mexico and had become familiar with the story of Quetzalcoatl and his alleged departure toward the east, identified him with Kukulcan, and that, following the notion of this assumed identity, numerous later writers have framed theories to account for the civilization of ancient Yucatan through colonies of "Toltec" immigrants.

It can, indeed, be shown beyond doubt that there were various points of contact between the Aztec and Maya civilizations. The complex and artificial method of reckoning time was one of these; certain architectural devices were others; a small number of words, probably a hundred all told, have been borrowed by the one tongue from the other. Mexican merchants traded with Yucatan, and bands of Aztec warriors with their families, from Tabasco, dwelt in Mayapan by invitation of its rulers, and after its destruction, settled in the province of Canul, on the western coast, where they lived strictly separate from the Maya-speaking population at the time the Spaniards conquered the country.[1]

[1: *El Libro de Chilan Balam de Chumayel*, MS.; Landa, *Relacion*, p. 54.]

But all this is very far from showing that at any time a race speaking the Aztec tongue ruled the Peninsula. There are very strong grounds to deny this. The traditions which point to a migration from the west or southwest may well have referred to the depopulation of Palenque, a city which undoubtedly was a product of Maya architects. The language of Yucatan is too absolutely dissimilar from the Nahuatl for it ever to have been moulded by leaders of that race. The details of Maya civilization are markedly its own, and show an evolution peculiar to the people and their surroundings.

How far they borrowed from the fertile mythology of their Nahuatl visitors is not easily answered. That the circular temple in Mayapan, with four doors, specified by Landa as different from any other in Yucatan, was erected to Quetzalcoatl, by or because of the Aztec colony there, may plausibly be supposed when we recall how peculiarly this form was devoted to his worship. Again, one of the Maya chronicles--that translated by Pio Perez and published by Stephens in his *Travels in Yucatan*--opens with a distinct reference to Tula and Nonoal, names inseparable from the Quetzalcoatl myth. A statue of a sleeping god holding a vase was disinterred by Dr. Le Plongeon at Chichen Itza, and it is too entirely similar to others found at Tlaxcala and near the city of Mexico, for us to doubt but that they represented the same divinity, and that the god of rains, fertility and the harvests.[1]

[1: I refer to the statue which Dr. LePlongeon was pleased to name "Chac Mool." See the *Estudio acerca de la Estatua llamada Chac-Mool o rey tigre*, by Sr. Jesus Sanchez, in the *Anales del Museo Nacional de Mexico*, Tom. i. p. 270. There was a divinity worshiped in Yucatan, called Cum-ahau, lord of the vase, whom the *Diccionario de Motul*, MS. terms, "Lucifer, principal de los demonios." The name is also given by Pio Perez in his manuscript dictionary in my possession, but is omitted in the printed copy. As Lucifer, the morning star, was identified with Quetzalcoatl in Mexican mythology, and as the word *cum*, vase, Aztec *comitl*, is the same in both tongues, there is good ground to suppose that this lord of the vase, the "prince of devils," was the god of fertility, common to both cults.]

The version of the tradition which made Kukulcan arrive from the West, and at his disappearance return to the West--a version quoted by Landa, and which evidently originally referred to the westward course of the sun, easily led to an identification of him with the Aztec Quetzalcoatl, by those acquainted with both myths.

The probability seems to be that Kukulcan was an original Maya divinity, one of their hero-gods, whose myth had in it so many similarities to that of Quetzalcoatl that the priests of the two nations came to regard the one as the same as the other. After the destruction of Mayapan, about the middle of the fifteenth century, when the Aztec mercenaries were banished to Canul, and the reigning family (the Xiu) who supported them became reduced in power, the worship of Kukulcan fell, to some extent, into disfavor. Of this we are informed by Landa, in an interesting passage.

He tells us that many of the natives believed that Kukulcan, after his earthly labors, had ascended into Heaven and become one of their gods. Previous to the destruction of Mayapan temples were built to him, and he was worshiped throughout the land, but after that event he was paid such honor only in the province of Mani (governed by the Xiu). Nevertheless, in gratitude for what all recognized they owed to him, the kings of the neighboring provinces sent yearly to Mani, on the occasion of his annual festival, which took place on the 16th of the month Xul (November 8th), either four or five magnificent feather banners. These were placed in his temple, with appropriate ceremonies, such as fasting, the burning of incense, dancing, and with simple offerings of food cooked without salt or pepper, and drink from beans and gourd seeds. This lasted five nights and five days; and, adds Bishop Landa, they said, and held it for certain, that on the last day of the festival Kukulcan himself descended from Heaven and personally received the sacrifices and offerings which were made in his honor. The celebration itself was called the Festival of the Founder[1], with reference, I suppose, to the alleged founding of the cities of Maya-pan and Chichen Itza by this hero-god. The five days and five sacred banners again bring to mind the close relation of this with the Quetzalcoatl symbolism.

[1: "Llamaban a esta fiesta **Chic Kaban**;" Landa, **Relacion**, p. 302. I take it this should read **Chiic u Kaba** (**Chiic**; fundar o poblar alguna cosa, casa, pueblo, etc. **Diccionario de Motul**, MS.)]

As Itzamna had disappeared without undergoing the pains of death, as Kukul-can had risen into the heavens and thence returned annually, though but for a moment, on the last day of the festival in his honor, so it was devoutly believed by the Mayas that the time would come when the worship of other gods should be done away with, and these mighty deities alone demand the adoration of their race. None of the American nations seems to have been more given than they to prognostics and prophecies, and of none other have we so large an amount of this kind of literature remaining. Some of it has been preserved by the Spanish missionaries, who used it with good effect for their own purposes of proselyting; but that it was not manufactured by them for this purpose, as some late writers have thought, is proved by the existence of copies of these prophecies, made by native writers themselves, at the time of the Conquest and at dates shortly subsequent.

These prophecies were as obscure and ambiguous as all successful prophets are accustomed to make their predictions; but the one point that is clear in them is, that they distinctly referred to the arrival of white and bearded strangers from the East, who should control the land and alter the prevailing religion.[1]

[1: Nakuk Pech, **Concixta yetel mapa**, 1562. MS.; **El Libro de Chilan Balam de Mani**, 1595, MS. The former is a history of the Conquest written in Maya, by a native noble, who was an adult at the time that Merida was founded (1542).]

Even that portion of the Itzas who had separated from the rest of their nation at the time of the destruction of Mayapan (about 1440-50) and wandered off to the far south, to establish a powerful nation around Lake Peten, carried with them a forewarning that at the "eighth age" they should be subjected to a white race and have to embrace their religion; and, sure enough, when that time came, and not till then, that is, at the close of the seventeenth century of our reckoning, they were driven from their island homes by Governor Ursua, and their numerous temples, filled with idols, leveled to the soil.[1]

[1: Juan de Villagutierre Sotomayor, ***Historia de la Provincia de el Itza***, passim (Madrid, 1701).]

The ground of all such prophecies was, I have no doubt, the expected return of the hero-gods, whose myths I have been recording. Both of them represented in their original forms the light of day, which disappears at nightfall but returns at dawn with unfailing certainty. When the natural phenomenon had become lost in its personification, this expectation of a return remained and led the priests, who more than others retained the recollection of the ancient forms of the myth, to embrace this expectation in the prognostics which it was their custom and duty to pronounce with reference to the future.

CHAPTER V.
THE QQUICHUA HERO-GOD VIRACOCHA.

VIRACOCHA AS THE FIRST CAUSE--HIS NAME, ILLA TICCI--QQUI-
CHUA PRAYERS--OTHER NAMES AND TITLES OF VIRACOCHA--
HIS WORSHIP A TRUE MONOTHEISM--THE MYTH OF THE FOUR
BROTHERS--MYTH OF THE TWIN BROTHERS.
VIRACOCHA AS TUNAPA, HE WHO PERFECTS--VARIOUS INCI-
DENTS IN HIS LIFE--RELATION TO MANCO CAPAC--HE DISAP-
PEARS IN THE WEST.
VIRACOCHA RISES FROM LAKE TITICACA AND JOURNEYS TO THE
WEST--DERIVATION OF HIS NAME--HE WAS REPRESENTED AS
WHITE AND BEARDED--THE MYTH OF CON AND PACHACAMAC-
-CONTICE VIRACOCHA--PROPHECIES OF THE PERUVIAN SEERS--
THE WHITE MEN CALLED VIRACOCHAS--SIMILARITIES TO AZTEC
MYTHS.

The most majestic empire on this continent at the time of its discovery was
that of the Incas. It extended along the Pacific, from the parallel of 2 deg.
north latitude to 20 deg. south, and may be roughly said to have been 1500
miles in length, with an average width of 400 miles. The official and principal tongue was the Qquichua, the two other languages of importance being the
Yunca, spoken by the coast tribes, and the Aymara, around Lake Titicaca and south
of it. The latter, in phonetics and in many root-words, betrays a relationship to the
Qquichua, but a remote one.

The Qquichuas were a race of considerable cultivation. They had a developed
metrical system, and were especially fond of the drama. Several specimens of their

poetical and dramatic compositions have been preserved, and indicate a correct taste. Although they did not possess a method of writing, they had various mnemonic aids, by which they were enabled to recall their verses and their historical traditions.

In the mythology of the Qquichuas, and apparently also of the Aymaras, the leading figure is *Viracocha*. His august presence is in one cycle of legends that of Infinite Creator, the Primal Cause; in another he is the beneficent teacher and wise ruler; in other words, he too, like Quetzalcoatl and the others whom I have told about, is at one time God, at others the incarnation of God.

As the first cause and ground of all things, Viracocha's distinctive epithet was *Ticci*, the Cause, the Beginning, or *Illa ticci*, the Ancient Cause[1], the First Beginning, an endeavor in words to express the absolute priority of his essence and existence. He it was who had made and moulded the Sun and endowed it with a portion of his own divinity, to wit, the glory of its far-shining rays; he had formed the Moon and given her light, and set her in the heavens to rule over the waters and the winds, over the queens of the earth and the parturition of women; and it was still he, the great Viracocha, who had created the beautiful Chasca, the Aurora, the Dawn, goddess of all unspotted maidens like herself, her who in turn decked the fields and woods with flowers, whose time was the gloaming and the twilight, whose messengers were the fleecy clouds which sail through the sky, and who, when she shakes her clustering hair, drops noiselessly pearls of dew on the green grass fields.[2]

[1: "*Ticci*, origen, principio, fundamento, cimiento, causa. *Ylla*; todo lo que es antiguo." Holguin, *Vocabulario de la Lengua Qquichua o del Inga* (Ciudad de los Reyes, 1608). *Ticci* is not to be confounded with *aticsi*, he conquers, from *atini*, I conquer, a term also occasionally applied to Viracocha.]

[2: *Relacion Anonyma, de los Costumbres Antiguos de los Naturales del Piru*, p. 138. 1615. (Published, Madrid, 1879).]

Invisible and incorporeal himself, so, also, were his messengers (the light-rays), called *huaminca*, the faithful soldiers, and *hayhuaypanti*, the shining ones, who conveyed his decrees to every part.[1] He himself was omnipresent, imparting motion and life, form and existence, to all that is. Therefore it was, says an old writer, with more than usual insight into man's moral nature, with more than usual charity for a persecuted race, that when these natives worshiped some swift river or pellucid spring, some mountain or grove, "it was not that they believed that some particular divinity was there, or that it was a living thing, but because they believed that the great God, Illa Ticci, had created and placed it there and impressed upon it some mark of distinction, beyond other objects of its class, that it might thus be designated as an appropriate spot whereat to worship the maker of all things; and this is manifest from the prayers they uttered when engaged in adoration, because they are not addressed to that mountain, or river, or cave, but to the great Illa Ticci Viracocha, who, they believed, lived in the heavens, and yet was invisibly present in that sacred object."[2]

[1: Ibid., p. 140.]

[2: Ibid., p. 147.]

In the prayers for the dead, Illa Ticci was appealed to, to protect the body, that it should not see corruption nor become lost in the earth, and that he should not allow the soul to wander aimlessly in the infinite spaces, but that it should be conducted to some secure haven of contentment, where it might receive the sacrifices and offerings which loving hands laid upon the tomb.[1] Were other gods also called upon, it was that they might intercede with the Supreme Divinity in favor of these petitions of mortals.

[1: Ibid., p. 154.]

To him, likewise, the chief priest at certain times offered a child of six years, with a prayer for the prosperity of the Inca, in such terms as these:--

"Oh, Lord, we offer thee this child, in order that thou wilt maintain us in comfort, and give us victory in war, and keep to our Lord, the Inca, his greatness and his state, and grant him wisdom that he may govern us righteously."[1]

[1: Herrera, ***Historia de las Indias***, Dec. v, Lib. iv, cap. i.]

Or such a prayer as this was offered up by the assembled multitude:--

"Oh, Viracocha ever present, Viracocha Cause of All, Viracocha the Helper, the Ceaseless Worker, Viracocha who gives the beginnings, Viracocha who encourages, Viracocha the always fortunate, Viracocha ever near, listen to this our prayer, send health, send prosperity to us thy people."[1]

[1: Christoval de Molina, ***The Fables and Rites of the Incas***, p. 29. Molina gives the original Qquichua, the translation of which is obviously incomplete, and I have extended it.]

Thus Viracocha was placed above and beyond all other gods, the essential First Cause, infinite, incorporeal, invisible, above the sun, older than the beginning, but omnipresent, accessible, beneficent.

Does this seem too abstract, too elevated a notion of God for a race whom we are accustomed to deem gross and barbaric? I cannot help it. The testimony of the earliest observers, and the living proof of language, are too strong to allow of doubt. The adjectives which were applied to this divinity by the native priests are still on record, and that they were not a loan from Christian theology is conclusively shown by the fact that the very writers who preserved them often did not know their meaning, and translated them incorrectly.

Thus even Garcilasso de la Vega, himself of the blood of the Incas, tells us that neither he nor the natives of that day could translate *Ticci*.[1] Thus, also, Garcia and Acosta inform us that Viracocha was surnamed *Usapu*, which they translate "admirable,"[2] but really it means "he who accomplishes all that he undertakes, he who is successful in all things;" Molina has preserved the term *Ymamana*, which means "he who controls or owns all things;"[3] the title *Pachayachachi*, which the Spanish writers render "Creator," really means the "Teacher of the World;" that of *Caylla* signifies "the Ever-present one;" *Taripaca*, which has been guessed to be the same as *tarapaca*, an eagle, is really a derivative of *taripani*, to sit in judgment, and was applied to Viracocha as the final arbiter of the actions and destinies of man. Another of his frequent appellations for which no explanation has been offered, was *Tokay* or *Tocapo*, properly *Tukupay*.[4] It means "he who finishes," who completes and perfects, and is antithetical to *Ticci*, he who begins. These two terms express the eternity of divinity; they convey the same idea of mastery over time and the things of time, as do those words heard by the Evangelist in his vision in the isle called Patmos, "I am Alpha and Omega; I am the Beginning and the End."

[1: "Dan (los Indios), otro nombre a Dios, que es Tici Viracocha, que yo no se que signifique, ni ellos tampoco." Garcilasso de la Vega, *Comentarios Reales*, Lib. ii, cap. ii.]

[2: Garcia, *Origen de los Indios*, Lib. iii, cap. vi; Acosta, *Historia, Natural y Moral de las Indias*, fol. 199 (Barcelona 1591).]

[3: Christoval de Molina, *The Fables and Rites of the Incas*, Eng. Trans., p. 6.]

[4: Melchior Hernandez, one of the earliest writers, whose works are now lost, but who is quoted in the *Relacion Anonima*, gives this name *Tocapu*; Christoval de Molina (ubi sup.) spells it *Tocapo*; La Vega *Tocay*; Molina gives its signification, "the maker." It is from the word *tukupay* or *tucuychani*, to finish, complete, perfect.]

Yet another epithet of Viracocha was *Zapala*.[1] It conveys strongly and positively the monotheistic idea. It means "The One," or, more strongly, "The Only One."

[1: Gomara, *Historia de las Indias*, p. 232 (ed. Paris, 1852).]

Nor must it be supposed that this monotheism was unconscious; that it was, for example, a form of "henotheism," where the devotion of the adorer filled his soul, merely to the forgetfulness of other deities; or that it was simply the logical law of unity asserting itself, as was the case with many of the apparently monotheistic utterances of the Greek and Roman writers.

No; the evidence is such that we are obliged to acknowledge that the religion of Peru was a consciously monotheistic cult, every whit as much so as the Greek or Roman Catholic Churches of Christendom.

Those writers who have called the Inca religion a "sun worship" have been led astray by superficial resemblances. One of the best early authorities, Christoval de Molina, repeats with emphasis the statement, "They did not recognize the Sun as their Creator, but as created by the Creator," and this creator was "not born of woman, but was unchangeable and eternal."[1] For conclusive testimony on this point, however, we may turn to an *Informacion* or Inquiry as to the ancient belief, instituted in 1571, by order of the viceroy Don Francisco de Toledo. The oldest Indians, especially those of noble birth, including many descendants of the Incas, were assembled at different times and in different parts of the country, and carefully questioned, through the official interpreter, as to just what the old religion was. The questions were not leading ones, and the replies have great uniformity. They all agreed that Viracocha was worshiped as creator, and as the ever-present active divinity; he alone answered prayers, and aided in time of need; he was the sole efficient god. All prayers to the Sun or to the deceased Incas, or to idols, were directed to them as intercessors only. On this point the statements were most positive[2]. The Sun was but one of Viracocha's creations, not itself the Creator.

[1: Christoval de Molina, *The Fables and Rites of the Incas*, pp. 8, 17. Eng. Trans.]

[2: "Ellos solo Viracocha tenian por hacedor de todas las cosas, y que el solo los podia socorrer, y que de todos los demas los tenian por sus intercesores, y que ansi los decian ellos en sus oraciones antiguas, antes que fuesen cristianos, y que ansi lo dicen y declaran por cosa muy cierta y verdadera." *Information de las Idolatras de los Incas e Indios*, in the *Coleccion de Documentos Ineditos del Archivo de Indias*, vol. xxi, p. 198. Other witnesses said: "Los dichos Ingas y sus antepasados tenian por criador al solo Viracocha, y que solo los podia socorrer," id. p. 184. "Adoraban a Viracocha por hacedor de todas las cosas, como a el sol y a Hachaccuna los adoraban porque los tenia por hijos de Viracocha y por cosa muy allegada suya," p. 133.]

It is singular that historians have continued to repeat that the Qquichuas adored the Sun as their principal divinity, in the face of such evidence to the contrary. If this Inquiry and its important statements had not been accessible to them, at any rate they could readily have learned the same lesson from the well known History of Father Joseph de Acosta. That author says, and repeats with great positiveness, that the Sun was in Peru a secondary divinity, and that the supreme deity, the Creator and ruler of the world, was Viracocha.[1]

[1: "Sientan y confiessan un supremo senor, y hazedor de todo, al qual los del Piru llamavan Viracocha. * * Despues del Viracocha, o supremo Dios, fui, y es en los infieles, el que mas comunmente veneran y adoran el sol." Acosta, *De la Historia Moral de las Indias*, Lib, v. cap. iii, iv, (Barcelona, 1591).]

Another misapprehension is that these natives worshiped directly their ancestors. Thus, Mr. Markham writes: "The Incas worshiped their ancestors, the *Pacarina*, or forefather of the *Ayllu*, or lineage, being idolized as the soul or essence of his descendants."[1] But in the *Inquiry* above quoted it is explained that the belief, in fact, was that the soul of the Inca went at death to the presence of the deity Viracocha, and its emblem, the actual body, carefully preserved, was paid divine honors in order that the soul might intercede with Viracocha for the fulfillment of the prayers.[2]

[1: Clements R. Markham, *Journal of the Royal Geographical Society*, 1871, p.

291. *Pacarina* is the present participle of *pacarini*, to dawn, to begin, to be born.]

[2: *Informacion*, etc., p. 209.]

We are compelled, therefore, by the best evidence now attainable, to adopt the conclusion that the Inca religion, in its purity, deserved the name of monotheism. The statements of the natives and the terms of their religious language unite in confirming this opinion.

It is not right to depreciate the force of these facts simply because we have made up our minds that a people in the intellectual stage of the Peruvians could not have mounted to such a pure air of religion. A prejudgment of this kind is unworthy of a scientific mind. The evidence is complete that the terms I have quoted did belong to the religious language of ancient Peru. They express the conception of divinity which the thinkers of that people had formed. And whether it is thought to be in keeping or not with the rest of their development, it is our bounden duty to accept it, and explain it as best we can. Other instances might be quoted, from the religious history of the old world, where a nation's insight into the attributes of deity was singularly in advance of their general state of cultivation. The best thinkers of the Semitic race, for example, from Moses to Spinoza, have been in this respect far ahead of their often more generally enlightened Aryan contemporaries.

The more interesting, in view of this lofty ideal of divinity they had attained, become the Peruvian myths of the incarnation of Viracocha, his life and doings as a man among men.

These myths present themselves in different, but to the reader who has accompanied me thus far, now familiar forms. Once more we meet the story of the four brothers, the first of men. They appeared on the earth after it had been rescued from the primeval waters, and the face of the land was divided between them. Manco Capac took the North, Colla the South, Pinahua the West, and the East, the region whence come the sun and the light, was given to Tokay or Tocapa, to Viracocha, under his name of the Finisher, he who completes and perfects.[1]

[1: Garcilasso de la Vega, *Comentarios Reales*, Lib. i, cap. xviii.]

The outlines of this legend are identical with another, where Viracocha appears under the name of Ayar Cachi. This was, in its broad outlines, the most general myth, that which has been handed down by the most numerous authorities, and which they tell us was taken directly from the ancient songs of the Indians, as repeated by those who could recall the days of the Incas Huascar and Atahualpa.[1]

[1: "Parece por los cantares de los Indios; * * * afirmaron los Orejones que quedaron de los tiempos de Guascar i de Atahualpa; * * * cuentan los Indios del Cuzco mas viejos, etc.," repeats the historian Herrera, *Historia de las Indias Occidentals*, Dec. v, Lib. iii, cap. vii, viii.]

It ran in this wise: In the beginning of things there appeared on the earth four brothers, whose names were, of the oldest, Ayar Cachi, which means he who gives Being, or who Causes;[1] of the youngest, Ayar Manco, and of the others, Ayar Aucca (the enemy), and Ayar Uchu. Their father was the Sun, and the place of their birth, or rather of their appearance on earth, was Paccari-tampu, which means *The House of the Morning* or the *Mansion of the Dawn*.[2] In after days a certain cave near Cuzco was so called, and pointed out as the scene of this momentous event, but we may well believe that a nobler site than any the earth affords could be correctly designated.

[1: "*Cachini*; dar el ser y hazer que sea; *cachi chiuachic*, el autor y causa de algo." Holguin, *Vocabvlario de la Lengva Qquichua, sub voce, cachipuni*. The names differ little in Herrera (who, however, omits Uchu), Montesinos, Balboa, Oliva, La Vega and Pachacuti; I have followed the orthography of the two latter, as both were native Qquichuas.]

[2: Holguin (*ubi supra*,) gives *paccarin*, the morning, *paccarini*, to dawn; *tampu, venta o meson*.]

These brothers were clothed in long and flowing robes, with short upper garments without sleeves or collar, and this raiment was worked with marvelous skill, and glittered and shone like light. They were powerful and proud, and determined to rule the whole earth, and for this purpose divided it into four parts, the North, the South, the East, and the West. Hence they were called by the people, *Tahuantin Suyu Kapac*, Lords of all four Quarters of the Earth.[1]

[1: *Tahuantin*, all four, from *tahua*, four; *suyu*, division, section; *kapac*, king.]

The most powerful of these was Ayar Cachi. He possessed a sling of gold, and in it a stone with which he could demolish lofty mountains and hurl aloft to the clouds themselves. He gathered together the natives of the country at Pacari tampu, and accumulated at the House of the Dawn a great treasure of yellow gold. Like the glittering hoard which we read of in the lay of the Nibelung, the treasure brought with it the destruction of its owner, for his brothers, envious of the wondrous pile, persuaded Ayar Cachi to enter the cave where he kept his hoard, in order to bring out a certain vase, and also to pray to their father, the Sun, to aid them to rule their domains. As soon as he had entered, they stopped the mouth of the cave with huge stones; and thus rid of him, they set about collecting the people and making a settlement at a certain place called *Tampu quiru* (the Teeth of the House).

But they did not know the magical power of their brother. While they were busy with their plans, what was their dismay to see Ayar Cachi, freed from the cave, and with great wings of brilliantly colored feathers, hovering like a bird in the air over their heads. They expected swift retribution for their intended fratricide, but instead of this they heard reassuring words from his lips.

"Have no fear," he said, "I left you in order that the great empire of the Incas might be known to men. Leave, therefore, this settlement of Tampu quiru, and descend into the Valley of Cuzco, where you shall found a famous city, and in it build a sumptuous temple to the Sun. As for me, I shall remain in the form in which you see me, and shall dwell in the mountain peak Guanacaure, ready to help you, and on that mountain you must build me an altar and make to me sacrifices. And the sign that you shall wear, whereby you shall be feared and respected of your subjects, is that you shall have your ears pierced, as are mine," saying which he showed them his ears pierced and carrying large, round plates of gold.

They promised him obedience in all things, and forthwith built an altar on the mountain Guanacaure, which ever after was esteemed a most holy place. Here again Ayar Cachi appeared to them, and bestowed on Ayar Manco the scarlet fillet which became the perpetual insignia of the reigning Inca. The remaining brothers were turned into stone, and Manco, assuming the title of *Kapac*, King, and the metaphorical surname of *Pirhua*, the Granary or Treasure house, founded the City of Cuzco, married his four sisters, and became the first of the dynasty of the Incas. He lived to a great age, and during the whole of his life never omitted to pay divine honors to his brothers, and especially to Ayar Cachi.

In another myth of the incarnation the infinite Creator Ticci Viracocha duplicates himself in the twin incarnation of *Ymamana Viracocha* and *Tocapu Viraco-*

cha, names which we have already seen mean "he who has all things," and "he who perfects all things." The legend was that these brothers started in the distant East and journeyed toward the West. The one went by way of the mountains, the other by the paths of the lowlands, and each on his journey, like Itzamna in Yucatecan story, gave names to the places he passed, and also to all trees and herbs of the field, and to all fruits, and taught the people which were good for food, which of virtue as medicines, and which were poisonous and to be shunned. Thus they journeyed westward, imparting knowledge and doing good works, until they reached the western ocean, the great Pacific, whose waves seem to stretch westward into infinity. There, "having accomplished all they had to do in this world, they ascended into Heaven," once more to form part of the Infinite Being; for the venerable authority whom I am following is careful to add, most explicitly, that "these Indians believed for a certainty that neither the Creator nor his sons were born of woman, but that they all were unchangeable and eternal."[1]

[1: Christoval de Molina, *Fables and Rites of the Incas*, p. 6.]

Still more human does Viracocha become in the myth where he appears under the surnames *Tunapa* and *Taripaca*. The latter I have already explained to mean He who Judges, and the former is a synonym of Tocapu, as it is from the verb *ttaniy* or *ttanini*, and means He who Finishes completes or perfects, although, like several other of his names, the significance of this one has up to the present remained unexplained and lost. The myth has been preserved to us by a native Indian writer, Joan de Santa Cruz Pachacuti, who wrote it out somewhere about the year 1600.[1]

[1: *Relacion de Antiguedades deste Reyno del Piru*, por Don Joan de Santacruz Pachacuti Yamqui, passim. Pachacuti relates the story of Tunapa as being distinctly the hero-myth of the Qquichuas. He was also the hero-god of the Aymaras, and about him, says Father Ludovico Bertonio, "they to this day relate many fables and follies." *Vocabulario de la Lengua Aymara*, s.v. Another name he bore in Aymara was *Ecaco*, which in that language means, as a common noun, an ingenious, shifty man of many plans (*Bertonio, Vocabulario*, s.v.). "Thunnupa," as Bertonio spells it, does not lend itself to any obvious etymology in Aymara, which is further evidence that the name was introduced from the Qquichua. This is by no means a singular example of the identity of religious thought and terms between these nations. In comparing the two tongues, M. Alcide D'Orbigny long since observed:

"On retrouve meme a peu pres un vingtieme des mots qui ont evidemment la meme origine, surtout ceux qui expriment les idees religieuses." ***L'Homme Americain, considere sous ses Rapports Physiologiques et Moraux***, Tome i, p. 322 (Paris, 1839). This author endeavors to prove that the Qquichua religion was mainly borrowed from the Aymaras, and of the two he regards the latter as the senior in civilization. But so far as I have been able to study the mythology of the Aymaras, which is but very superficially, on account of the lack of sources, it does not seem to be entitled to this credit.]

He tells us that at a very remote period, shortly after the country of Peru had been populated, there came from Lake Titicaca to the tribes an elderly man with flowing beard and abundant white hair, supporting himself on a staff and dressed in wide-spreading robes. He went among the people, calling them his sons and daughters, relieving their infirmities and teaching them the precepts of wisdom.

Often, however, he met the fate of so many other wise teachers, and was rejected and scornfully entreated by those whom he was striving to instruct. Swift retribution sometimes fell upon such stiff-necked listeners. Thus he once entered the town of Yamquesupa, the principal place in the province of the South, and began teaching the inhabitants; but they heeded him not, and seized him, and with insult and blows drove him from the town, so that he had to sleep in the open fields. Thereupon he cursed their town, and straightway it sank into the earth with all its inhabitants, and the depression was filled with water, and all were drowned. To this day it is known as the lake of Yamquesupa, and all the people about there well know that what is now a sheet of water was once the site of a flourishing city.

At another time he visited Tiahuanaco, where may yet be seen the colossal ruins of some ancient city, and massive figures in stone of men and women. In his time this was a populous mart, its people rich and proud, given to revelry, to drunkenness and dances. Little they cared for the words of the preacher, and they treated him with disdain. Then he turned upon them his anger, and in an instant the dancers were changed into stone, just as they stood, and there they remain to this day, as any one can see, perpetual warnings not to scorn the words of the wise.

On another occasion he was seized by the people who dwelt by the great lake of Carapaco, and tied hands and feet with stout cords, it being their intention to put him to a cruel death the next day. But very early in the morning, just at the time of the dawn, a beautiful youth entered and said, "Fear not, I have come to call you in the name of the lady who is awaiting you, that you may go with her to the place of joys." With that he touched the fetters on Tunapa's limbs, and the ropes snapped asunder, and they went forth untouched by the guards, who stood around. They descended to the lake shore, and just as the dawn appeared, Tunapa spread his mantle on the waves, and he and his companion stepping upon it, as upon a raft, were wafted rapidly away into the rays of the morning light.

The cautious Pachacuti does not let us into the secret of this mysterious assignation, either because he did not know or because he would not disclose the mysteries of his ancestral faith. But I am not so discreet, and I vehemently suspect that the lady who was awaiting the virtuous Tunapa, was Chasca, the Dawn Maiden, she of the beautiful hair which distills the dew, and that the place of joys whither she invited him was the Mansion of the Sky, into which, daily, the Light-God, at the hour of the morning twilight, is ushered by the chaste maiden Aurora.

As the anger of Tunapa was dreadful, so his favors were more than regal. At the close of a day he once reached the town of the chief Apotampo, otherwise Pacari tampu, which means the House or Lodgings of the Dawn, where the festivities of a wedding were in progress. The guests, intent upon the pleasures of the hour, listened with small patience to the words of the old man, but the chief himself heard them with profound attention and delight. Therefore, as Tunapa was leaving he presented to the chief, as a reward for his hospitality and respect, the staff which had assisted his feeble limbs in many a journey. It was of no great seemliness, but upon it were inscribed characters of magic power, and the chief wisely cherished it among his treasures. It was well he did, for on the day of the birth of his next child the staff turned into fine gold, and that child was none other than the far-famed Manco Capac, destined to become the ancestor of the illustrious line of the Incas, Sons of the Sun, and famous in all countries that it shines upon; and as for the golden staff, it became, through all after time until the Spanish conquest, the sceptre of the Incas and the sign of their sovereignty, the famous and sacred *tupa yauri*, the royal wand.[1]

[1: "***Tupa yauri***; El cetro real, vara insignia real del Inca." Holguin, ***Vocabvlario de la Lengva Qquichua o del Inca***, s.v.]

It became, indeed, to Manco Capac a mentor and guide. His father and mother having died, he started out with his brothers and sisters, seven brothers and seven sisters of them, to seek new lands, taking this staff in his hand. Like the seven brothers who, in Mexican legend, left Aztlan, the White Land, to found nations and cities, so the brothers of Manco Capac, leaving Pacari tampu, the Lodgings of the Dawn, became the *sinchi*, or heads of various noble houses and chiefs of tribes in the empire of the Incas. As for Manco, it is well known that with his golden wand he journeyed on, overcoming demons and destroying his enemies, until he reached the mountain over against the spot where the city of Cuzco now stands. Here the sacred wand sunk of its own motion into the earth, and Manco Capac, recognizing the divine monition, named the mountain **Huanacauri**, the Place of Repose. In the valley at the base he founded the great city which he called **Cuzco**, the Navel. Its inhabitants ever afterwards classed Huanacauri as one of their principal deities.[1]

[1: Don Gavino Pacheco Zegarra derives Huanacauri from **huanaya**, to rest oneself, and **cayri**, here; "c'est ici qu'il faut se reposer." **Ollantai**, Introd., p. xxv. It was distinctly the **huzca**, or sacred fetish of the Incas, and they were figuratively said to have descended from it. Its worship was very prominent in ancient Peru. See the **Information de las Idolatras de los Incas y Indios**, 1671, previously quoted.]

When Manco Capac's work was done, he did not die, like other mortals, but rose to heaven, and became the planet Jupiter, under the name **Pirua**. From this, according to some writers, the country of Peru derived its name.[2]

[2: The identification of Manco Capac with the planet Jupiter is mentioned in the **Relacion Anonima**, on the authority of Melchior Hernandez.]

It may fairly be supposed that this founder of the Inca dynasty was an actual historical personage. But it is evident that much that is told about him is imagery drawn from the legend of the Light-God.

And what became of Tunapa? We left him sailing on his outspread mantle, into the light of the morning, over Lake Carapace. But the legend does not stop there. Whereever he went that day, he returned to his toil, and pursued his way down the river Chacamarca till he reached the sea. There his fate becomes obscure; but, adds Pachacuti, "I understand that he passed by the strait (of Panama) into the other sea (back toward the East). This is what is averred by the most ancient sages of the Inca line, (*por aquellos ingas antiquissimos*)." We may well believe he did; for the light of day, which is quenched in the western ocean, passes back again, by the straits or in some other way, and appears again the next morning, not in the West, where we watched its dying rays, but in the East, where again it is born to pursue its daily and ever recurring journey.

According to another, and also very early account, Viracocha was preceded by a host of attendants, who were his messengers and soldiers. When he reached the sea, he and these his followers marched out upon the waves as if it had been dry land, and disappeared in the West.[1]

[1: Garcia, *Origen de los Indios*, Lib. v, Cap. vii.]

These followers were, like himself, white and bearded. Just as, in Mexico, the natives attributed the erection of buildings, the history of which had been lost, to the white Toltecs, the subjects of Quetzalcoatl (see above, chapter iii, Sec.2), so in Peru various ancient ruins, whose builders had been lost to memory, were pointed out to the Spaniards as the work of a white and bearded race who held the country in possession long before the Incas had founded their dynasty.[1] The explanation in both cases is the same. In both the early works of art of unknown origin were supposed to be the productions of the personified light rays, which are the source of skill, because they supply the means indispensable to the acquisition of knowledge.

[2: Speaking of certain "grandes y muy antiquissimos edificios" on the river Vinaque, Cieza de Leon says: "Preguntando a los Indios comarcanos quien hizo aquella antigualla, responden que otras gentes barbadas y blancas como nosotros: los cuales, muchos tiempos antes que los Ingas reinasen, dicen que vinieron a estas partes y hicieron alli su morada." *La Cronica del Peru*, cap. lxxxvi.]

The versions of these myths which have been preserved to us by Juan de Betanzos, and the documents on which the historian Herrera founded his narrative, are in the main identical with that which I have quoted from the narrative of Pachacuti. I shall, however, give that of Herrera, as it has some interesting features.

He tells us that the traditions and songs which the Indians had received from their remote ancestors related that in very early times there was a period when there was no sun, and men lived in darkness. At length, in answer to their urgent prayers, the sun emerged from Lake Titicaca, and soon afterwards there came a man from the south, of fair complexion, large in stature, and of venerable presence, whose power was boundless. He removed mountains, filled up valleys, caused fountains to burst from the solid rocks, and gave life to men and animals. Hence the people called him the "Beginning of all Created Things," and "Father of the Sun." Many good works he performed, bringing order among the people, giving them wise counsel, working miracles and teaching. He went on his journey toward the north, but until the latest times they bore his deeds and person in memory, under the names of Tici Viracocha and Tuapaca, and elsewhere as Arnava. They erected many temples to him, in which they placed his figure and image as described.

They also said that after a certain length of time there re-appeared another like this first one, or else he was the same, who also gave wise counsel and cured the sick. He met disfavor, and at one spot the people set about to slay him, but he called down upon them fire from heaven, which burned their village and scorched the mountains into cinders. Then they threw away their weapons and begged of him to deliver them from the danger, which he did[1]. He passed on toward the West until he reached the shore of the sea. There he spread out his mantle, and seating himself upon it, sailed away and was never seen again. For this reason, adds the chronicler, "the name was given to him, **Viracocha**, which means Foam of the Sea, though afterwards it changed in signification."[2]

[1: This incident is also related by Pachacuti and Betanzos. All three locate the scene of the event at Carcha, eighteen leagues from Cuzco, where the Canas tribe lived at the Conquest. Pachacuti states that the cause of the anger of Viracocha was that upon the Sierra there was the statue of a woman to whom human victims were sacrificed. If this was the tradition, it would offer another point of identity with that of Quetzalcoatl, who was also said to have forbidden human sacrifices.]

[2: Herrera, **Historia de las Indias Occidentales**, Dec. v, Lib. iii, cap. vi.]

This leads me to the etymology of the name. It is confessedly obscure. The translation which Herrera gives, is that generally offered by the Spanish writers, but it is not literal. The word **uira** means fat, and **cocha**, lake, sea, or other large body of water; therefore, as the genitive must be prefixed in the Qquichua tongue, the translation must be "Lake or Sea of Fat." This was shown by Garcilasso de la Vega, in his **Royal Commentaries**, and as he could see no sense or propriety in applying such a term as "Lake of Grease" to the Supreme Divinity, he rejected this derivation, and contented himself by saying that the meaning of the name was totally unknown.[1] In this Mr. Clements R. Markham, who is an authority on Peruvian matters, coincides, though acknowledging that no other meaning suggests itself.[2] I shall not say anything about the derivations of this name from the Sanskrit,[3] or the ancient Egyptian;[4] these are etymological amusements with which serious studies have nothing to do.

[1: "Donde consta claro no ser nombre compuesto, sino proprio de aquella fantasma que dijo llamarse Viracocha y que era hijo del Sol." **Com, Reales**, Lib. v, cap. xxi.]

[2: Introduction to **Narratives of the Rites and Laws of the Incas**, p. xi.]

[3: "Le nom de Viracocha dont la physionomie sanskrite est si frappante," etc. Desjardins, **Le Perou avant la Conquete Espagnole**, p. 180 (Paris 1858).]

[4: Viracocha "is the Il or Ra of the Babylonian monuments, and thus the Ra of Egypt," etc. Professor John Campbell, **Compte-Rendu du Congres International des Americanistes**, Vol. i, p. 362 (1875).]

The first and accepted derivation has been ably and to my mind successfully defended by probably the most accomplished Qquichua scholar of our age, Senor Gavino Pacheco Zegarra, who, in the introduction to his most excellent edition of the Drama of **Ollantai**, maintains that Viracocha, literally "Lake of Fat," was a simile applied to the frothing, foaming sea, and adds that as a personal name in this signification it is in entire conformity with the genius of the Qquichua tongue[1].

[1: **Ollantai, Drame en vers Quechuas**, Introd., p. xxxvi (Paris, 1878). There was a class of diviners in Peru who foretold the future by inspecting the fat of animals; they were called Vira-piricuc. Molina, **Fables and Rites**, p. 13.]

To quote his words:--"The tradition was that Viracocha's face was extremely white and bearded. From this his name was derived, which means, taken literally, 'Lake of Fat;' by extension, however, the word means 'Sea-Foam,' as in the Qquichua language the foam is called *fat*, no doubt on account of its whiteness."

It had a double appropriateness in its application to the hero-god. Not only was he supposed in the one myth to have risen from the waves of Lake Titicaca, and in another to have appeared when the primeval ocean left the land dry, but he was universally described as of fair complexion, *a white man*. Strange, indeed, it is that these people who had never seen a member of the white race, should so persistently have represented their highest gods as of this hue, and what is more, with the flowing beard and abundant light hair which is their characteristic.

There is no denying, however, that such is the fact. Did it depend on legend alone we might, however strong the consensus of testimony, harbor some doubt about it. But it does not. The monuments themselves attest it. There is, indeed, a singular uniformity of statement in the myths. Viracocha, under any and all his surnames, is always described as white and bearded, dressed in flowing robes and of imposing mien. His robes were also white, and thus he was figured at the entrance of one of his most celebrated temples, that of Urcos. His image at that place was of a man with a white robe falling to his waist, and thence to his feet; by him, cut in stone, were his birds, the eagle and the falcon.[1] So, also, on a certain occasion when he was said to have appeared in a dream to one of the Incas who afterwards adopted his name, he was said to have come with beard more than a span in length, and clothed in a large and loose mantle, which fell to his feet, while with his hand he held, by a cord to its neck, some unknown animal. And thus in after times he was represented in painting and statue, by order of that Inca.[2]

[1: Christoval de Molina, ***ubi supra***, p. 29.]

[2: Garcilasso de la Vega, ***Comentarios Reales***, Lib. iv, cap. xxi.]

An early writer tells us that the great temple of Cuzco, which was afterwards chosen for the Cathedral, was originally that of Illa Ticci Viracocha. It contained only one altar, and upon it a marble statue of the god. This is described as being, "both as to the hair, complexion, features, raiment and sandals, just as painters represent the Apostle, Saint Bartholomew."[1]

[1: ***Relacion anonima***, p. 148.]

Misled by the statements of the historian Garcilasso de la Vega, some later writers, among whom I may note the eminent German traveler Von Tschudi, have supposed that Viracocha belonged to the historical deities of Peru, and that his worship was of comparatively recent origin.[1] La Vega, who could not understand the name of the divinity, and, moreover, either knew little about the ancient religion, or else concealed his knowledge (as is shown by his reiterated statement that human sacrifices were unknown), pretended that Viracocha first came to be honored through a dream of the Inca who assumed his name. But the narrative of the occurrence that he himself gives shows that even at that time the myth was well known and of great antiquity.[2]

[1: "La principal de estas Deidades historicas era ***Viracocha***. * * * Dos siglos contaba el culto de Viracocha a la llegada de los Espanoles." J. Diego de Tschudi, ***Antiguedades Peruanas***, pp. 159, 160 (Vienna, 1851).]

[2: Compare the account in Garcilasso de la Vega, ***Comentarios Reales***, Lib. ii, cap. iv; Lib. iv, cap. xxi, xxiii, with that in Acosta, ***Historia Natural y Moral de las Indias***, Lib. vi, cap. xxi.]

The statements which he makes on the authority of Father Blas Valera, that the Inca Tupac Yupanqui sought to purify the religion of his day by leading it toward the contemplation of an incorporeal God,[3] is probably, in the main, correct. It is supported by a similar account given by Acosta, of the famous Huayna Capac. Indeed, they read so much alike that they are probably repetitions of teachings familiar to the nobles and higher priests. Both Incas maintained that the Sun could not be the chief god, because he ran daily his accustomed course, like a slave, or an animal that is led. He must therefore be the subject of a mightier power than himself.

[3: ***Comentarios Reales***, Pt. i, Lib. viii, cap. viii.]

We may reasonably suppose that these expressions are proof of a growing sense of the attributes of divinity. They are indications of the evolution of religious thought, and go to show that the monotheistic ideas which I have pointed out in the titles and names of the highest God, were clearly recognized and publicly announced.

Viracocha was also worshiped under the title ***Con-ticci-Viracocha***. Various explanations of the name ***Con*** have been offered. It is not positively certain that it belongs to the Qquichua tongue. A myth preserved by Gomara treats Con as a distinct deity. He is said to have come from the north, to have been without bones, muscles or members, to have the power of running with infinite swiftness, and to have leveled mountains, filled up valleys, and deprived the coast plains of rain. At the same time he is called a son of the Sun and the Moon, and it was owing to his good will and creative power that men and women were formed, and maize and fruits given them upon which to subsist.

Another more powerful god, however, by name Pachacamac, also a son of the Sun and Moon, and hence brother to Con, rose up against him and drove him from the land. The men and women whom Con had formed were changed by Pachacamac into brutes, and others created who were the ancestors of the present race.

These he supplied with what was necessary for their support, and taught them the arts of war and peace. For these reasons they venerated him as a god, and constructed for his worship a sumptuous temple, a league and a half from the present city of Lima.[1]

[1: Francisco Lopez de Gomara, ***Historia de las Indias***, p. 233 (Ed. Paris, 1852).]

This myth of the conflict of the two brothers is too similar to others I have quoted for its significance to be mistaken. Unfortunately it has been handed down in so fragmentary a condition that it does not seem possible to assign it its proper relations to the cycle of Viracocha legends.

As I have hinted, we are not sure of the meaning of the name Con, nor whether it is of Qquichua origin. If it is, as is indeed likely, then we may suppose that it is a transcription of the word ***ccun***, which in Qquichua is the third person singular, present indicative, of ***ccuni***, I give. "He Gives;" the Giver, would seem an appropriate name for the first creator of things. But the myth itself, and the description of the deity, incorporeal and swift, bringer at one time of the fertilizing rains, at another of the drought, seems to point unmistakably to a god of the winds. Linguistic analogy bears this out, for the name given to a whirlwind or violent wind storm was ***Conchuy***, with an additional word to signify whether it was one of rain or merely a dust storm.[1] For this reason I think M. Wiener's attempt to make of Con (or ***Qquonn***, as he prefers to spell it) merely a deity of the rains, is too narrow.[2]

[1: A whirlwind with rain was ***paria conchuy*** (***paria***, rain), one with clouds of dust, ***allpa conchuy*** (***allpa***, earth, dust); Holguin, ***Vocabulario Qquichua***, s.v. ***Antay conchuy***.]

[2: ***Le Perou et Bolivie***, p. 694. (Paris, 1880.)]

The legend would seem to indicate that he was supposed to have been defeated and quite driven away. But the study of the monuments indicates that this was not the case. One of the most remarkable antiquities in Peru is at a place called ***Concacha***, three leagues south of Abancay, on the road from Cuzco to Lima. M. Leonce Angrand has observed that this "was evidently one of the great religious centres of the primitive peoples of Peru." Here is found an enormous block of granite, very curiously carved to facilitate the dispersion of a liquid poured on its summit into varied streams and to quaint receptacles. Whether the liquid was the blood of victims, the intoxicating beverage of the country, or pure water, all of which have been suggested, we do not positively know, but I am inclined to believe, with M. Wiener, that it was the last mentioned, and that it was as the beneficent deity of the rains that Con was worshiped at this sacred spot. Its name *con cacha*, "the Messenger of Con," points to this.[1]

[1: These remains are carefully described by Charles Wiener, *Perou et Bolivie*, p. 282, seq; from the notes of M. Angrand, by Desjardins, *Le Perou avant la Conquete Espagnole*, p. 132; and in a superficial manner by Squier, *Peru*, p. 555.]

The words *Pacha camac* mean "animating" or "giving life to the world." It is said by Father Acosta to have been one of the names of Viracocha,[1] and in a sacred song preserved by Garcilasso de la Vega he is appealed to by this title.[2] The identity of these two divinities seems, therefore, sufficiently established.

[1: *Historia Natural y Moral de las Indias*, Lib. v, cap. iii.]

[2: *Comentarios Reales*, Lib. ii, cap. xxviii.]

The worship of Pachacamac is asserted by competent antiquarian students to have been more extended in ancient Peru than the older historians supposed. This is indicated by the many remains of temples which local tradition attribute to his worship, and by the customs of the natives.[1] For instance, at the birth of a child it was formally offered to him and his protection solicited. On reaching some arduous height the toiling Indian would address a few words of thanks to Pachacamac; and the piles of stones, which were the simple signs of their gratitude, are still visible in all parts of the country.

[1: Von Tschudi, who in one part of his work maintains that sun-worship was the prevalent religion of Peru, modifies the assertion considerably in the following passage: "El culto de Pachacamac se hallaba mucho mas extendido de lo que suponen los historiadores; y se puede sin error aventurar la opinion de que era la Deidad popular y acatada por las masas peruanas; mientras que la religion del Sol era la de la corte, culto que, por mas adoptado que fuese entre los Indios, nunca llego a desarraigar la fe y la devocion al Numen primitivo. En effecto, en todas las relaciones de la vida de los Indios, resalta la profunda veneracion que tributavan a Pachacamac." *Antiguedades Peruanas*, p. 149. Inasmuch as elsewhere this author takes pains to show that the Incas discarded the worship of the Sun, and instituted in place of it that of Viracocha, the above would seem to diminish the sphere of

Sun-worship very much.]

This variation of the story of Viracocha aids to an understanding of his mythical purport. The oft-recurring epithet "Contice Viracocha" shows a close relationship between his character and that of the divinity Con, in fact, an identity which deserves close attention. It is explained, I believe, by the supposition that Viracocha was the Lord of the Wind as well as of the Light. Like all the other light gods, and deities of the cardinal points, he was at the same time the wind from them. What has been saved from the ancient mythology is enough to show this, but not enough to allow us to reconcile the seeming contradictions which it suggests. Moreover, it must be ever remembered that all religions repose on contradictions, contradictions of fact, of logic, and of statement, so that we must not seek to force any one of them into consistent unity of form, even with itself.

I have yet to add another point of similarity between the myth of Viracocha and those of Quetzalcoatl, Itzamna and the others, which I have already narrated. As in Mexico, Yucatan and elsewhere, so in the realms of the Incas, the Spaniards found themselves not unexpected guests. Here, too, texts of ancient prophecies were called to mind, words of warning from solemn and antique songs, foretelling that other Viracochas, men of fair complexion and flowing beards, would some day come from the Sun, the father of existent nature, and subject the empire to their rule. When the great Inca, Huayna Capac, was on his death-bed, he recalled these prophecies, and impressed them upon the mind of his successor, so that when De Soto, the lieutenant of Pizarro, had his first interview with the envoy of Atahuallpa, the latter humbly addressed him as Viracocha, the great God, son of the Sun, and told him that it was Huayna Capac's last command to pay homage to the white men when they should arrive.[1]

[1: Garcilasso de La Vega, **Comentarios Reales**, Lib. ix, caps. xiv, xv; Cieza de Leon, **Relacion**, MS. in Prescott, **Conquest of Peru**, Vol. i, p. 329. The latter is the second part of Cieza de Leon.]

We need no longer entertain about such statements that suspicion or incredulity which so many historians have thought it necessary to indulge in. They are too generally paralleled in other American hero-myths to leave the slightest doubt as to their reality, or as to their significance. They are again the expression of the expected return of the Light-God, after his departure and disappearance in the western horizon. Modifications of what was originally a statement of a simple occurrence of daily routine, they became transmitted in the limbeck of mythology to the story of the beneficent god of the past, and the promise of golden days when again he should return to the people whom erstwhile he ruled and taught.

The Qquichuas expected the return of Viracocha, not merely as an earthly ruler to govern their nation, but as a god who, by his divine power, would call the dead to life. Precisely as in ancient Egypt the literal belief in the resurrection of the body led to the custom of preserving the corpses with the most sedulous care, so in Peru the cadaver was mummied and deposited in the most secret and inaccessible spots, so that it should remain undisturbed to the great day of resurrection.

And when was that to be?

We are not left in doubt on this point. It was to be when Viracocha should return to earth in his bodily form. Then he would restore the dead to life, and they should enjoy the good things of a land far more glorious than this work-a-day world of ours.[1]

[1: "Dijeron quellos oyeron decir a sus padres y pasados que un Viracocha habia de revolver la tierra, y habia de resucitar esos muertos, y que estos habian de bibir en esta tierra.". *Information de las Idolatras de los Incas e Indios*, in the *Coll. de Docs. ineditos del Archivo de Indias*, vol. xxi, p. 152.]

As at the first meeting between the races the name of the hero-god was applied to the conquering strangers, so to this day the custom has continued. A recent traveler tells us, "Among *Los Indios del Campo*, or Indians of the fields, the llama herdsmen of the *punas*, and the fishermen of the lakes, the common salutation to strangers of a fair skin and blue eyes is '*Tai-tai Viracocha*.'"[1] Even if this is used now, as M. Wiener seems to think,[2] merely as a servile flattery, there is no doubt but that at the beginning it was applied because the white strangers were identified with the white and bearded hero and his followers of their culture myth, whose return had been foretold by their priests.

[1: E.G. Squier, *Travels in Peru*, p. 414.]

[2: C. Wiener, *Perou et Bolivie*, p. 717.]

Are we obliged to explain these similarities to the Mexican tradition by supposing some ancient intercourse between these peoples, the arrival, for instance, and settlement on the highlands around Lake Titicaca, of some "Toltec" colony, as has been maintained by such able writers on Peruvian antiquities as Leonce Angrand and J.J. von Tschudi?[1] I think not. The great events of nature, day and night, storm and sunshine, are everywhere the same, and the impressions they produced on the minds of this race were the same, whether the scene was in the forests of the north temperate zone, amid the palms of the tropics, or on the lofty and barren plateaux of the Andes. These impressions found utterance in similar myths, and were represented in art under similar forms. It is, therefore, to the oneness of cause and of racial psychology, not to ancient migrations, that we must look to explain the identities of myth and representation that we find between such widely sundered nations.

[1: L. Angrand, *Lettre sur les Antiquites de Tiaguanaco et l'Origine presumable de la plus ancienne civilisation du Haut-Perou*. Extrait du 24eme vol. de la *Revue Generale d'Architecture*, 1866. Von Tschudi, *Das Ollantadrama*, p. 177-9. The latter says: "Der von dem Plateau von Anahuac ausgewanderte Stamm verpflanzte seine Gesittung und die Hauptzuege seiner Religion durch das westliche Suedamerica, etc."]

CHAPTER VI.
THE EXTENSION AND INFLUENCE OF
THE TYPICAL HERO-MYTH.

THE TYPICAL MYTH FOUND IN MANY PARTS OF THE CONTINENT-
-DIFFICULTIES IN TRACING IT--RELIGIOUS EVOLUTION IN AMERI-
CA SIMILAR TO THAT IN THE OLD WORLD--FAILURE OF CHRISTI-
ANITY IN THE RED RACE.
THE CULTURE MYTH OF THE TARASCOS OF MECHOACAN--THAT
OF THE RICHES OF GUATEMALA--THE VOTAN MYTH OF THE
TZENDALS OF CHIAPAS--A FRAGMENT OF A MIXE MYTH--THE
HERO-GOD OF THE MUYSCAS OF NEW GRANADA--OF THE TUPI-
GUARANAY STEM OF PARAGUAY AND BRAZIL--MYTHS OF THE
DENE OF BRITISH AMERICA.
SUN WORSHIP IN AMERICA--GERMS OF PROGRESS IN AMERI-
CAN RELIGIONS--RELATION OF RELIGION AND MORALITY--THE
LIGHT-GOD A MORAL AND BENEFICENT CREATION--HIS WOR-
SHIP WAS ELEVATING--MORAL CONDITION OF NATIVE SOCIETIES
BEFORE THE CONQUEST--PROGRESS IN THE DEFINITION OF THE
IDEA OF GOD IN PERU, MEXICO, AND YUCATAN--ERRONEOUS
STATEMENTS ABOUT THE MORALS OF THE NATIVES--EVOLUTION
OF THEIR ETHICAL PRINCIPLES.

In the foregoing chapters I have passed in review the hero-myths of five nations widely asunder in location, in culture and in language. I have shown the
strange similarity in their accounts of their mysterious early benefactor and
teacher, and their still more strange, because true, presentiments of the arrival

of pale-faced conquerors from the East.

I have selected these nations because their myths have been most fully recorded, not that they alone possessed this striking legend. It is, I repeat, the fundamental myth in the religious lore of American nations. Not, indeed, that it can be discovered in all tribes, especially in the amplitude of incident which it possesses among some. But there are comparatively few of the native mythologies that do not betray some of its elements, some fragments of it, and, often enough to justify us in the supposition that had we the complete body of their sacred stories, we should find this one in quite as defined a form as I have given it.

The student of American mythology, unfortunately, labors under peculiar disadvantages. When he seeks for his material, he finds an extraordinary dearth of it. The missionaries usually refused to preserve the native myths, because they believed them harmful, or at least foolish; while men of science, who have had such opportunities, rejected all those that seemed the least like a Biblical story, as they suspected them to be modern and valueless compositions, and thus lost the very life of the genuine ancient faiths.

A further disadvantage is the slight attention which has been paid to the aboriginal American tongues, and the sad deficiency of material for their study. It is now recognized on all hands that the key of a mythology is to be found in the language of its believers. As a German writer remarks, "the formation of the language and the evolution of the myth go hand in hand."[1] We must know the language of a tribe, at least we must understand the grammatical construction and have facilities to trace out the meaning and derivation of names, before we can obtain any accurate notion of the foundation in nature of its religious beliefs. No convenient generality will help us.

[1: "In der Sprache herrscht immer und erneut sich stets die sinnliche Anschauung, die vor Jahrtausenden mit dem glaeubigen Sinn vermaehlt die Mythologien schuf, und gerade durch sie wird es am klarsten, wie Sprachenschoepfung und mythologische Entwicklung, der Ausdruck des Denkens und Glaubens, einst Hand in Hand gegangen." Dr. F.L.W. Schwartz, ***Der Ursprung der Mythologie dargelegt an Griechischer und Deutscher Sage***, p. 23 (Berlin, 1860).]

I make these remarks as a sort of apology for the shortcomings of the present study, and especially for the imperfections of the fragments I have still to present.

They are, however, sufficiently defined to make it certain that they belonged to cycles of myths closely akin to those already given. They will serve to support my thesis that the seemingly confused and puerile fables of the native Americans are fully as worthy the attention of the student of human nature as the more poetic narratives of the Veda or the Edda. The red man felt out after God with like childish gropings as his white brother in Central Asia. When his course was interrupted, he was pursuing the same path toward the discovery of truth. In the words of a thoughtful writer: "In a world wholly separated from that which it is customary to call the Old World, the religious evolution of man took place precisely in the same manner as in those surroundings which produced the civilization of western Europe."[1]

[1: Girard de Rialle, *La Mythologie Comparee*, vol. I, p. 363 (Paris, 1878).]

But this religious development of the red man was violently broken by the forcible imposition of a creed which he could not understand, and which was not suited to his wants, and by the heavy yoke of a priesthood totally out of sympathy with his line of progress. What has been the result? "Has Christianity," asks the writer I have just quoted, "exerted a progressive action on these peoples? Has it brought them forward, has it aided their natural evolution? We are obliged to answer, No."[1] This sad reply is repeated by careful observers who have studied dispassionately the natives in their homes.[2] The only difference in the results of the two great divisions of the Christian world seems to be that on Catholic missions has followed the debasement, on Protestant missions the destruction of the race.

[1: Girard de Rialle, *ibid*, p. 862.]

[2: Those who would convince themselves of this may read the work of Don Francisco Pimentel, *Memoria sobre las Causas que han originado la Situation Actual de la Raza Indigena de Mexico* (Mexico, 1864), and that of the Licentiate Apolinar Garcia y Garcia, *Historia de la Guerra de Castas de Yucatan*, Prologo (Merida, 1865). That the Indians of the United States have directly and positively degenerated in moral sense as a race, since the introduction of Christianity, was also very decidedly the opinion of the late Prof. Theodor Waitz, a most competent ethnologist. See *Die Indianer Nordamerica's. Eine Studie*, von Theodor Waitz, p. 39, etc. (Leipzig, 1865). This opinion was also that of the visiting committee of the Society of Friends who reported on the Indian Tribes in 1842; see the *Report of a*

Visit to Some of the Tribes of Indians West of the Mississippi River, by John D. Lang and Samuel Taylor, Jr. (New York, 1843). The language of this Report is calm, but positive as to the increased moral degradation of the tribes, as the, direct result of contact with the whites.]

It may be objected to this that it was not Christianity, but its accompaniments, the greedy horde of adventurers, the profligate traders, the selfish priests, and the unscrupulous officials, that wrought the degradation of the native race. Be it so. Then I merely modify my assertion, by saying that Christianity has shown itself incapable of controlling its inevitable adjuncts, and that it would have been better, morally and socially, for the American race never to have known Christianity at all, than to have received it on the only terms on which it has been possible to offer it.

With the more earnestness, therefore, in view of this acknowledged failure of Christian effort, do I turn to the native beliefs, and desire to vindicate for them a dignified position among the faiths which have helped to raise man above the level of the brute, and inspired him with hope and ambition for betterment.

For this purpose I shall offer some additional evidence of the extension of the myth I have set forth, and then proceed to discuss its influence on the minds of its believers.

The Tarascos were an interesting nation who lived in the province of Michoacan, due west of the valley of Mexico. They were a polished race, speaking a sonorous, vocalic language, so bold in war that their boast was that they had never been defeated, and yet their religious rites were almost bloodless, and their preference was for peace. The hardy Aztecs had been driven back at every attempt they made to conquer Michoacan, but its ruler submitted himself without a murmur to Cortes, recognizing in him an opponent of the common enemy, and a warrior of more than human powers.

Among these Tarascos we find the same legend of a hero-god who brought them out of barbarism, gave them laws, arranged their calendar, which, in principles, was the same as that of the Aztecs and Mayas, and decided on the form of their government. His name was ***Surites*** or ***Curicaberis***, words which, from my limited resources in that tongue, I am not able to analyze. He dwelt in the town Cromuscuaro, which name means the Watch-tower or Look-out, and the hour in which he gave his instructions was always at sunrise, just as the orb of light appeared on the eastern horizon. One of the feasts which he appointed to be celebrated in his honor was called *Zitacuarencuaro*, which melodious word is said by the Spanish missionaries to mean "the resurrection from death." When to this it is added that he distinctly predicted that a white race of men should arrive in the country, and that he himself should return,[1] his identity with the light-gods of similar American myths is too manifest to require argument.

[1: P. Francisco Xavier Alegre, *Historia de la Compania de Jesus en la Nueva Espana*, Tomo i, pp. 91, 92 (Mexico, 1841). The authorities whom Alegre quotes are P.P. Alonso de la Rea, *Cronica de Mechoacan* (Mexico, 1648), and D. Basalenque, *Cronica de San Augustin de Mechoacan* (Mexico, 1673). I regret that I have been unable to find either of these books in any library in the United States. It is a great pity that the student of American history is so often limited in his investigations in this country, by the lack of material. It is sad to think that such an opulent and intelligent land does not possess a single complete library of its own history.]

The king of the Tarascos was considered merely the vicegerent of the absent hero-god, and ready to lay down the sceptre when Curicaberis should return to earth.

We do not know whether the myth of the Four Brothers prevailed among the Tarascos; but there is hardly a nation on the continent among whom the number Four was more distinctly sacred. The kingdom was divided into four parts (as also among the Itzas, Qquichuas and numerous other tribes), the four rulers of which constituted, with the king, the sacred council of five, in imitation, I can hardly doubt, of the hero-god, and the four deities of the winds.

The goddess of water and the rains, the female counterpart of Curicaberis, was the goddess *Cueravaperi*. "She is named," says the authority I quote, "in all their fables and speeches. They say that she is the mother of all the gods of the earth, and that it is she who bestows the harvests and the germination of seeds." With her ever went four attendant goddesses, the personifications of the rains from the four cardinal points. At the sacred dances, which were also dramatizations of her supposed action, these attendants were represented by four priests clad respectively in white, yellow, red and black, to represent the four colors of the clouds.[1] In other words, she doubtless bore the same relation to Curicaberis that Ixchel did to Itzamna in the mythology of the Mayas, or the rainbow goddess to Arama in the religious legends of the Moxos.[2] She was the divinity that presided over the rains, and hence over fertility and the harvests, standing in intimate relation to the god of the sun's rays and the four winds.

[1: *Relacion de las Ceremonias y Ritos, etc., de Mechoacan*, in the *Coleccion de Documentos para la Historia de Espana*, vol. liii, pp. 13, 19, 20. This account is anonymous, but was written in the sixteenth century, by some one familiar with the subject. A handsome MS. of it, with colored illustrations (these of no great value, however), is in the Library of Congress, obtained from the collection of the late Col. Peter Force.]

[2: See above, chapter iv, Sec.1]

The Kiches of Guatemala were not distant relatives of the Mayas of Yucatan, and their mythology has been preserved to us in a rescript of their national book, the *Popol Vuh*. Evidently they had borrowed something from Aztec sources, and a flavor of Christian teaching is occasionally noticeable in this record; but for all that it is one of the most valuable we possess on the subject.

It begins by connecting the creation of men and things with the appearance of light. In other words, as in so many mythologies, the history of the world is that of the day; each begins with a dawn. Thus the *Popol Vuh* reads:--

"This is how the heaven exists, how the Heart of Heaven exists, he, the god, whose name is Qabauil."

"His word came in the darkness to the Lord, to Gucumatz, and it spoke with the Lord, with Gucumatz."

"They spoke together; they consulted and planned; they understood; they united in words and plans."

"As they consulted, the day appeared, the white light came forth, mankind was produced, while thus they held counsel about the growth of trees and vines, about life and mankind, in the darkness, in the night (the creation was brought about), by the Heart of Heaven, whose name is Hurakan."[1]

[1: *Popol Vuh, le Livre Sacre des Quiches*, p. 9 (Paris, 1861).]

But the national culture-hero of the Kiches seems to have been *Xbalanque*, a name which has the literal meaning, "Little Tiger Deer," and is a symbolical appellation referring to days in their calendar. Although many of his deeds are recounted in the ***Popol Vuh***, that work does not furnish us his complete mythical history. From it and other sources we learn that he was one of the twins supposed to have been born of a virgin mother in Utatlan, the central province of the Kiches, to have been the guide and protector of their nation, and in its interest to have made a journey to the Underworld, in order to revenge himself on his powerful enemies, its rulers. He was successful, and having overcome them, he set free the Sun, which they had seized, and restored to life four hundred youths whom they had slain, and who, in fact, were the stars of heaven. On his return, he emerged from the bowels of the earth and the place of darkness, at a point far to the east of Utatlan, at some place located by the Kiches near Coban, in Vera Paz, and came again to his people, looking to be received with fitting honors. But like Viracocha, Quetzalcoatl, and others of these worthies, the story goes that they treated him with scant courtesy, and in anger at their ingratitude, he left them forever, in order to seek a nobler people.

I need not enter into a detailed discussion of this myth, many points in which are obscure, the less so as I have treated them at length in a monograph readily accessible to the reader who would push his inquiries further. Enough if I quote the conclusion to which I there arrive. It is as follows:--

"Suffice it to say that the hero-god, whose name is thus compounded of two signs in the calendar, who is one of twins born of a virgin, who performs many surprising feats of prowess on the earth, who descends into the world of darkness and sets free the sun, moon and stars to perform their daily and nightly journeys through the heavens, presents in these and other traits such numerous resemblances to the Divinity of Light, the Day-maker of the northern hunting tribes, reappearing in so many American legends, that I do not hesitate to identify the narrative of Xbalanque and his deeds as but another version of this wide-spread, this well-nigh universal myth."[1]

[1: ***The Names of the Gods in the Kiche Myths, Central America***, by Daniel G. Brinton, M.D., in the ***Proceedings of the American Philosophical Society*** for 1881.]

Few of our hero-myths have given occasion for wilder speculation than that of Votan. He was the culture hero of the Tzendals, a branch of the Maya race, whose home was in Chiapas and Tabasco. Even the usually cautious Humboldt suggested that his name might be a form of Odin or Buddha! As for more imaginative writers, they have made not the least difficulty in discovering that it is identical with the Odon of the Tarascos, the Oton of the Othomis, the Poudan of the East Indian Tamuls, the Vaudoux of the Louisiana negroes, etc. All this has been done without any attempt having been made to ascertain the precise meaning and derivation of the name Votan. Superficial phonetic similarities have been the only guide.

We are not well acquainted with the Votan myth. It appears to have been written down some time in the seventeenth century, by a Christianized native. His manuscript of five or six folios, in the Tzendal tongue, came into the possession of Nunez de la Vega, Bishop of Chiapas, about 1690, and later into the hands of Don Ramon Ondonez y Aguiar, where it was seen by Dr. Paul Felix Cabrera, about 1790. What has become of it is not known.

No complete translation of it was made; and the extracts or abstracts given by the authors just named are most unsatisfactory, and disfigured by ignorance and prejudice. None of them, probably, was familiar with the Tzendal tongue, especially in its ancient form. What they tell us runs as follows:--

At some indefinitely remote epoch, Votan came from the far East. He was sent by God to divide out and assign to the different races of men the earth on which they dwell, and to give to each its own language. The land whence he came was vaguely called ***ualum uotan***, the land of Votan.

His message was especially to the Tzendals. Previous to his arrival they were ignorant, barbarous, and without fixed habitations. He collected them into villages, taught them how to cultivate the maize and cotton, and invented the hieroglyphic signs, which they learned to carve on the walls of their temples. It is even said that he wrote his own history in them.

He instituted civil laws for their government, and imparted to them the proper ceremonials of religious worship. For this reason he was also called "Master of the Sacred Drum," the instrument with which they summoned the votaries to the ritual dances.

They especially remembered him as the inventor of their calendar. His name stood third in the week of twenty days, and was the first Dominical sign, according to which they counted their year, corresponding to the ***Kan*** of the Mayas.

As a city-builder, he was spoken of as the founder of Palenque, Nachan, Huehuetlan--in fact, of any ancient place the origin of which had been forgotten. Near the last mentioned locality, Huehuetlan in Soconusco, he was reported to have constructed an underground temple by merely blowing with his breath. In this gloomy mansion he deposited his treasures, and appointed a priestess to guard it, for whose assistance he created the tapirs.

Votan brought with him, according to one statement, or, according to another, was followed from his native land by, certain attendants or subordinates, called in the myth *tzequil*, petticoated, from the long and flowing robes they wore. These aided him in the work of civilization. On four occasions he returned to his former home, dividing the country, when he was about to leave, into four districts, over which he placed these attendants.

When at last the time came for his final departure, he did not pass through the valley of death, as must all mortals, but he penetrated through a cave into the under-earth, and found his way to "the root of heaven." With this mysterious expression, the native myth closes its account of him.[1]

[1: The references to the Votan myth are Nunez de la Vega, *Constituciones Diocesanas, Prologo* (Romae, 1702); Boturini, *Idea de una Nueva Historia de la America septentrional*, pp. 114, et seq., who discusses the former; Dr. Paul Felix Cabrera, *Teatro Critico Americano*, translated, London, 1822; Brasseur de Bourbourg, *Hist. des Nations Civilisees de Mexique*, vol. i, chap, ii, who gives some additional points from Ordonez; and H. de Charencey, *Le Mythe de Votan; Etude sur les Origines Asiatiques de la Civilization Americaine*. (Alencon, 1871).]

He was worshiped by the Tzendals as their principal deity and their beneficent patron. But he had a rival in their religious observances, the feared *Yalahau* Lord of Blackness, or Lord of the Waters. He was represented as a terrible warrior, cruel to the people, and one of the first of men.[1]

[1: *Yalahau* is referred to by Bishop Nunez de la Vega as venerated in Occhuc and other Tzendal towns of Chiapas. He translates it "Senor de los Negros." The terminal *ahau* is pure Maya, meaning king, ruler, lord; *Yal* is also Maya, and means water. The god of the waters, of darkness, night and blackness, is often one and the same in mythology, and probably had we the myth complete, he would prove to be Votan's brother and antagonist.]

According to an unpublished work by Fuentes, Votan was one of four brothers, the common ancestors of the southwestern branches of the Maya family.[1]

[1: Quoted in Emeterio Pineda, ***Descripcion Geografica de Chiapas y Soconusco***, p. 9 (Mexico, 1845).]

All these traits of this popular hero are too exactly similar to those of the other representatives of this myth, for them to leave any doubt as to what we are to make of Votan. Like the rest of them, he and his long-robed attendants are personifications of the eastern light and its rays. Though but uncritical epitomes of a fragmentary myth about him remain, they are enough to stamp it as that which meets us so constantly, no matter where we turn in the New World.[1]

[1: The title of the Tzendal MSS., is said by Cabrera to be "Proof that I am a Chan." The author writes in the person of Votan himself, and proves his claim that he is a Chan, "because he is a Chivim." Chan has been translated ***serpent***; on ***chivim*** the commentators have almost given up. Supposing that the serpent was a totem of one of the Tzendal clans, then the effort would be to show that their hero-god was of that totem; but how this is shown by his being proved a ***chivim*** is not obvious. The term ***ualum chivim***, the land of the ***chivim***. appears to be that applied, in the MS., to the country of the Tzendals, or a part of it. The words ***chi uinic*** would mean, "men of the shore," and might be a local name applied to a clan on the coast. But in default of the original text we can but surmise as to the precise meaning of the writer.]

It scarcely seems necessary for me to point out that his name Votan is in no way akin to Othomi or Tarasco roots, still less to the Norse Wodan or the Indian Buddha, but is derived from a radical in pure Maya. Yet I will do so, in order, if possible, to put a stop to such visionary etymologies.

As we are informed by Bishop Nunez de la Vega, ***uotan*** in Tzendal means ***heart***. Votan was spoken of as "the heart or soul of his people." This derivation has been questioned, because the word for the heart in the other Maya dialects is different, and it has been suggested that this was but an example of "otosis," where a foreign proper name was turned into a familiar common noun. But these objections do not hold good.

In regard to derivation, ***uotan*** is from the pure Maya root-word ***tan***, which means primarily "the breast," or that which is in front or in the middle of the body;

with the possessive prefix it becomes **utan**. In Tzendal this word means both **breast** and **heart**. This is well illustrated by an ancient manuscript, dating from 1707, in my possession. It is a guide to priests for administering the sacraments in Spanish and Tzendal. I quote the passage in point[1]:--

[1: **Modo de Administrar los Sacramentos en Castellano y Tzendal**, 1707. 4to MS., p. 13.]

"Con todo tu corazon, hiriendote en los pechos, di, conmigo."

Ta zpizil auotan, xatigh zny auotan, zghoyoc, alagh ghoyoc.--

Here, **a** is the possessive of the second person, and **uotan** is used both for heart and breast. Thus the derivation of the word from the Maya radical is clear.

The figure of speech by which the chief divinity is called "the heart of the earth," "the heart of the sky," is common in these dialects, and occurs repeatedly in the **Popol Vuh**, the sacred legend of the Kiches of Guatemala.[2]

[2: Thus we have (**Popol Vuh**, Part i, p. 2) **u qux cho**, Heart of the Lakes, and **u qux palo**, Heart of the Ocean, as names of the highest divinity; later, we find **u qux cah**, Heart of the Sky (p. 8), **u qux uleu**, Heart of the Earth, p. 12, 14, etc.

I may here repeat what I have elsewhere written on this figurative expression in the Maya languages: "The literal or physical sense of the word heart is not that which is here intended. In these dialects this word has a richer metaphorical meaning than in our tongue. It stands for all the psychical powers, the memory, will and reasoning faculties, the life, the spirit, the soul. It would be more correct to render these names the 'Spirit' or 'Soul' of the lake, etc., than the 'Heart.' They indicate a dimly understood sense of the unity of spirit or energy in all the various manifestations of organic and inorganic existence." **The Names of the Gods in the Kiche Myths, Central America**, by Daniel G. Brinton, in **Proceedings of the American Philosophical Society**, vol. xix, 1881, p. 623.]

The immediate neighbors of the Tzendals were the Mixes and Zoques, the former resident in the central mountains of the Isthmus of Tehuantepec, the latter rather in the lowlands and toward the eastern coast. The Mixes nowadays number but a few villages, whose inhabitants are reported as drunken and worthless, but the time was when they were a powerful and warlike nation. They are in nowise akin to the Maya stock, although they are so classed in Mr. H.H. Bancroft's excellent work.[1] They have, however, a distinct relationship with the Zoques, about thirty per cent of the words in the two languages being similar.[2] The Zoques, whose mythology we unfortunately know little or nothing about, adjoined the Tzendals, and were in constant intercourse with them.

[1: "Mijes, Maya nation," *The Native Races of the Pacific States*, Vol. v, p. 712.]

[2: *Apuntes sobre la Lengua Mije*, por C.H. Berendt, M.D., MS., in my hands. The comparison is made of 158 words in the two languages, of which 44 have marked affinity, besides the numerals, eight out of ten of which are the same. Many of the remaining words are related to the Zapotec, and there are very few and faint resemblances to Maya dialects. One of them may possibly be in this name, Votan (*uotan*), heart, however. In Mixe the word for heart is *hot*. I note this merely to complete my observations on the Votan myth.]

We have but faint traces of the early mythology of these tribes; but they preserved some legends which show that they also partook of the belief, so general among their neighbors, of a beneficent culture-god.

This myth relates that their first father, who was also their Supreme God, came forth from a cave in a lofty mountain in their country, to govern and direct them. He covered the soil with forests, located the springs and streams, peopled them with fish and the woods with game and birds, and taught the tribe how to catch them. They did not believe that he had died, but that after a certain length of time, he, with his servants and captives, all laden with bright gleaming gold, retired into the cave and closed its mouth, not to remain there, but to reappear at some other part of the world and confer similar favors on other nations.

The name, or one of the names, of this benefactor was Condoy, the meaning of which my facilities do not enable me to ascertain.[1]

[1: Juan B. Carriedo, *Estudios Historicos y Estadisticos del Estado Libre de Oaxaca*, p. 3 (Oaxaca, 1847).]

There is scarcely enough of this to reveal the exact lineaments of their hero; but if we may judge from these fragments as given by Carriedo, it appears to be of precisely the same class as the other hero-myths I have collected in this volume. Historians of authority assure us that the Mixes, Zoques and Zapotecs united in the expectation, founded on their ancient myths and prophecies, of the arrival, some time, of men from the East, fair of hue and mighty in power, masters of the lightning, who would occupy the land.[1]

[1: Ibid., p. 94, **note**, quoting from the works of Las Casas and Francisco Burgoa.]

On the lofty plateau of the Andes, in New Granada, where, though nearly under the equator, the temperature is that of a perpetual spring, was the fortunate home of the Muyscas. It is the true El Dorado of America; every mountain stream a Pactolus, and every hill a mine of gold. The natives were peaceful in disposition, skilled in smelting and beating the precious metal that was everywhere at hand, lovers of agriculture, and versed in the arts of spinning, weaving and dying cotton. Their remaining sculptures prove them to have been of no mean ability in designing, and it is asserted that they had a form of writing, of which their signs for the numerals have alone been preserved.

The knowledge of these various arts they attributed to the instructions of a wise stranger who dwelt among them many cycles before the arrival of the Spaniards. He came from the East, from the llanos of Venezuela or beyond them, and it was said that the path he made was broad and long, a hundred leagues in length, and led directly to the holy temple at his shrine at Sogamoso. In the province of Ubaque his footprints on the solid rock were reverently pointed out long after the Conquest. His hair was abundant, his beard fell to his waist, and he dressed in long and flowing robes. He went among the nations of the plateaux, addressing each in its own dialect, taught them to live in villages and to observe just laws. Near the village of Coto was a high hill held in special veneration, for from its prominent summit he was wont to address the people who gathered round its base. Therefore it was esteemed a sanctuary, holy to the living and the dead. Princely families from a distance carried their dead there to be interred, because this teacher had said that man does not perish when he dies, but shall rise again. It was held that this would be more certain to occur in the very spot where he announced this doctrine. Every sunset, when he had finished his discourse, he retired into a cave in the mountain, not to reappear again until the next morning.

For many years, some said for two thousand years, did he rule the people with equity, and then he departed, going back to the East whence he came, said some authorities, but others averred that he rose up to heaven. At any rate, before he left, he appointed a successor in the sovereignty, and recommended him to pursue the paths of justice.[1]

[1: "Afirman que fue trasladado al cielo, y que al tiempo de su partida dexo al Cacique de aquella Provincia por heredero de su santidad i poderio." Lucas Fernaudez Piedrahita, ***Historia General de las Conquistas del Nueoo Reyno de Granada***, Lib. i, cap. iii (Amberes, 1688).]

What led the Spanish missionaries to suspect that this was one of the twelve apostles, was not only these doctrines, but the undoubted fact that they found the symbol of the cross already a religious emblem among this people. It appeared in their sacred paintings, and especially, they erected one over the grave of a person who had died from the bite of a serpent.

A little careful investigation will permit us to accept these statements as quite true, and yet give them a very different interpretation.

That this culture-hero arrives from the East and returns to the East are points that at once excite the suspicion that he was the personification of the Light. But when we come to his names, no doubt can remain. These were various, but one of the most usual was ***Chimizapagua***, which, we are told, means "a messenger from ***Chiminigagua***." In the cosmogonical myths of the Muyscas this was the home or source of Light, and was a name applied to the demiurgic force. In that mysterious dwelling, so their account ran, light was shut up, and the world lay in primeval gloom. At a certain time the light manifested itself, and the dawn of the first morning appeared, the light being carried to the four quarters of the earth by great black birds, who blew the air and winds from their beaks. Modern grammarians profess themselves unable to explain the exact meaning of the name ***Chiminigagua***, but it is a compound, in which, evidently, appear the words ***chie***, light, and ***gagua***, Sun. [1]

[1: Uricoechea says, "al principio del mundo la luz estaba encerrada en una cosa que no podian describir i que llamaban ***Chiminigague***, o El Criador." ***Gramatica de la Lengua Chibcha***, Introd., p. xix. ***Chie*** in this tongue means light, moon, month, honor, and is also the first person plural of the personal pronoun. ***Ibid***., p. 94. Father Simon says ***gagua*** is "el nombre del mismo sol," though ordinarily Sun is ***Sua***.]

Other names applied to this hero-god were Nemterequeteba, Bochica, and Zuhe, or Sua, the last mentioned being also the ordinary word for the Sun. He was reported to have been of light complexion, and when the Spaniards first arrived they were supposed to be his envoys, and were called *sua* or *gagua*, just as from the memory of a similar myth in Peru they were addressed as Viracochas.

In his form as Bochica, he is represented as the supreme male divinity, whose female associate is the Rainbow, Cuchaviva, goddess of rains and waters, of the fertility of the fields, of medicine, and of child-bearing in women, a relationship which I have already explained.[1]

[1: The principal authority for the mythology of the Mayscas, or Chibchas, is Padre Pedro Simon, *Noticias Historiales de las Conquistas de Tierra Firme en el Nuevo Reyno de Granada*, Pt. iv, caps. ii, iii, iv, printed in Kingsborough, *Mexican Antiquities*, vol. viii, and Piedrahita as above quoted.]

Wherever the widespread Tupi-Guaranay race extended--from the mouth of the Rio de la Plata and the boundless plains of the Pampas, north to the northern-most islands of the West Indian Archipelago--the early explorers found the natives piously attributing their knowledge of the arts of life to a venerable and benevolent old man whom they called "Our Ancestor," *Tamu*, or *Tume*, or *Zume*.

The early Jesuit missionaries to the Guaranis and affiliated tribes of Paraguay and southern Brazil, have much to say of this personage, and some of them were convinced that he could have been no other than the Apostle St. Thomas on his proselytizing journey around the world.

The legend was that Pay Zume, as he was called in Paraguay (*Pay* = magician, diviner, priest), came from the East, from the Sun-rising, in years long gone by. He instructed the people in the arts of hunting and agriculture, especially in the culture and preparation of the manioc plant, their chief source of vegetable food. Near the city of Assumption is situated a lofty rock, around which, says the myth, he was accustomed to gather the people, while he stood above them on its summit, and delivered his instructions and his laws, just as did Quetzalcoatl from the top of the mountain Tzatzitepec, the Hill of Shouting. The spot where he stood is still marked by the impress of his feet, which the pious natives of a later day took pride in pointing out as a convincing proof that their ancestors received and remembered the preachings of St. Thomas.[1] This was not a suggestion of their later learning, but merely a christianized term given to their authentic ancient legend. As early as 1552, when Father Emanuel Nobrega was visiting the missions of Brazil, he heard the legend, and learned of a locality where not only the marks of the feet, but also of the hands of the hero-god had been indelibly impressed upon the hard rock. Not satisfied with the mere report, he visited the spot and saw them with his own eyes, but indulged in some skepticism as to their origin.[2]

[1: "Juxta Paraquariae metropolim rupes utcumque cuspidata, sed in modicam planitiem desinens cernitur, in cujus summitate vestigia pedum humanorum saxo impressa adhuc manent, affirmantibus constanter indigenis, ex eo loco Apostolum Thomam multitudini undequaque ad eum audiendum confluenti solitum fuisse legem divinam tradere: et addunt mandiocae, ex qua farinam suam ligneam conficiunt, plantandae rationem ab eodem accepisse." P. Nicolao del Techo, **Historia Provincial Paraquariae Societatis Jesu**, Lib. vi, cap. iv (folio, Leodii, 1673).]

[2: "Ipse abii," he writes in his well known Letter, "et propriis oculis inspexi, quatuor pedum et digitorum satis alte impressa vestigia, quae nonnunquam aqua excrescens cooperit." The reader will remember the similar event in the history of Quetzalcoatl (see above, chapter iii, Sec.3)]

The story was that wherever this hero-god walked, he left behind him a well-marked path, which was permanent, and as the Muyscas of New Granada pointed out the path of Bochica, so did the Guaranays that of Zume, which the missionaries regarded "not without astonishment."[1] He lived a certain length of time with his people and then left them, going back over the ocean toward the East, according to some accounts. But according to others, he was driven away by his stiff-necked and unwilling auditors, who had become tired of his advice. They pursued him to the bank of a river, and there, thinking that the quickest riddance of him was to kill him, they discharged their arrows at him. But he caught the arrows in his hand and hurled them back, and dividing the waters of the river by his divine power he walked between them to the other bank, dry-shod, and disappeared from their view in the distance.

[1: "E Brasilia in Guairaniam euntibus spectabilis adhuc semita viditur, quam ab Sancto Thoma ideo incolae vocant, quod per eam Apostolus iter fecisse credatur; quae semita quovis anni tempore eumdem statum conservat, modice in ea crescentibus herbis, ab adjacenti campo multum herbescenti prorsus dissimilibus, praebetque speciem viae artificiose ductae; quam Socii nostri Guairaniam excolentes persaepe non sine stupore perspexisse se testantur." Nicolao del Techo, **ubi supra**, Lib. vi, cap. iv.

The connection of this myth with the course of the sun in the sky, "the path of the bright God," as it is called in the Veda, appears obvious. So also in later legend we read of the wonderful slot or trail of the dragon Fafnir across the Glittering Heath, and many cognate instances, which mythologists now explain by the same reference.]

Like all the hero-gods, he left behind him the well-remembered promise that at some future day he should return to them, and that a race of men should come in time, to gather them into towns and rule them in peace.[1] These predictions were carefully noted by the missionaries, and regarded as the "unconscious prophecies of heathendom" of the advent of Christianity; but to me they bear too unmistakably the stamp of the light-myth I have been following up in so many localities of the New World for me to entertain a doubt about their origin and meaning.

[1: "Ilium quoque pollicitum fuisse, se aliquando has regiones revisurum." Father Nobrega, **ubi supra**. For the other particulars I have given see Nicolao del Techo, **Historia Provinciae Paraquariae**, Lib. vi, cap. iv, "De D. Thomae Apostoli itineribus;" and P. Antonio Ruiz, **Conquista Espiritual hecha por los Religiosos de la Compania de Jesus en las Provincias del Paraguay, Parana, Uruguay y Tape**, fol. 29, 30 (4to., Madrid, 1639). The remarkable identity of the words relating to their religious beliefs and observances throughout this widespread group of tribes has been demonstrated and forcibly commented on by Alcide D'Orbigny, **L'Homme Americain**, vol. ii, p. 277. The Vicomte de Porto Seguro identifies Zume with the **Cemi** of the Antilles, and this etymology is at any rate not so fanciful as most of those he gives in his imaginative work, **L'Origine Touranienne des Americaines Tupis-Caribes**, p. 62 (Vienna, 1876).]

I have not yet exhausted the sources from which I could bring evidence of the widespread presence of the elements of this mythical creation in America. But probably I have said enough to satisfy the reader on this point. At any rate it will be sufficient if I close the list with some manifest fragments of the myth, picked out from the confused and generally modern reports we have of the religions of the

Athabascan race. This stem is one of the most widely distributed in North America, extending across the whole continent south of the Eskimos, and scattered toward the warmer latitudes quite into Mexico. It is low down in the intellectual scale, its component tribes are usually migratory savages, and its dialects are extremely synthetic and of difficult phonetics, requiring as many as sixty-five letters for their proper orthography. No wonder, therefore, that we have but limited knowledge of their mental life.

Conspicuous in their myths is the tale of the Two Brothers. These mysterious beings are upon the earth before man appears. Though alone, they do not agree, and the one attacks and slays the other. Another brother appears on the scene, who seems to be the one slain, who has come to life, and the two are given wives by the Being who was the Creator of things. These two women were perfectly beautiful, but invisible to the eyes of mortals. The one was named, The Woman of the Light or The Woman of the Morning; the other was the Woman of Darkness or the Woman of Evening. The brothers lived together in one tent with these women, who each in turn went out to work. When the Woman of Light was at work, it was daytime; when the Woman of Darkness was at her labors, it was night.

In the course of time one of the brothers disappeared and the other determined to select a wife from one of the two women, as it seems he had not yet chosen. He watched what the Woman of Darkness did in her absence, and discovered that she descended into the waters and enjoyed the embraces of a monster, while the Woman of Light passed her time in feeding white birds. In course of time the former brought forth black man-serpents, while the Woman of Light was delivered of beautiful boys with white skins. The master of the house killed the former with his arrows, but preserved the latter, and marrying the Woman of Light, became the father of the human race, and especially of the Dene Dindjie, who have preserved the memory of him.[1]

[1: ***Monographie des Dene Dindjie, par*** C.R.P.E. Petitot, pp. 84-87 (Paris, 1876). Elsewhere the writer says: "Tout d'abord je dois rappeler mon observation que presque toujours, dans les traditions Dene, le couple primitif se compose de ***deux freres***." Ibid., p. 62.]

In another myth of this stock, clearly a version of the former, this father of the race is represented as a mighty bird, called ***Yel***, or ***Yale***, or ***Orelbale***, from the root *ell*, a term they apply to everything supernatural. He took to wife the daughter of the Sun (the Woman of Light), and by her begat the race of man. He formed the dry land for a place for them to live upon, and stocked the rivers with salmon, that they might have food. When he enters his nest it is day, but when he leaves it it is night; or, according to another myth, he has the two women for wives, the one of whom makes the day, the other the night.

In the beginning Yel was white in plumage, but he had an enemy, by name **Cannook**, with whom he had various contests, and by whose machinations he was turned black. Yel is further represented as the god of the winds and storms, and of the thunder and lightning.[1]

[1: For the extent and particulars of this myth, many of the details of which I omit, see Petitot, **ubi supra**, pp. 68, 87, note; Matthew Macfie. *Travels in Vancouver Island and British Columbia*, pp. 452-455 (London, 1865); and J.K. Lord, *The Naturalist in Vancouver Island and British Columbia* (London, 1866). It is referred to by Mackenzie and other early writers.]

Thus we find, even in this extremely low specimen of the native race, the same basis for their mythology as in the most cultivated nations of Central America. Not only this; it is the same basis upon which is built the major part of the sacred stories of all early religions, in both continents; and the excellent Father Petitot, who is so much impressed by these resemblances that he founds upon them a learned argument to prove that the Dene are of oriental extraction,[1] would have written more to the purpose had his acquaintance with American religions been as extensive as it was with those of Asiatic origin.

[1: See his "Essai sur l'Origine des Dene-Dindjie," in his *Monographie*, above quoted.]

There is one point in all these myths which I wish to bring out forcibly. That is, the distinction which is everywhere drawn between the God of Light and the Sun. Unless this distinction is fully comprehended, American mythology loses most of its meaning.

The assertion has been so often repeated, even down to the latest writers, that the American Indians were nearly all sun-worshipers, that I take pains formally to contradict it. Neither the Sun nor the Spirit of the Sun was their chief divinity.

Of course, the daily history of the appearance and disappearance of light is intimately connected with the apparent motion of the sun. Hence, in the myths there is often a seeming identification of the two, which I have been at no pains to avoid. But the identity is superficial only; it entirely disappears in other parts of the myth, and the conceptions, as fundamentally distinct, must be studied separately, to reach accurate results. It is an easy, but by no means a profound method of treating these religions, to dismiss them all by the facile explanations of "animism," and "sun and moon worship."

I have said, and quoted strong authority to confirm the opinion, that the native tribes of America have lost ground in morals and have retrograded in their religious life since the introduction of Christianity. Their own faiths, though lower in form, had in them the germs of a religious and moral evolution, more likely, with proper regulation, to lead these people to a higher plane of thought than the Aryan doctrines which were forced upon them.

This may seem a daring, even a heterodox assertion, but I think that most modern ethnologists will agree that it is no more possible for races in all stages of culture and of widely different faculties to receive with benefit any one religion, than it is for them to thrive under one form of government, or to adopt with advantage one uniform plan of building houses. The moral and religious life is a growth, and the brash wood of ancient date cannot be grafted on the green stem. It is well to remember that the heathendoms of America were very far from wanting living seeds of sound morality and healthy mental education. I shall endeavor to point this out in a few brief paragraphs.

In their origin in the human mind, religion and morality have nothing in common. They are even antagonistic. At the root of all religions is the passionate desire for the widest possible life, for the most unlimited exercise of all the powers. The basis of all morality is self-sacrifice, the willingness to give up our wishes to the will of another. The criterion of the power of a religion is its ability to command this sacrifice; the criterion of the excellence of a religion is the extent to which its commands coincide with the good of the race, with the lofty standard of the "categorical imperative."

With these axioms well in mind, we can advance with confidence to examine the claims of a religion. It will rise in the scale just in proportion as its behests, were they universally adopted, would permanently increase the happiness of the human race.

In their origin, as I have said, morality and religion are opposites; but they are opposites which inevitably attract and unite. The first lesson of all religions is that we gain by giving, that to secure any end we must sacrifice something. This, too, is taught by all social intercourse, and, therefore, an acute German psychologist has set up the formula," All manners are moral,"[1] because they all imply a subjection of the personal will of the individual to the general will of those who surround him, as expressed in usage and custom.

[1: "Alle Sitten sind sittlich." Lazarus, *Ursprung der Sitte*, S. 5, quoted by Roskoff. I hardly need mention that our word *morality*, from *mos*, means by etymology, simply what is customary and of current usage. The moral man is he who conforms himself to the opinions of the majority. This is also at the basis of Robert Browning's definition of a people: "A people is but the attempt of many to rise to the completer life of one" (*A Soul's Tragedy*).]

Even the religion which demands bloody sacrifices, which forces its votaries to futile and abhorrent rites, is at least training its adherents in the virtues of obedience and renunciation, in endurance and confidence.

But concerning American religions I need not have recourse to such a questionable vindication. They held in them far nobler elements, as is proved beyond cavil by the words of many of the earliest missionaries themselves. Bigoted and bitter haters of the native faiths, as they were, they discovered in them so much that was good, so much that approximated to the purer doctrines that they themselves came to teach, that they have left on record many an attempt to prove that there must, in some remote and unknown epoch, have come Christian teachers to the New World, St. Thomas, St. Bartholomew, monks from Ireland, or Asiatic disciples, to acquaint the natives with such salutary doctrines. It is precisely in connection with the myths which I have been relating in this volume that these theories were put forth, and I have referred to them in various passages.

The facts are as stated, but the credit of developing these elevated moral conceptions must not be refused to the red race. They are its own property, the legitimate growth of its own religious sense.

The hero-god, the embodiment of the Light of Day, is essentially a moral and beneficent creation. Whether his name be Michabo, Ioskeha, or Quetzalcoatl, Itzamna, Viracocha or Tamu, he is always the giver of laws, the instructor in the arts of social life, the founder of commonwealths, the patron of agriculture. He casts his influence in favor of peace, and against wars and deeds of violence. He punishes those who pursue iniquity, and he favors those who work for the good of the community.

In many instances he sets an example of chaste living, of strict temperance, of complete subjection of the lusts and appetites. I have but to refer to what I have already said of the Maya Kukulcan and the Aztec Quetzalcoatl, to show this. Both are particularly noted as characters free from the taint of indulgence.

Thus it occurred that the early monks often express surprise that these, whom they chose to call savages and heathens, had developed a moral law of undeniable purity. "The matters that Bochica taught," says the chronicler Piedrahita, "were certainly excellent, inasmuch as these natives hold as right to do just the same that we do." "The priests of these Muyscas," he goes on to say, "lived most chastely and with great purity of life, insomuch that even in eating, their food was simple and of small quantity, and they refrained altogether from women and marriage. Did one transgress in this respect, he was dismissed from the priesthood."[1]

[1: "Las cosas que el Bochica les ensenaba eran buenas, siendo assi, que tenian por malo lo mismo que nosotros tenemos por tal." Piedrahita, ***Historia General de las Conquistas del Nuevo Reyno de Granada***, Lib. i, Cap. iii.]

The prayers addressed to these deities breathe as pure a spirit of devotion as many now heard in Christian lands. Change the names, and some of the formulas preserved by Christobal de Molina and Sahagun would not jar on the ears of a congregation in one of our own churches.

Although sanguinary rites were common, they were not usual in the worship of these highest divinities, but rather as propitiations to the demons of the darkness, or the spirits of the terrible phenomena of nature. The mild god of light did not demand them.

To appreciate the effect of all this on the mind of the race, let it be remembered that these culture-heroes were also the creators, the primal and most potent of divinities, and that usually many temples and a large corps of priests were devoted to their worship, at least in the nations of higher civilization. These votaries were engaged in keeping alive the myth, in impressing the supposed commands of the deity on the people, and in imitating him in example and precept. Thus they had formed a lofty ideal of man, and were publishing this ideal to their fellows. Certainly this could not fail of working to the good of the nation, and of elevating and purifying its moral conceptions.

That it did so we have ample evidence in the authentic accounts of the ancient society as it existed before the Europeans destroyed and corrupted it, and in the collections of laws, all distinctly stamped with the seal of religion, which have been preserved, as they were in vogue in Anahuac, Utatlan, Peru and other localities. [1] Any one who peruses these will see that the great moral principles, the radical doctrines of individual virtue, were clearly recognized and deliberately enforced as divine and civil precepts in these communities. Moreover, they were generally and cheerfully obeyed, and the people of many of these lands were industrious, peaceable, moral, and happy, far more so than they have ever been since.

[1: The reader willing to pursue the argument further can find these collections of ancient American laws in Sahagun, *Historia de Nueva Espana*, for Mexico; in Geronimo Roman, *Republica de las Indias Occidentales*, for Utatlan and other nations; for Peru in the *Relacion del Origen, Descendencia, Politica, y Gobierno de los Incas, por el licenciado Fernando de Santillan* (published at Madrid. 1879); and for the Muyscas, in Piedrahita, *Hist. Gen. del Nuevo Reyno de Granada*, Lib. ii, cap. v.]

There was also a manifest progress in the definition of the idea of God, that is, of a single infinite intelligence as the source and controlling power of phenomena. We have it on record that in Peru this was the direct fruit of the myth of Viracocha. It is related that the Inca Yupangui published to his people that to him had appeared Viracocha, with admonition that he alone was lord of the world, and creator of all things; that he had made the heavens, the sun, and man; and that it was not right that these, his works, should receive equal homage with himself. Therefore, the Inca decreed that the image of Viracocha should thereafter be assigned supremacy to those of all other divinities, and that no tribute nor sacrifice should be paid to him, for He was master of all the earth, and could take from it as he chose.[1] This was evidently a direct attempt on the part of an enlightened ruler to lift his people from a lower to a higher form of religion, from idolatry to theism. The Inca even went so far as to banish all images of Viracocha from his temples, so that this, the greatest of gods, should be worshiped as an immaterial spirit only.

[1: P. Joseph de Acosta, ***Historia Natural y Moral de las Indias***, Lib. vi, cap. 31 (Barcelona, 1591).]

A parallel instance is presented in Aztec annals. Nezahualcoyotzin, an enlightened ruler of Tezcuco, about 1450, was both a philosopher and a poet, and the songs which he left, seventy in number, some of which are still preserved, breathe a spirit of emancipation from the idolatrous superstition of his day. He announced that there was one only god, who sustained and created all things, and who dwelt above the ninth heaven, out of sight of man. No image was fitting for this divinity, nor did he ever appear bodily to the eyes of men. But he listened to their prayers and received their souls.[1]

[1: See Fernando de Alva Ixtlilxochitl, ***Historica Chichimeca***, cap. xlix; and Joseph Joaquin Granados y Galvez, ***Tardes Americanas***, p. 90 (Mexico, 1778).]

These traditions have been doubted, for no other reason than because it was assumed that such thoughts were above the level of the red race. But the proper names and titles, unquestionably ancient and genuine, which I have analyzed in the preceding pages refute this supposition.

We may safely affirm that other and stronger instances of the kind could be quoted, had the early missionaries preserved more extensively the sacred chants and prayers of the natives. In the Maya tongue of Yucatan a certain number of them have escaped destruction, and although they are open to some suspicion of having been colored for proselytizing purposes, there is direct evidence from natives who were adults at the time of the Conquest that some of their priests had predicted the time should come when the worship of one only God should prevail. This was nothing more than another instance of the monotheistic idea finding its expression, and its apparition is not more extraordinary in Yucatan or Peru than in ancient Egypt or Greece. The actual religious and moral progress of the natives was designedly ignored and belittled by the early missionaries and conquerors. Bishop Las Casas directly charges those of his day with magnifying the vices of the Indians and the cruelties of their worship; and even such a liberal thinker as Roger Williams tells us that he would not be present at their ceremonies, "Lest I should have been partaker of Satan's Inventions and Worships."[1] This same prejudice completely blinded the first visitors to the New World, and it was only the extravagant notion that Christianity had at some former time been preached here that saved us most of the little that we have on record.

[1: Roger Williams, *A Key Into the Language of America*, p. 152.]

Yet now and then the truth breaks through even this dense veil of prejudice. For instance, I have quoted in this chapter the evidence of the Spanish chroniclers to the purity of the teaching attributed to Bochica. The effect of such doctrines could not be lost on a people who looked upon him at once as an exemplar and a deity. Nor was it. The Spaniards have left strong testimony to the pacific and virtuous character of that nation, and its freedom from the vices so prevalent in lower races.[1]

[1: See especially the *Noticias sobre el Nuevo Reino de Granada*, in the *Colleccion de Documentos ineditos del Archivo de Indias*, vol. v, p. 529.]

Now, as I dismiss from the domain of actual fact all these legendary instructors, the question remains, whence did these secluded tribes obtain the sentiments of justice and morality which they loved to attribute to their divine founders, and, in a measure, to practice themselves?

The question is pertinent, and with its answer I may fitly close this study in American native religions. If the theory that I have advocated is correct, these myths had to do at first with merely natural occurrences, the advent and departure of the daylight, the winds, the storm and the rains. The beneficent and injurious results of these phenomena were attributed to their personifications. Especially was the dispersal of darkness by the light regarded as the transaction of all most favorable to man. The facilities that it gave him were imputed to the goodness of the personified Spirit of Light, and by a natural association of ideas, the benevolent emotions and affections developed by improving social intercourse were also brought into relation to this kindly Being. They came to be regarded as his behests, and, in the national mind, he grew into a teacher of the friendly relations of man to man, and an ideal of those powers which "make for righteousness." Priests and chieftains favored the acceptance of these views, because they felt their intrinsic wisdom, and hence the moral evolution of the nation proceeded steadily from its mythology. That the results achieved were similar to those taught by the best religions of the eastern world should not excite any surprise, for the basic principles of ethics are the same everywhere and in all time.

The Codes Of Hammurabi And Moses
W. W. Davies

QTY

The discovery of the Hammurabi Code is one of the greatest achievements of archaeology, and is of paramount interest, not only to the student of the Bible, but also to all those interested in ancient history...

Religion   **ISBN:** *1-59462-338-4*   **Pages:132**
MSRP $12.95

The Theory of Moral Sentiments
Adam Smith

QTY

This work from 1749. contains original theories of conscience amd moral judgment and it is the foundation for systemof morals.

Philosophy **ISBN:** *1-59462-777-0*   **Pages:536**
MSRP $19.95

Jessica's First Prayer
Hesba Stretton

QTY

In a screened and secluded corner of one of the many railway-bridges which span the streets of London there could be seen a few years ago, from five o'clock every morning until half past eight, a tidily set-out coffee-stall, consisting of a trestle and board, upon which stood two large tin cans, with a small fire of charcoal burning under each so as to keep the coffee boiling during the early hours of the morning when the work-people were thronging into the city on their way to their daily toil...

Pages:84

Childrens   **ISBN:** *1-59462-373-2*   *MSRP $9.95*

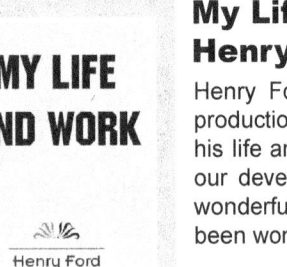

My Life and Work
Henry Ford

QTY

Henry Ford revolutionized the world with his implementation of mass production for the Model T automobile. Gain valuable business insight into his life and work with his own auto-biography... "We have only started on our development of our country we have not as yet, with all our talk of wonderful progress, done more than scratch the surface. The progress has been wonderful enough but..."

Pages:300

Biographies/   **ISBN:** *1-59462-198-5*   *MSRP $21.95*

The Art of Cross-Examination
Francis Wellman

QTY

I presume it is the experience of every author, after his first book is published upon an important subject, to be almost overwhelmed with a wealth of ideas and illustrations which could readily have been included in his book, and which to his own mind, at least, seem to make a second edition inevitable. Such certainly was the case with me; and when the first edition had reached its sixth impression in five months, I rejoiced to learn that it seemed to my publishers that the book had met with a sufficiently favorable reception to justify a second and considerably enlarged edition. ..

Reference   **ISBN: *1-59462-647-2***

Pages:412
MSRP $19.95

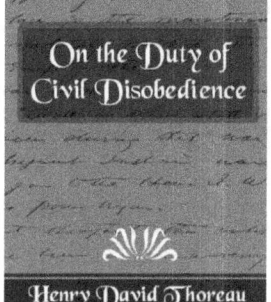

On the Duty of Civil Disobedience
Henry David Thoreau

QTY

Thoreau wrote his famous essay, On the Duty of Civil Disobedience, as a protest against an unjust but popular war and the immoral but popular institution of slave-owning. He did more than write—he declined to pay his taxes, and was hauled off to gaol in consequence. Who can say how much this refusal of his hastened the end of the war and of slavery ?

Law   **ISBN: *1-59462-747-9***

Pages:48
MSRP $7.45

Dream Psychology Psychoanalysis for Beginners
Sigmund Freud

QTY

Sigmund Freud, born Sigismund Schlomo Freud (May 6, 1856 - September 23, 1939), was a Jewish-Austrian neurologist and psychiatrist who co-founded the psychoanalytic school of psychology. Freud is best known for his theories of the unconscious mind, especially involving the mechanism of repression; his redefinition of sexual desire as mobile and directed towards a wide variety of objects; and his therapeutic techniques, especially his understanding of transference in the therapeutic relationship and the presumed value of dreams as sources of insight into unconscious desires.

Psychology   **ISBN: *1-59462-905-6***

Pages:196
MSRP $15.45

The Miracle of Right Thought
Orison Swett Marden

QTY

Believe with all of your heart that you will do what you were made to do. When the mind has once formed the habit of holding cheerful, happy, prosperous pictures, it will not be easy to form the opposite habit. It does not matter how improbable or how far away this realization may see, or how dark the prospects may be, if we visualize them as best we can, as vividly as possible, hold tenaciously to them and vigorously struggle to attain them, they will gradually become actualized, realized in the life. But a desire, a longing without endeavor, a yearning abandoned or held indifferently will vanish without realization.

Self Help   **ISBN: *1-59462-644-8***

Pages:360
MSRP $25.45

The Rosicrucian Cosmo-Conception Mystic Christianity *by Max Heindel*   ISBN: *1-59462-188-8*   **$38.95**
The Rosicrucian Cosmo-conception is not dogmatic, neither does it appeal to any other authority than the reason of the student. It is: not controversial, but is: sent forth in the, hope that it may help to clear...   New Age/Religion Pages 646

Abandonment To Divine Providence *by Jean-Pierre de Caussade*   ISBN: *1-59462-228-0*   **$25.95**
"The Rev. Jean Pierre de Caussade was one of the most remarkable spiritual writers of the Society of Jesus in France in the 18th Century. His death took place at Toulouse in 1751. His works have gone through many editions and have been republished...   Inspirational/Religion Pages 400

Mental Chemistry *by Charles Haanel*   ISBN: *1-59462-192-6*   **$23.95**
Mental Chemistry allows the change of material conditions by combining and appropriately utilizing the power of the mind. Much like applied chemistry creates something new and unique out of careful combinations of chemicals the mastery of mental chemistry...   New Age Pages 354

The Letters of Robert Browning and Elizabeth Barret Barrett 1845-1846 vol II   ISBN: *1-59462-193-4*   **$35.95**
by Robert Browning and Elizabeth Barrett   Biographies Pages 596

Gleanings In Genesis (volume I) *by Arthur W. Pink*   ISBN: *1-59462-130-6*   **$27.45**
Appropriately has Genesis been termed "the seed plot of the Bible" for in it we have, in germ form, almost all of the great doctrines which are afterwards fully developed in the books of Scripture which follow...   Religion/Inspirational Pages 420

The Master Key *by L. W. de Laurence*   ISBN: *1-59462-001-6*   **$30.95**
In no branch of human knowledge has there been a more lively increase of the spirit of research during the past few years than in the study of Psychology, Concentration and Mental Discipline. The requests for authentic lessons in Thought Control, Mental Discipline and...   New Age/Business Pages 422

The Lesser Key Of Solomon Goetia *by L. W. de Laurence*   ISBN: *1-59462-092-X*   **$9.95**
This translation of the first book of the "Lernegton" which is now for the first time made accessible to students of Talismanic Magic was done, after careful collation and edition, from numerous Ancient Manuscripts in Hebrew, Latin, and French...   New Age/Occult Pages 92

Rubaiyat Of Omar Khayyam *by Edward Fitzgerald*   ISBN:*1-59462-332-5*   **$13.95**
Edward Fitzgerald, whom the world has already learned, in spite of his own efforts to remain within the shadow of anonymity, to look upon as one of the rarest poets of the century, was born at Bredfield, in Suffolk, on the 31st of March, 1809. He was the third son of John Purcell...   Music Pages 172

Ancient Law *by Henry Maine*   ISBN: *1-59462-128-4*   **$29.95**
The chief object of the following pages is to indicate some of the earliest ideas of mankind, as they are reflected in Ancient Law, and to point out the relation of those ideas to modern thought.   Religion/History Pages 452

Far-Away Stories *by William J. Locke*   ISBN: *1-59462-129-2*   **$19.95**
"Good wine needs no bush, but a collection of mixed vintages does. And this book is just such a collection. Some of the stories I do not want to remain buried for ever in the museum files of dead magazine-numbers an author's not unpardonable vanity..."   Fiction Pages 272

Life of David Crockett *by David Crockett*   ISBN: *1-59462-250-7*   **$27.45**
"Colonel David Crockett was one of the most remarkable men of the times in which he lived. Born in humble life, but gifted with a strong will, an indomitable courage, and unremitting perseverance...   Biographies/New Age Pages 424

Lip-Reading *by Edward Nitchie*   ISBN: *1-59462-206-X*   **$25.95**
Edward B. Nitchie, founder of the New York School for the Hard of Hearing, now the Nitchie School of Lip-Reading, Inc, wrote "LIP-READING Principles and Practice". The development and perfecting of this meritorious work on lip-reading was an undertaking...   How-to Pages 400

A Handbook of Suggestive Therapeutics, Applied Hypnotism, Psychic Science   ISBN: *1-59462-214-0*   **$24.95**
by Henry Munro   Health/New Age/Health/Self-help Pages 376

A Doll's House: and Two Other Plays *by Henrik Ibsen*   ISBN: *1-59462-112-8*   **$19.95**
Henrik Ibsen created this classic when in revolutionary 1848 Rome. Introducing some striking concepts in playwriting for the realist genre, this play has been studied the world over.   Fiction/Classics/Plays 308

The Light of Asia *by sir Edwin Arnold*   ISBN: *1-59462-204-3*   **$13.95**
In this poetic masterpiece, Edwin Arnold describes the life and teachings of Buddha. The man who was to become known as Buddha to the world was born as Prince Gautama of India but he rejected the worldly riches and abandoned the reigns of power when...   Religion/History/Biographies Pages 170

The Complete Works of Guy de Maupassant *by Guy de Maupassant*   ISBN: *1-59462-157-8*   **$16.95**
"For days and days, nights and nights, I had dreamed of that first kiss which was to consecrate our engagement, and I knew not on what spot I should put my lips..."   Fiction/Classics Pages 240

The Art of Cross-Examination *by Francis L. Wellman*   ISBN: *1-59462-309-0*   **$26.95**
Written by a renowned trial lawyer, Wellman imparts his experience and uses case studies to explain how to use psychology to extract desired information through questioning.   How-to/Science/Reference Pages 408

Answered or Unanswered? *by Louisa Vaughan*   ISBN: *1-59462-248-5*   **$10.95**
Miracles of Faith in China   Religion Pages 112

The Edinburgh Lectures on Mental Science (1909) *by Thomas*   ISBN: *1-59462-008-3*   **$11.95**
This book contains the substance of a course of lectures recently given by the writer in the Queen Street Hail, Edinburgh. Its purpose is to indicate the Natural Principles governing the relation between Mental Action and Material Conditions...   New Age/Psychology Pages 148

Ayesha *by H. Rider Haggard*   ISBN: *1-59462-301-5*   **$24.95**
Verily and indeed it is the unexpected that happens! Probably if there was one person upon the earth from whom the Editor of this, and of a certain previous history, did not expect to hear again...   Classics Pages 380

Ayala's Angel *by Anthony Trollope*   ISBN: *1-59462-352-X*   **$29.95**
The two girls were both pretty, but Lucy who was twenty-one who supposed to be simple and comparatively unattractive, whereas Ayala was credited, as her Bombwhat romantic name might show, with poetic charm and a taste for romance. Ayala when her father died was nineteen...   Fiction Pages 484

The American Commonwealth *by James Bryce*   ISBN: *1-59462-286-8*   **$34.45**
An interpretation of American democratic political theory. It examines political mechanics and society from the perspective of Scotsman James Bryce   Politics Pages 572

Stories of the Pilgrims *by Margaret P. Pumphrey*   ISBN: *1-59462-116-0*   **$17.95**
This book explores pilgrims religious oppression in England as well as their escape to Holland and eventual crossing to America on the Mayflower, and their early days in New England...   History Pages 268

www.bookjungle.com *email: sales@bookjungle.com fax: 630-214-0564 mail: Book Jungle PO Box 2226 Champaign, IL 61825*

QTY

The Fasting Cure *by Sinclair Upton* ISBN: *1-59462-222-1* **$13.95**
In the Cosmopolitan Magazine for May, 1910, and in the Contemporary Review (London) for April, 1910, I published an article dealing with my experiences in fasting. I have written a great many magazine articles, but never one which attracted so much attention... New Age/Self Help/Health Pages 164

Hebrew Astrology *by Sepharial* ISBN: *1-59462-308-2* **$13.45**
In these days of advanced thinking it is a matter of common observation that we have left many of the old landmarks behind and that we are now pressing forward to greater heights and to a wider horizon than that which represented the mind-content of our progenitors... Astrology Pages 144

Thought Vibration or The Law of Attraction in the Thought World ISBN: *1-59462-127-6* **$12.95**
by William Walker Atkinson *Psychology/Religion Pages 144*

Optimism *by Helen Keller* ISBN: *1-59462-108-X* **$15.95**
Helen Keller was blind, deaf, and mute since 19 months old, yet famously learned how to overcome these handicaps, communicate with the world, and spread her lectures promoting optimism. An inspiring read for everyone... Biographies/Inspirational Pages 84

Sara Crewe *by Frances Burnett* ISBN: *1-59462-360-0* **$9.45**
In the first place, Miss Minchin lived in London. Her home was a large, dull, tall one, in a large, dull square, where all the houses were alike, and all the sparrows were alike, and where all the door-knockers made the same heavy sound... Childrens/Classic Pages 88

The Autobiography of Benjamin Franklin *by Benjamin Franklin* ISBN: *1-59462-135-7* **$24.95**
The Autobiography of Benjamin Franklin has probably been more extensively read than any other American historical work, and no other book of its kind has had such ups and downs of fortune. Franklin lived for many years in England, where he was agent... Biographies/History Pages 332

Name	
Email	
Telephone	
Address	
City, State ZIP	

☐ **Credit Card**   ☐ **Check / Money Order**

Credit Card Number	
Expiration Date	
Signature	

Please Mail to: Book Jungle
PO Box 2226
Champaign, IL 61825
or Fax to: 630-214-0564

ORDERING INFORMATION

web: *www.bookjungle.com*
email: *sales@bookjungle.com*
fax: *630-214-0564*
mail: *Book Jungle PO Box 2226 Champaign, IL 61825*
or PayPal *to sales@bookjungle.com*

Please contact us for bulk discounts

DIRECT-ORDER TERMS

**20% Discount if You Order
Two or More Books**
Free Domestic Shipping!
Accepted: Master Card, Visa,
Discover, American Express

www.ingramcontent.com/pod-product-compliance
Lightning Source LLC
Chambersburg PA
CBHW080909020726
47502CB00008B/2403